Making Lemonade

Making Lemonade

Karen Ramsey

One

In this small sitting room, the nurse's voice is booming as she calls a name from the side door and a young couple a few chairs down rises. I track the girl as she waddles to the back. Grimacing, I think, *Do all women look that way at the end of pregnancy?*

Once the door closes, I shift my focus back to the only other patient. He's in the center of the room, slouching in a chair and scrolling through his phone. His eyes flick up, catching me staring. I quickly look away, but when I chance a glance back over at him, he's squinting, looking like he's trying to solve a puzzle.

I ignore him and close my eyes. Leaning back, I take a deep breath. This isn't the worst thing in the world, is it? Oh, who am I kidding? It is.

Instead of focusing on my situation, I try and guess why a guy would come to the clinic. The obvious is for a sexually transmitted infection, or maybe he's here to get condoms? They also do vasectomies and screenings for certain cancers, which I thought was interesting.

Fingers snap. "Maclaren!"

My eyes fly open. Blue eyes are staring right at me.

"Come on, I know you know me." He winks.

Oh my gosh, this is now my worst nightmare. John from Mesquite High, John from Molly Shepard's party Saturday, John— the guy my best friend Andi begged me to be her wing woman for— is sitting in the same waiting room as me. I'm going to barf.

"Ah, there it is. So, Maclaren, what brings you in today?" John gets up, walks over, and plops down in the chair beside me.

"I could ask you the same question," I retort. Truthfully, I don't want to know. I wonder what Andi will think. However, if I tell her I saw John at the clinic, she will immediately wonder why *I'm* at the clinic, and I'm not ready for her to know. I'm not ready for anyone to know. There's a reason I'm here alone. This pregnancy opens the door to a whole world of secrets that I'm not ready to share. A tear slips down my cheek.

John swears. The chair creaks beside me and then John's extending a tissue toward me.

I glance over and John smiles. I take it, quickly wiping my eyes.

"So, wanna talk about it?"

I shake my head.

"Cool, cool."

Silence. I sit there fiddling with the cuff of my sweater sleeve.

"It's Mac, by the way."

"Huh?"

"Just Mac, not Maclaren."

"All right, just Mac. Did you have fun Saturday?"

The party was all right. I had been feeling queasy all afternoon and still wasn't feeling awesome. Andi had been whining about me being a party pooper. When she spotted John, I figured that was my chance. If I could hook her up, she'd leave me alone. Suddenly, I realize her and John had hit it off. He could easily spill that he saw me here today.

"Lookin' a little green there, Mac."

"You can't say anything, okay? Please promise you won't say anything about me or this morning to anyone. Especially Andi!"

"I won't," he says casually.

I try to breathe. I knew eventually everything would be
out in the open, but I wasn't expecting that day to be this soon. It was
hard enough trying to wrap my head around having a baby. The
minute this pregnancy is revealed there will be so many questions.
Who is the father? How did this happen? When did you start dating?
Was this a one-night stand? How could I be so irresponsible? I mean,
my parents still think I'm their perfect little angel who has never
once thought about sex, let alone actually *had* sex.

I close my eyes but it's too late—my nerves are fried. I can't
hold it any longer. The chair beside me scratches on the tile. I clamp
my mouth shut, trying not to puke all over the floor. John thrusts a
plastic trash can in front of me before the miniscule breakfast I ate
finds its way out.

"Yo, Mr. Chivalrous. Let's go!" someone calls out as a door
clicks shut.

"You good?" John asks me instead.

I don't answer. My stomach tightens, and I feel more liquid
crawl up my throat.

"Dude!" a guy yells.

"Holy…ugh," John mumbles from beside me. There's a jingling,
I'm assuming keys. The sound is quickly stifled. "Go, I'll see you
later," John says.

"Whatever."

When I'm finished, I sit up. John is beside me with a paper towel
and a little paper cup of water.

Taking the paper towel, I wipe my mouth, glancing over. "So,
how you getting home?" I take a small sip of water from the cup
John hands me. He shrugs.

"Wait, you were just someone's ride?"

"Yep."

"Not fair," I whisper.

John chuckles. Just then, my name is called. I stand, grab the trash can, and take it with me.

"Good luck," John calls out.

I give a little wave to John and an apologetic smile to the nurse as I hold the trash can.

When I walk back out to the lobby, John's gone. I walk to my car holding the pamphlets the doctor gave me. I'm officially near the end of my first trimester. The nausea and fatigue should subside in the next couple weeks. By that time, I'll be able to schedule an ultrasound to check the heartbeat and see how everything is progressing.

I contemplate if John will mention anything to anyone. I'm putting a lot of trust in someone I met at a party. Hopefully, me puking my guts out obscured my face from his friend. Was his friend at the party? If he did catch a glimpse of me, did he know who I was? Did John walk out and tell him? I need this to be my secret for a bit longer.

I drive home and head straight to my room. I hide the pamphlets in my desk drawer and then change for work. Work is currently the worst part of any day. The smell of the dough and mozzarella cheese makes me gag, and breathing it in for at least six hours a day is unbearable. Thankfully, our fountain drink station has lemonade which, surprisingly, I can tolerate. The only downside is since I'm constantly guzzling it, I'm frequently making trips to the bathroom. The other day my manager, Mr. Cruz, gave me the stink eye as I made my who-knows-what-number trip to the bathroom. When I returned to the register, I just flashed him a smile.

Walking into work today, Mr. Cruz steps out of his office. "Mac, can I see you for a moment?"

"Um, sure." He steps back into his office and I follow, taking a seat in one of the plastic chairs. "Is there a problem?" I ask innocently.

"You tell me. I've noticed you are constantly stepping away from the register. Yesterday, I had to jump in for you several times. If this continues, I'll have to take disciplinary action. So, anything you want to divulge?"

"I promise, I'll be better." I'm not sure how true that statement is, but I don't want to tell him the reason I keep disappearing.

"Consider this your warning. If I have to call you in here again, it will be a write-up. Do you understand?"

I nod and rise from the chair.

"Mac, don't make me write you up. You're one of my best."

"I won't." I step out of his office and head straight to the fountain station, grabbing a cup. I fill it with lemonade and take my place at the register. I'm close to the end of my shift when a large group walks in reeking of sunscreen and chlorine. A large gentleman approaches the counter, and the smell becomes overwhelming. I try to breathe through my mouth as he places his order. Luckily, I'm able to repeat it back to him without gagging. As soon as he joins his group I beeline it for the bathroom. When I come back, Mr. Cruz is standing there taking an order. He glances over, disappointment evident on his face.

"Chris, can you sub on the register for a moment?" Mr. Cruz calls.

Chris walks up to the front, looking between me and our manager. Tears well in my eyes. I turn and head to the office.

"We just had a conversation not four hours ago. Maclaren, this is not like you. So, before I draw up the paperwork, is there anything going on that I should know about?"

I sniffle. "I'm…"

He leans on the desk, patiently waiting for an explanation.

"My stomach's been upset; I just threw up."

He sighs. "Grab your stuff and go home. Do you work tomorrow?"

I nod.

"I'll get your shift covered. Rest, and I'll see you next week."

"That's not necessary. I can work."

"Either I chalk today up to you being sick and I send you home, or I write you up. Which would you prefer?"

"Being sick," I mutter.

"Have a good night. Feel better."

"Thank you." I walk out of his office, grab my belongings from the front, and head home.

Waking up instantly feeling nauseous is not the way I wish to start my day, but it's how my Thursday begins. I skip lunch, texting Kyle and Andi that I have homework to finish and they can find me in the library. Before my next class, I turn the corner to see Kyle leaning against my locker.

"Hey." He steps aside as I unlock my locker and open the door. I slip my backpack off my shoulder and suddenly the world tilts. I grab ahold of the bottom of my locker to steady myself.

"Woah, are you okay?"

I close my eyes for a moment, hoping the dizzy spell will pass. I open my eyes and then proceed to exchange books.

"Mac? What's up?"

I turn. Kyle is staring at me, concern flickering across his face. I open my mouth to tell him. I know we are standing in the middle of senior hall, and this is the last place he should find out he's going to be a father, but I'm so tired of hiding this from him. Right now, I'm just tired.

"I'm…"

Andi appears behind Kyle, slinging her arm around his shoulders. "I'm not graduating," she states.

Kyle and I stare at her, perplexed; she has straight A's.

"—is all I heard about from Jace Miller today during homeroom. He begged me to tutor him. Like any help he receives is going to save him this late in the year. Also, he's a giant—" She scrunches her nose, trying to come up with the correct terminology. It's not that she doesn't have it, there are probably too many options.

"Bag of crap?" I offer.

She shakes her head. "Worse, but we'll go with it."

The woozy feeling has dissipated. I close my locker and Kyle wraps his arm around my shoulders, holding me a little tighter, still worried about what he just witnessed at the locker.

The three of us make our way down the hall, toward the double doors where Kyle will turn left to go to government, and Andi and I will turn right and head for English. Kyle gives me one last look as we part ways. *I'm fine*, I mouth.

Saturday, Andi throws a party at her house while her parents are out of town. Stepping out onto the back patio, I pull my sweater sleeves down, thankful there is still a slight chill in the air. Soon, the nice weather will be replaced by stifling heat. The whicker creaks as I lie down on one of the couches. I've been trying to pretend that I have all the energy in the world and can last all night, when in truth, I was ready for bed hours ago.

The back door opens, and I hold my breath. *Please don't let it be Andi.*

"Hey there," John says, taking a seat across from me.

Breathing a sigh of relief, I stay where I am, closing my eyes.

Rustling leaves from nearby palm trees fill the silence until John clears his throat. "How've you been?"

Fine is the response at the tip of my tongue, but what comes out is, "Exhausted."

"That's sucky. Why aren't you at home?"

I turn my head toward him. "Then Kyle and Andi would wonder what's up," I explain.

John opens his mouth to reply when the back door opens.

"Oh, hey." Andi steps to the back of the couch I'm on, briefly glancing down. "I was looking for you. We're going to play Never Have I Ever. I already grabbed you a drink." I sit up and she hands me a cup filled with Coke mixed with a lot of rum. The smell makes me want to vomit. John furrows his brow.

"Here, you can take this one. I'll go grab one more." Andi holds out the second cup to John as people begin to congregate on the patio.

"It's cool. I'll go grab something." John disappears inside.

Andi begins to rearrange the patio furniture so everyone is able to sit in a circle. A few dining room chairs are brought out for extra seating. Across the circle, Kyle takes a seat on the other couch, chatting with a few others. John comes back out, sitting beside me.

"Trade ya."

I glance over at him.

"Sparkling water with a splash of lime." He holds the cup out. "Thanks."

We switch beverages. John's nose wrinkles at the smell of the alcohol.

"She's not a light pourer," I mutter.

Andi claps her hands twice to get everyone's attention. "Okay, rules are simple. If you've done the thing that someone says, you drink. If you haven't you don't. Please be creative here, people. We want this to be fun. I'll go first. Never have I ever used my

rudimentary French to get out of a speeding ticket." Andi throws a wicked grin my way.

I take a tiny sip of my drink, thankful it doesn't make me gag. John's eyebrows lift in surprise.

"Okay, never have I ever skinny dipped in Fremont pool," I say.

Andi rolls her eyes, taking a swig of her drink.

The thing about playing Never Have I Ever with your friends is they know everything you've done, so they can target you. If I had alcohol in my cup, I'd probably be tipsy by now.

Crystal, one of the partygoers, finishes taking a sip of her drink and then says, "Never have I ever kissed Kyle."

Andi and I both drink.

"No, not like some innocent kiss on the cheek," Crystal protests. "Like a real kiss, on the mouth."

Kyle's eyes dart to me. My fingers tighten on my cup, but I don't lift it to my lips. From the corner of my eye, I see John watching me. For a moment, I panic, thinking Crystal is going to call me out. Instead, she frowns. Andi glances over at me, rolling her eyes. For years people have tried to use various techniques to get us to admit that our little trio isn't really a trio. People always assume one or both of us has had a fling with Kyle. And…well…

Crystal points to John. He thinks for a moment. "Never have I ever broken a bone."

I take a sip of my drink.

Andi stumbles over. "There has to be a more creative question," she slurs.

"Sorry, I'll try to think of something better for the next round."

Andi pats his shoulder. I slide over, making room for her to sit. Instead, she takes a seat on the chair beside the couch. My eyes bounce between her and John. When Andi is dating someone, she loves physical contact—hand holding, sitting on laps, giving kisses.

Tonight, she and John haven't been very affectionate toward each other. I'm going to have to ask Andi about it once she's sober.

Two

After nearly passing out at my locker last week, Kyle seems more watchful. Even though I feel miserable I make myself sit through another lunch. Andi asks if I'm ready for our Galentine's sleepover. I give her a weak smile. She presented this idea to me while visiting me on my break at work Monday evening.

She grins. "It should be fun." Her eyes shift to Kyle and she gives him a quick wink. I'm curious to know what they are in cahoots about, but I'm too tired to care.

Nausea and vomiting seem to be the last of the first trimester symptoms that don't want to let up. I spend the next couple hours hunched over my toilet. I'm praying everything is expelled from my system before my evening with Andi. If I don't pig out on junk food, she'll know something is up. Kneeling on my hard tile bathroom floor, I debate if I should text Kyle and invite him over tonight. It would ruin our Galentine's Day, but at least they would both know. Checking the time, I have thirty minutes before I'm supposed to be over at Andi's. I clean myself up a little and head out.

Walking into Andi's room, it looks like a tornado hit. Clothes are everywhere. Several outfits have been abandoned on her bed. I notice a pair of jeans and a black sequined top hanging over her computer chair. This can only mean one thing. I groan.

"Hey lady, no time to stand there. The guys are gonna be here any minute." She gives me a playful swat on the butt.

"What happened to staying in?"

"I decided staying in was no fun." Andi walks over to her bed and shuffles some clothes around; a few pieces slide to the floor. "Hey, chop, chop! Like, seriously, they will be here any minute. What's up with you?"

"Nothing."

"That's yours." She points to the computer chair.

I reluctantly start to change. When I go to button the jeans, I cannot get them closed. I've been living in sweats, but I didn't think clothes would stop fitting already. Sucking in a little, I can almost get them closed, but then I wouldn't be able to breathe or sit all night. I'm sure pants digging into my stomach isn't good for the baby. I search her cluttered dresser and find a hair tie. Now let's hope the shirt is long enough to cover.

I'm not surprised to see John standing in Andi's living room. I assume the guy next to him is my date. That is until Andi walks in, nods at John, and then kisses the new guy on the cheek.

"Ta-da! You can't even call it a blind date. You two know each other." Andi beams. John turns and his eyes widen.

On the ride over I get to know Andi's date, Eric. He was at her party last weekend. They went out for coffee earlier this week. This is date number two. I cringe at the fact Andi made this a double date. What if I ruin the night? My stomach somersaults and I take a deep breath. John glances over at me, brows furrowed.

Andi chooses Applebee's for dinner. The hostess seats us at a booth against the wall. Eric is a gentleman and gestures for Andi to slide in first. John glances at me and slides in first, no doubt anticipating I might need a quick exit. The table has a faint scent of disinfectant which makes my stomach turn. I try to breathe through my mouth, but it's not helping much.

The waitress comes to the table and takes our drink order.

"Oh, can we also get the sampler platter?" Andi asks.

The waitress nods. "Be right back," she says cheerfully.

"Just FYI, you will have to fight Mac for the mozzarella sticks. Those are her favorite." Andi winks at John.

John looks over at me and I give him a slight grin. Just the thought of food is enough to make me want to gag. "Yep, they are a favorite, but I had a big lunch, so I guess I'll share."

Andi gives me a curious look. A small frown accompanies John's furrowed brow. I want to ask what he's thinking. After all, he's the only person who knows my secret and undoubtedly has thoughts about this situation.

The waitress returns with our drinks and then sets down the platter in the center of the table. The smell of fried mozzarella and wings pushes me over the edge.

"Excuse me." I bolt from the table.

I'm hunched over the toilet when I hear the bathroom door creak. "Mac?" Andi calls. My stomach tightens. I have nothing left in my system. I dry heave a few times and then sit back on my heels. I reach up to flush the toilet. As I watch the water swirl down all I can think of are string lights.

Sitting on Andi's back porch, I watched as the weathered string lights spun, like water circling a drain. I closed my eyes and let myself slowly sink into the wicker couch. A dried-up leaf flattened against the back door screeched along the metal frame. I threw my hands over my ears to dull the sound.

"You live," Andi proclaimed as she plopped down on the wicker sofa across from me.

"That might be a premature statement," I muttered.

"Maybe next time set a limit. You're so tiny, one drink is probably more than enough," Andi remarked.

She was probably right. My five-foot-three frame could only tolerate so much alcohol.

"So, what happened last night?"

Andi's question stumped me. I tried to think back to the beginning of the night. I ran a flat iron over my honey blonde hair, and threw on some eyeliner and mascara before heading out the door. My parents were arguing in the kitchen. This had been the third audible fight in a week and I wasn't sure what to do. My parents had fought before but this time something felt different. It was almost like I was waiting for a bomb to detonate. I could hear the ticking of the timer but couldn't see the clock to know how much time was left. So, when I arrived at Andi's, I grabbed a beer. One became two and two became three.

At some point, Kyle found me. He offered to take me home but that was the last place I wanted to be. I vaguely remembered stumbling to his car. We sat in the front seat and talked for a bit. Once we were out of things to say I leaned over and kissed him. His lips moved slowly at first but then he embraced it. After a minute he pulled away.

"What are we doing?" he asked.

"You're distracting me," I stated, leaning forward again.

Kyle backed off. "We can't do this."

"We were doing just fine." I stared at him.

He looked up, his eyes meeting mine. "If we do this, it's just a distraction. Just for tonight."

"Never to be brought up again. This night never happened," I affirmed.

That was all the assurance Kyle needed. His lips found mine. I clenched my eyes closed, praying that what came next was just a dream.

*"You look freaked," Andi said, interrupting my
turbulent thoughts. "Hopefully you remember something because I'm
sure there are some good stories."*

I walk out of the stall, my mind swirling as much as my stomach.

"Oh my gosh! Are you okay?" Andi asks, pushing off the wall
and starting toward me.

I nod.

She places a hand on my dewy forehead. "No fever, that's weird.
You notoriously run a fever when you're sick."

I walk over to the sink and scoop some water into my mouth.

"When did you start feeling sick? Maybe the fever is coming.
Either way—why are you shaking your head?"

"This isn't the flu."

"Oh, was it something from lunch? The non-existent lunch you
ate. Did you snack when you got home?"

I shake my head.

"It doesn't matter. If you weren't feeling good, why didn't you
say something?"

I don't want to break the news in the bathroom of an Applebee's
while our dates are waiting at the table. Kyle doesn't even know yet,
but Andi is going to do everything to make sure I feel better and am
back to one hundred percent. Unfortunately, this isn't a twenty-four-
hour bug. I can tell Andi is waiting for an answer while
simultaneously making a list of cold and flu medicines to pick up
from the pharmacy.

I take a deep breath, steeling myself before saying, "I'm
pregnant."

Andi blinks. Once. Twice. "Say that again."

"Um, see, the night of your party, I had a few drinks and the
night was a little hazy, but…"

"Yeah, Kyle filled me in. He said he kept you company for a bit."

Suddenly, the puzzle pieces click, and she begins shaking her head. Before I can get a word out Andi's moving toward the door. She rips the door open, scaring an elderly lady walking up. She sidesteps the woman and storms back to the table.

As I approach, Andi's face darkens to a deep shade of red. I slide into my seat and take a small sip of water.

"Is everything okay?" Eric asks.

Andi glares at me. "Nope."

"I'm sorry," I whisper.

"Sorry! You're sorry?" Andi shouts, slamming her hands on the table, causing the silverware to rattle. "Wow, well, that makes me feel *so* much better." Andi's words drip with sarcasm. "How long have you known?"

Eric glances around the restaurant and I know people are quieting down to hear the drama. "Maybe we should finish this outside," he suggests.

"No, Miss Thing is finally talking, so spill."

I bite my lip as tears well in my eyes. I take a ragged breath. "Look, I wasn't sure exactly how long I would be pregnant."

"What does that even mean?" She throws her hands in the air. The restaurant chatter dims and a few tables turn toward ours.

My lip quivers. "The success rate of a pregnancy in my family, especially a first pregnancy, is slim to none. So, I thought that in a few weeks…" I can't finish. I hear a hushed "oh" from beside me.

"Does Kyle know?" Andi asks.

I shake my head.

"So, what exactly was your plan? Go on like nothing's happening?"

"No." My voice breaks.

Andi rolls her eyes. "Okay, so are you hoping you miscarry? What if you don't? Are you getting an abortion? That way no one ever has to know. How's that working?"

"I don't know, okay? I don't know." At this point I'm sure we've captured the attention of the whole restaurant. I can't sit at the table anymore. I walk out, leaving the others behind.

It's not like I haven't thought about what to do, try to formulate some sort of plan. I was afraid to say anything if I was going to miscarry. Maybe deep down I'm still hoping to. Then I wouldn't have to look my best friend in the face and tell her that I hooked up with our best friend.

I mean, Andi and I met in second grade and had been inseparable. At the start of sixth grade, Kyle was put at our little group of desks. The three of us have been thick as thieves since. We are now in our senior year. It always seemed there was an unspoken rule—Kyle was off limits. I broke the rule that night and now I feel like I have to explain the whole evening, all the events leading up to the drinks and the car and then both of them will know World War III is breaking out at my house. I didn't intend to drink as much as I did. I thought one or two would make me briefly drown out the fighting I had left behind. Now, war is still waging and I'm holding a grenade that will make everything worse.

"Hey," John whispers.

I look up. John's face blurs from my tears. I wipe them away. "Hi."

"Ready to go?"

I catch a glimpse of Andi and Eric walking to the car.

"I guess." I shrug, not moving.

"Yeah, I'm not looking forward to the car ride either. Try not to puke on me." He smiles, but my eyes fill with tears again. "Too soon?" John studies me a minute. "I could grab you a Sprite or ginger ale for—" I shake my head vigorously. "Okay."

The tension in the car is suffocating. Every so often I catch Andi glare at me through the rearview mirror. I'm trying to breathe and praying my stomach settles enough to make it home. I feel a light tap on my knee and peek over.

You okay? John mouths.

I shake my head.

John reaches over, giving my knee a light squeeze. Even though it's a small gesture, it loosens some of the knots in my stomach. John turns back to the window. I pull my phone out and send a text to Kyle, asking if it's okay to come over.

Date night go bad? he responds.

You knew?!?

Yeah, Andi told me earlier this week.

When we get back to Andi's house, I'm the first out of the car. I move over to the edge of her driveway, the knot in my stomach tightening instantly. John walks around the car and joins me. "Hey, are you all right?"

I ignore his question. "Why did you come tonight?" I whisper.

"I didn't know it was you. Right before the party last week, Andi told me she didn't think we were working but knew the perfect person for me. She didn't give a name. I was intrigued."

I nod.

"Even if I knew it was you, what was I supposed to do?"

I look up at him. "I don't know. Say no."

"Yeah, but it's Andi. She's persistent. She would have kept trying and what reason could I give her?"

"Good point." I look over at the car where Andi and Eric are still sitting.

"Maybe it's better I didn't know who she set me up with." He shrugs. "So, now what?"

My throat tightens. "I have to tell Kyle."

I stop talking when the window rolls down.

"We're gonna go grab food," Andi explains, glowering at me.

"Okay."

Andi looks at John. "Sorry your night was ruined. I feel like I owe you dinner and a new date." She throws another scowl my way.

"Don't worry about it," John says.

Andi is still boiling as she rolls up the window and backs out of the driveway.

"Well, I better go." I begin making my way to my car.

He smirks. "Thanks for making the night interesting."

"I don't know if I would call it that. It's kind of like my worst nightmare. Right up there with recognizing someone at the clinic."

"You survived. You'll get through this."

"Let's hope." I cross my fingers, then give a small wave. "Night, John."

"Night, Mac."

Kyle's sprawled out on his bed in sweats and a T-shirt, his mahogany brown hair disheveled.

"Uh-oh, it must have been really bad if you're crying." He reaches for the remote and turns the television off. "It's still early. What happened?"

"I have to tell you something." My voice cracks.

Kyle sits up straighter. "Okay…"

"You remember that night at Andi's?"

"Yeah."

"Well, we were stupid, and we didn't think things through."

He quirks a brow. "I thought we agreed to never speak of it."

"Yeah, but—"

"Mac, c'mon—"

"I'm pregnant," I blurt out.

He stills immediately. "Pregnant?"

"Yeah."

He sits there like a statue for a few minutes, the silence stretching on. Little wrinkles appear on his forehead. He holds up his index finger. "So, wait, her party was like two, three months ago."

"About thirteen weeks ago," I state.

"How long have you known about this?"

"About three-ish."

"*What*?" Kyle leaps off his bed.

"I didn't want everyone freaking out if there was nothing to freak out about. There's a high rate of miscarriages in my family, so I wasn't sure how long I'd actually be pregnant."

"And you didn't think I had a right to know at all? What the hell, Mac?"

"You have a right to know. I just—you have a scholarship and college plans. We aren't even a couple. I didn't want you worrying."

"You are such an idiot," he snaps.

"Hey!"

"So, last week, when I asked if you were doing all right, what was that? Was that related to the pregnancy?" I don't even get a chance to answer the question. "It was, wasn't it? I knew something was wrong. I can't believe this. Does Andi know?"

I bite my lip.

"*Andi knows!*"

"I'm sorry. We were out and I got sick at the restaurant. You know Andi. She went into nurse mode and I just… I…" A tear slides down my cheek. I wipe it away quickly.

He inhales deeply before letting it out. "Pregnant."

I nod, hot tears continuing to roll down my cheeks. "I'm really sorry. I handled this all wrong."

"You think?" he snarls.

I start crying harder, burying my face in my hands. His arms wrap around me. "I want to kill you right now."

"I know," I sob.

"It's okay." He holds me until I settle down. "So, what now?" he asks.

"I have an ultrasound on Monday and then I scheduled a doctor's appointment Thursday. You can come to one or both. Or none." I step away from him.

"Which ones do you want me at?" He backs up and sits on his bed.

I shrug. "It's up to you. Everything is after school. I planned around my work schedule."

"I'll come to both."

I nod and bite my nail. Kyle picks at a piece of lint on his sheet. "Mac, I shouldn't have to say this, but I will *always* worry when it comes to you." He looks up at me. "You and Andi are my girls. I will be there for you no matter what. You *have* to tell me what is going on. If you feel like you might…" He swallows. "You call me. Don't text me, *call* me. Got it?"

I nod.

On the way to my car I send a message to Andi, letting her know I've talked to Kyle. I'm not surprised when I don't receive a response.

Three

Monday morning, Kyle's waiting by my locker.

"How are you?" he asks.

"Fine." I unlock my locker and shove my backpack inside.

He leans in close to me. "Any morning sickness?"

"In my case, it's like afternoon-evening sickness," I reply. I look around the hall and spot Andi, her locker three down from mine. Her eyes narrow when she sees me. She doesn't even venture over, just turns and heads toward her class. Tears begin to sting my eyes. I shut them tight, willing myself not to cry.

"What's wrong?" Kyle asks, a bit panicked.

"Andi's never going to speak to me again."

Kyle glances over his shoulder in the direction Andi had just been. He looks back at me. "We majorly messed up. She'll be mad for a while, but she'll talk to you again."

I shake my head, tears forcing their way out.

Kyle wraps me in a hug. "This is weird. You've always been the quiet, stoic one. Andi is the one who wears her emotions on her sleeve."

"I know." I sniffle.

By lunch I'm feeling nauseous and exhausted. It's a relief not having to pretend at school. Home is a different story. Kyle's seated at our usual table. I pull out a chair, cross my arms, and rest my head on them.

"How is she?" I hear Andi ask from behind me.

"She just came over and laid down. I don't know."

The chair next to me scratches on the linoleum. "You gonna survive?"

I open my eyes to see Andi with her head in the same position as mine, staring at me. Stupid tears. I turn and bury my head in my arms.

"Holy cow. Who is this chick?" Andi rubs my back.

"It's alternate universe Mac," Kyle says, to which I smile. I sit up and Andi drops her hand.

"Seriously, how are you?" There's still an edge to her voice, but there's also genuine concern.

My stomach chooses this time to twist. I clamp my jaw shut and wait for my stomach to settle. No such luck. "I'm going to be sick," I say through gritted teeth. I grab my backpack and head out of the cafeteria.

Andi follows me to the bathroom, taking my backpack as I rush to the closest stall. When I step out, she's leaning against one of the sinks.

"I have study hall, I have to check with Mr. Upstill on an assignment, I had a big breakfast, I'm just not super hungry…" She continues listing excuses I've made the past few weeks of why I wouldn't be at the table or why I wasn't eating. "I can't believe I didn't catch on sooner."

"There was one day I thought you were gonna start grilling me," I admit.

She scrunches up her nose, thinking for a moment, then chuckles. "You were acting so weird. It was your favorite lunch and you wouldn't touch it. That was the day you got up from the table and proclaimed you had to finish your English paper."

"I would have much rather been in the library, word vomiting on the page than actually…"

Andi wrinkles her nose.

"Come on, it stinks in here." I grab my backpack and we head out of the bathroom toward the cafeteria. The bell rings and a flood of students barrels toward us. I move over to the wall and wait for the halls to clear.

Kyle spots us and makes his way over. "You good?"

I nod.

"Can I get you anything?"

I shake my head.

"I'll meet you after school?"

"What's after school?" Andi asks.

"The ultrasound," Kyle says, eyes still on me.

"Wait, I wanna come."

I turn toward her. "You do?"

"Uh, yeah. If I'm going to be an aunt, I wanna see the little tyke."

Kyle's body goes rigid. We haven't discussed if we're keeping it. My focus last night was telling Kyle that there was a baby, that's it. What if I walk into the appointment today and there's no heartbeat? I haven't let myself fully consider the options yet. There definitely hasn't been a discussion between Kyle and me.

"What? Can I not come?" Andi asks, offended.

I bite my lip. "What if you come to the next one?" *If there is a next one*, I think.

Andi shakes her head. "Whatever." She turns and heads to class.

"I'll see you later," Kyle mumbles and walks off in the opposite direction.

I stay leaning against the wall until the bell rings, signaling class has started, then walk out to my car. It dawns on me while I'm

scrolling Google looking at all the exciting things to expect
at the beginning of the second trimester that the school will alert my
parents if I miss attendance. I quickly call my mom and tell her I had
to leave school because I'm sick.

"Oh no. Well, look, I have a light day here. Let me just wrap up
one thing and I can come home."

"No!"

"No?"

"I mean, that's not necessary. I was able to schedule a doctor's
appointment. Guess they had a cancelation or something. I'll just go
rest and then head to the doctor." My heart is beating a million miles
a minute. I sit, silently begging her not to leave work.

"All right, but if you need anything, call me."

I have my chair leaned back and the radio blasting when I hear a
faint knock on the passenger window. I peek over and spot Kyle.

I unlock my car and he climbs inside, turning down the volume
of the stereo.

"You want me to drive?" he asks.

I don't answer, I just climb out of the car and round to the
passenger side.

Kyle's adjusting the seat and the mirrors when he asks, "How
long have you been out here?"

"Since lunch."

He nods. He backs out of the parking spot. I pull up the
directions and let him know to turn left out of the parking lot.

"So, do you still feel gross?" he asks as we wait in the line of
cars.

"Kinda."

"Is there anything that helps? We can stop somewhere."

I think for a moment. "I could go for a lemonade. And not just
any lemonade. Tropicana lemonade, and something salty."

"Not just any lemonade, huh?"

"I can't really explain it. There's just something about Tropicana that doesn't make me want to puke my guts out. I've just been rolling with it."

"Gotcha."

Kyle stops at the convenience store and grabs a bottle of Tropicana lemonade and three different types of salty snacks. I go for the classic potato chips first, but a few chips in I start to feel queasy.

"This was a mistake." I set the bag of chips down.

"Do I need to pull over?"

I shake my head. He glances over and I shake it again. I take a swig of my lemonade and wait until we reach the doctor's office.

Lying on the table, cold jelly on my exposed midsection, I watch the little wand as the ultrasound technician glides it around my belly. She pauses a moment, hits a few buttons, and then moves the wand. After several minutes, she looks over. "Would you like to hear the heartbeat?"

"There's a heartbeat?" I squeeze Kyle's hand.

"There's a heartbeat." Her words are chipper.

"Yeah," Kyle replies.

It's silent in the room.

"Yes, we would like to hear the heartbeat," Kyle clarifies.

Suddenly, a rapid pulsing sound fills the space.

"Is that normal?" I feel myself starting to panic. I grip Kyle's hand tighter. He leans in closer, overlapping my hand with both of his.

"It's beautiful and strong," the tech informs us.

I breathe a sigh of relief. Kyle examines the monitor that the tech has turned toward us.

"See that little flutter there?" She points at the screen. "That's the heartbeat."

Walking out of the doctor's office, I send a message to Andi, giving her an update. She replies with a thumbs-up emoji. At school the next day, she avoids the lunch table and barely acknowledges me when I walk into English. When I check in with Kyle, he says he's received the same amount of communication, probably less.

Now, dressed in another paper gown, I look over at Kyle sitting in the vinyl chair next to me and give him a small smile. "Are you okay?"

He glances up. "Yeah. You?"

I don't get a chance to answer before the obstetrician walks in.

"Hello, my name is Dr. Lisa Huff. How are we doing today?"

I introduce myself and Kyle. She begins with questions about everything I've experienced so far. When I mention my concerns for miscarrying, she listens patiently and then conducts an exam, reassuring me everything looks completely normal. She gives me a couple pamphlets and a list of symptoms to watch for.

"Please call my office anytime, for anything. My job during this pregnancy is to take care of you and your baby."

I cringe at the term "your baby." I don't know if this will be my baby. I smile and thank her for her time anyway.

"So, now what?" Kyle asks when we get in the car.

"I don't want to be a parent," I state.

"So, I think we still have a few weeks, right? To…"

"I'm not getting an abortion."

He stares at me. "So, what?"

"There are women out there who would kill to be in my position. Women who want a baby, want a family. I think we should consider adoption."

"Are you sure?"

I shrug. I'm not sure of anything. "It just seems like the most logical option."

"If that's what you want."

"What do you want?" I ask.

"I don't know." He rubs his hand over his face. "You're right. I don't want to be a parent, but look at you. Pregnancy is taking its toll. Are you sure you want to put your body through another six months of this?"

"Yes." *No*, my mind counters. Throwing up daily is one thing. The expanding midsection, wild mood swings, swollen ankles, hemorrhoids, backaches, and all the other joyous symptoms I'd read about are not anything to look forward to. Not to mention labor. Especially if there's no reward at the end, like keeping the baby. That's what every woman says makes the whole pregnancy worth it: looking into that new little face. I try to keep my expression neutral.

"Well, then I guess we are doing the adoption thing."

"Kyle, are you…?"

"Stop asking," he barks. "I'm not sure about any of this, okay?"

"Okay." My voice breaks.

He sighs. "I'm sorry. It's just a lot."

I nod. He takes my hand. "If you're sure, then I'll support you."

Four

The next day, Kyle and I are sitting at the lunch table. I'm nibbling on a slice of pizza when Andi pulls out a chair and takes a seat next to me. "You're eating."

"Yep. Finally getting my appetite back." She gives me a slight grin, then begins to unpack her lunch. I glance over at Kyle, who looks at Andi and then back at me.

"So, do you have plans this weekend?" he asks.

Andi shakes her head. "You?" she asks, finally turning her attention to Kyle.

"Not really. Thinking of going to the batting cages."

Andi nods. "Cool, cool."

Lunch is tense and when we go our separate ways, Andi and I walk silently to English.

When I arrive home that afternoon, my mom tells me she has some things she wants to discuss. Since we are sitting down to dinner as a family, I figure now is as good a time as any to give them my life update. I sit at the table, Chinese food in front of me, thankful I'm ravenous. As soon as my dad takes his seat, I grab the container of fried rice and pile it on my plate. I go for the orange chicken next. Mid-scoop, I glance at my parents. Neither of them has made a move for the food. They exchange a look.

I set the orange chicken down, sticking the spoon inside. "What's going on?"

"Your dad has decided to move out," my mom bites.

My dad throws a disapproving look at my mom then turns his attention to me. "I've found an apartment a few blocks from here," he says, his tone gentle. "It's a two bedroom, so you'll have a room. It's still in your school district, so there are no major disruptions to your schedule."

"Wait, slow down. What?" I ask as my brain catches up to the fact my dad is moving out. Suddenly the mound of food on my plate seems unappealing. Pushing my plate away, I glance at my parents. "How often will I be over there?"

"We are still working out some details, but for now we are thinking the weekdays here and then Friday, Saturday, and Sunday will be spent with your dad," my mom answers.

"Is it a ground-floor apartment?" I ask.

"No, it's a third story." My dad gives me a quizzical look.

Stairs to a third-story apartment at nine months pregnant is going to suck.

My parents are silent. My dad opens his mouth but then quickly closes it. Now is my time.

"Well, since we are sharing life altering news, I have to tell you…" I have no idea how to deliver this news. I fill my lungs with air.

"Yes?" my dad asks.

"I'm pregnant," I breathe out.

My dad inhales sharply. My mom's face instantly hardens.

"Maclaren Fay Young. This better be a joke," my mom says, gritting her teeth.

I chuckle. "Why would I joke about this?"

That's a bad response. Her eyes narrow and she glares at me. "How far along?"

"I'm pretty much out of my first trimester," I answer.

"Go to your room." Her glare turns icy.

"Mom—"

"Maclaren, get out of my kitchen," she snaps. When I don't move, she pushes her chair back and walks out of the room, slamming her bedroom door.

"Peanut—"

"Don't. I just figured you guys should know."

I slide my chair away from the table, grab my keys off the hutch by our front door, and leave the house. Music plays as I drive around town replaying the conversation over and over again. My dad is moving out. When did they decide this? Now that I think about it, they haven't had an audible fight in over a week. Is this why?

The fights I've overheard range from my dad working too many hours to my mom being too uptight. The ones I hate are when they argue about me or how to raise me. *Have they ever been on the same page?* This thought crosses my mind and I chuckle. "Guess not," I say to myself. If they were then they wouldn't be getting divorced. Are they getting divorced? Or is my dad moving out while they work on things? I highly doubt they are staying together.

And just like that, the timer is up. The bomb has gone off and I'm now standing in the midst of the rubble, my ears ringing.

After an hour or so of just driving, I find myself parking in front of Kyle's. I catch Kyle pulling the black trash can to the street. He drops the can in the street and then spots my car. He walks over and I roll my window down.

"What are you doing here?"

"I figured I'd stop by and say my final goodbyes." I crack a half-smile.

"What does that mean?"

"It means my parents are aware of my situation and they are furious."

From the entrance of Kyle's house we hear his name. Kyle peeks over the roof of my car.

"Who's that?" Kyle's dad asks.

"It's Maclaren," he calls back.

"Perfect. Can you two come inside?"

I stare up at Kyle. What if his parents know? What if my parents called them? Except that doesn't make any sense because they don't know who the father is. I didn't even get to that piece.

I climb out of the car and follow Kyle inside. Kyle stays by my side as we trail his dad into the living room.

His dad gestures for us to sit, his mom already in the recliner. I take a seat on the couch and Kyle sits beside me. Both of his parents focus on me.

"Sweetie, your dad called us. He said they were looking for you, that you weren't answering your phone."

Of course I wasn't answering my phone. It's sitting on my bed, right next to my wallet.

"Your dad's very worried. He mentioned there was a bit of an argument and he wanted to make sure you were okay."

Argument? There was barely a conversation. I shake my head. "That's not exactly accurate."

"Um, Maclaren shared some news today that her parents may have taken badly," Kyle starts. He wipes his hands down the side of his pants. "Um, okay." He glances at me, seemingly getting permission. I nod, and he looks back to his parents. "Maclaren is pregnant." He pauses. "And…and I'm the father."

His mom sits up. "I didn't realize you two had gotten together," she says.

Kyle's dad chuckles. "How do you think they made a baby?"

"No, I mean, I didn't know they had started dating. I thought they were just friends. When did that change?"

"It hasn't really changed," I answer.

"We're not a couple. It was a one-night thing," Kyle says.

"If you're not a couple, how does a baby fit into the picture?" Kyle's dad asks.

I peek over at Kyle. "Well, we've discussed giving it up for adoption. We know that neither of us are ready for parenthood."

"Pregnancy and adoption are big commitments," Kyle's mom says.

"I know. We haven't taken any of this lightly."

It's silent as the Harts process. "The announcement is quite shocking. How did your parents take the news?"

Tears sting my eyes. Kyle laces his fingers with mine. "Still weird," he murmurs.

"Well, my mom opened our family discussion with the announcement that they are separating and then I concluded the evening by telling them I was pregnant."

Kyle's grip on my hand tightens. "Wait, separating?" he whispers.

I nod. I know the tears that start to fall are not just hormones. My dad's moving out. They have already figured out a schedule of where I'll be spending my time. The numb feeling from the car is slowly dissipating. Now that I've had time to digest the news, my heart starts to break. I pull my hand from Kyle's and bury my face in my palms, beginning to sob.

"Oh, sweetheart," Kyle's mom breathes.

"I'm sorry," I blubber. Kyle pulls me to his side and holds tight. I turn and bury my face on his shoulder.

"You're okay. I'm right here," Kyle whispers.

Once I've collected myself, I lean back, realizing we're alone. I smooth my hands over my barely-there baby bump and catch Kyle studying my belly.

"You didn't have to tell them," I say.

Kyle shrugs, leaning back. "Eventually you'll be too big not to notice. They were going to find out."

"They were so calm. Like, they just sat here and listened."

"Yeah, I doubt the conversation is over. And I'm sure there's a lecture waiting for me once you're gone," Kyle sighs.

Suddenly, we hear the front door open and Andi runs into the living room. She spots us on the couch before she doubles over, gasping for air.

I sit up. "What's wrong?"

She points at me, but no words come out of her mouth. She holds up her phone and then points to Kyle.

"You're going to have to use your words." I look her over. "I don't see any blood. You came racing in here so you still have your motor function."

"911," she gasps, straightening and taking a few deep breaths. "He texted 911."

911 was our code for any crisis. When Andi's dog Misty was going to be put down, she texted 911 and Kyle and I both hurried to her house. When Kyle's grandpa had a heart attack, he sent the code and we met him at the hospital. If two of us were together and we needed the third we would say, *911-M* or *911-D*, using the first initial of one of our names, letting the other know who was experiencing the catastrophe.

"You guys are just relaxing on the couch. Is everything okay? Is the baby okay?"

I nod. "I'm fine."

"Then what's with the 911?" She wiggles her way between me and Kyle.

Kyle explains what transpired before the text was sent.

"We are going to have to change our system. Especially when referring to this one." She points at me. "Now that she's prego, 911 takes on a whole new meaning."

"Sorry," Kyle says.

She turns to me. "That's intense."

Since I didn't eat dinner, I'm starving. I ask for a snack and Kyle jumps up, heading for the kitchen. Andi and I follow.

"Um, we have leftover pasta, leftover meatloaf…" He shifts some items around. "Ham and turkey, if you want a sandwich." He closes the fridge and goes to the pantry. "Peanut butter, an assortment of chips or crackers. Anything sound good?"

I stand there for a moment, thinking. "Do you have grape jelly?"

"I think so."

"Can I get a PB&J?"

"Absolutely." He heads toward the fridge, then pauses. "Andi, do you want anything?"

I glance at Andi. Her jaw is clenched. She takes a deep breath and then lets it out slowly. I take in her stance, all muscles tense.

"Are you okay?" I ask.

"Nope. I'm good," she answers Kyle. She pulls out a chair and sits at the table. I take a seat next to her and catch her slide her chair a bit away from mine. I open my mouth to say something when she turns toward me.

"How was the appointment?"

"We don't have to talk about it." I look over at Kyle and then at the table.

Andi takes another deep breath. She is pissed and I have no idea how to make it better. I glance back up at her.

"It's fine. I want to know."

"Andi, I didn't mean to mess things up. You have to know that, okay? I just…" Just what? Tears pool in my eyes and I blink hard.

"You guys made a choice." Her blurry form shrugs. "I'm not particularly thrilled, but doesn't mean I stopped caring."

"I know." I wipe my eyes and square my shoulders. Right now, I'm just grateful that she even showed up. "You have to tell me if it's too much."

She rolls her eyes, turning toward Kyle, who has taken a seat on my right. He slides the sandwich in front of me.

"Well?"

Kyle swallows. "The baby has a strong heartbeat. Mac's good. Everything is progressing smoothly."

"Good." Andi leans forward and rips off a corner of my PB&J.

"Andi, we're not keeping it," I say.

We give Andi the lowdown on our baby plan, which she supports one hundred percent.

When I walk into my house, the lights in the kitchen are on. I set my keys on the hutch and brace for the grounding of a lifetime. When I round the corner, both my parents are sitting at the table. My dad seems to breathe a sigh of relief when he sees me, but then I catch his eyes shift to my mom, whose face is stern.

"Take a seat."

I do as instructed.

My mom takes a deep breath.

"Here's the plan. Since you know you are almost out of your first trimester, I'm assuming you've been to the doctor?"

She waits for me to confirm. When I nod, she continues. "You will maintain all of your doctor's appointments and ultrasounds. We will make sure to stock up on all your prenatal vitamins and double-check to see if there are any other supplements you may need. Some women become anemic during pregnancy, so it may be beneficial to

take an iron supplement. It's a good question for your doctor. When's your next appointment?"

I glare at her, not answering.

"Maclaren, keeping up with your medical care is extremely important right now."

"Okay," I quip.

"Along with keeping up with all appointments, you may want to limit your activities. I'll be calling the school Monday to see if there are options for online, or maybe you can have a condensed schedule and come home early."

"Wait, what?"

"Honey, eight hours of school is a lot and I know some of your classes are nowhere near each other. I'm afraid it will be too much stress on you. It would be good for you to be able to come home and rest, take naps. Being home will limit the amount of physical exertion as well."

"You can't just pull me out of school," I snap.

"I'm not pulling you out of school. You need your education. I'm just examining all our options." She sighs before adding, "I'm also thinking we should reach out to Mr. Cruz and limit your hours at work."

"Forget it!" I shove my chair away from the table and stalk to my room, slamming the door and locking it. I kick off my shoes, grab my phone, and then curl up under my covers. I immediately text Andi and Kyle.

You okay? Andi responds.

I send the little shrug emoji to the group then switch to a private conversation with Andi.

I know you are trying to be supportive. I don't think I will ever say I'm sorry enough, but I meant what I said. If you don't want to talk about stuff with me, I get it.

Three little dots dance at the bottom of my screen, disappear, then start dancing again.

Mac, IDK what to feel right now. I'm simultaneously furious and panicky. I want to strangle you and Kyle for what you 2 did. Our whole dynamic has shifted now. However, sitting across from you telling me this is high risk and having Kyle text 911, I thought my heart was going to explode. You're my best friend and have been for like 10+ years now. I can't just drop you and move on with my life. I'd never do that.

I know that. I'm sry!!!!

You have to stop apologizing. We're moving on. If I don't want to know something or don't want to talk of course I'll let you know. It's me. I'm very outspoken. A winky face emoji follows.

You are. I luv u, I respond, along with a heart emoji.

So, can I ask a question?

Yes...

My phone buzzes and Andi's name appears on my screen. I swipe the green phone icon. "Texting not good enough anymore?"

"Why didn't you tell me about your parents?" she blurts out.

Leave it Andi to be direct. "I don't know," I mumble.

"Oh, please. Yes you do. Did you think I wouldn't be able to relate?"

I'm sure Andi would have understood. She has heard her parents fight. However, her parents always make up. Every time I'm in a room with them, they seem so in love. It's hard to fathom them ever fighting. Same with Kyle's parents. If Andi's parents seem perfect, Kyle's parents are saints. Kyle has never mentioned any marital problems between them, ever. I didn't want to be the kid whose parents couldn't make their relationship work.

"You should have talked to me," Andi states.

"I think I was hoping everything would work out." I shake my head. "That's stupid."

"It's not stupid. What's stupid is thinking you had to deal with it alone."

"I did not think that," I say defensively.

"Okay, then why didn't you talk to me? Or talk to us? Why did you choose to hook up with Kyle?" There's an edge to her voice.

I don't have answers to these questions. She's right. If I had just been honest about what was going on maybe I wouldn't have gotten drunk. Maybe Kyle and I wouldn't have ended up in the back of his car and I wouldn't be trying to figure out how to not get emotionally attached to the baby growing inside me. Sniffling, I try to answer, but what comes out instead is a little hiccup. Large hot tears begin rolling down my cheeks.

Andi mutters a few curses. "Mac, ugh. Maybe this wasn't a good night to have this conversation."

"I'm really sorry," I stutter between sobs.

"I know," Andi murmurs. "I know."

She sits on the phone with me until I've stopped crying. As I say goodbye to her, I hear a knock on my door.

"I'm not talking," I yell.

"Peanut, please open the door."

"Not tonight. I'm tired." Which isn't a lie. I listen to my dad's retreating footsteps before I move and begin getting ready for bed. When I open my door, I see the light from the living room lamp illuminating the end of the hallway. I lean out to see who is still awake and spot my dad sitting in his recliner, reading a book.

"Good night," I say.

He closes his book. "Before you go, mind if we talk?"

I take a seat on the couch.

"Tonight was intense and I wanted to know, how are you feeling about everything?"

"You're really moving out?" I meet his eyes.

"It wasn't an easy decision."

I scoff.

"Peanut, you know we've been fighting."

"Yeah, I know. I didn't think you'd do anything without telling me first."

"Maybe we could have handled things a bit differently. It doesn't change the final outcome though."

I stare at the carpet. A tear slides from the corner of my eye and follows my nose down. I hear the pop of the recliner before my dad joins me on the couch.

"What if I don't want to split my time?" I sniffle.

"That is something we can discuss. Given your current predicament, staying in one place might be easier."

I glance up to see him frowning at me.

"This wasn't a planned thing," I say, biting my nail.

"It may not have been planned, but it's happening. You said you were out of your first trimester. How far out?"

"I'll be fourteen weeks on Tuesday." I drop my hands to my belly.

"Oh, wow. Why didn't you say anything sooner?"

"You guys have always talked about how long it took to get me and how you guys always wanted more kids, but it never worked. Aunt Julie had issues conceiving and then had multiple miscarriages before she and Seth stopped trying all together. What if I made the announcement and then something happened?"

"I can understand that. Did you tell anyone about what was happening? I hate to think you've been dealing with this all alone."

I flash back to the waiting room and John. "Someone knew," I whisper.

"Good."

It's quiet for a moment.

"Dad, would it be okay if I wanted to move in with you?" I go back to biting my nail.

"Honey, you are established here. I think staying with your mom would be the best option."

"She has everything planned out. I'll be miserable. I don't want that."

He sighs. "We'll work something out."

"Well, I want to live with you. If I can."

"I know your mom came on strong this evening." My eyes narrow. He holds up his hands. "Peanut, your mom has good intentions. Just think about what she said and some points she made. If you feel like you will be able to manage everything, we can have a discussion." My dad leans over, kisses my forehead, and then stands. "Sleep well."

Five

Now that all the important people know, I feel it's safe to tell Mr. Cruz about my situation. I knock on the office doorframe and Mr. Cruz looks up from the mound of papers on his desk.

"Can I come in?"

He gestures to the plastic chairs in front of his desk. I take a seat and then square my shoulders. "I'm pregnant," I say. No better way to break the news.

He leans back in his chair.

"I know the last few weeks have been rough, but I promise, I'm feeling better, and I will do my best to make sure the pregnancy doesn't affect my work. I know some of my shifts are long and being on my feet might get a little challenging, but I need this job. I promise I will work really hard."

"Woah, woah, woah." He holds up his hands.

"Sorry, I just really need you to know—"

"Maclaren, stop talking for a moment." He sits up. "Let me process this." I take a deep breath while he rubs his hand over his face. "Why didn't you say something sooner?"

"I…" I don't have a reason. I put my job in jeopardy because I didn't say anything.

"I'm glad you finally told me."

I startle at that.

"Maclaren, I eventually put things together. Actually, that's not true. I mentioned my concern to my wife, and she put it together. I didn't want to be the first to say anything, especially if I was wrong."

"Oh."

"Moving forward, I need you to communicate with me. I don't know how to help if I don't know what's going on. Deal?"

"Deal."

"You mentioned long shifts. Do I need to adjust this week's schedule?"

I shake my head.

"Let me know if I do. We can schedule shorter shifts or give you an extra break. If being on your feet becomes an issue, we may be able to bring a stool up front so you can sit. Okay?"

"That sounds reasonable."

"I'm going to let you steer this ship. I'll try to accommodate the best I can. You just let me know what you need."

I nod. "Thanks."

That evening, I'm sitting in my room sketching on my iPad when there's a knock on the door. My mom peeks in. "Hey hon, you should probably think about heading for bed."

"I will in a few minutes."

"Maclaren, it's important to make sure you get plenty of sleep, especially at this stage."

I don't respond, rolling my eyes.

"Don't cop an attitude, young lady," she reprimands. "Are you working on homework?"

I shake my head.

"Then wrap it up. I'll be back in five minutes." She turns, walking away. "Five minutes," she calls.

I let out a little growl but continue to sketch. I try to ignore the time at the top left of my screen, except now it's all I can focus on. Peeling my eyes away from the time, I stare at my unfinished sketch for a minute, then hit the trash icon. The little pop-up asking if I'm sure appears in the center of my screen. I'm about to hit yes when another knock comes at my door. I glance at the time and grit my teeth.

"Hey, peanut." My dad walks in, looking over my shoulder. "What's wrong with that?"

"I don't know. Nothing."

My dad leans over and hits no. "Keep it for a while. If you still hate it tomorrow, then you can delete it."

"Thanks."

He places a kiss on my temple. "How was today? How are you feeling?"

"Eh, to both."

The next knock on the doorframe is the one I didn't want. I roll my eyes. My dad catches me, giving me a disapproving look.

"Bedtime," my mom says.

"I'm honestly not really tired," I remark.

"Maclaren, I'm not arguing with you. Please just trust me. It's not just about you anymore."

"Oh my gosh." I shake my head and crawl off my bed. I force past my parents and head toward the bathroom. As I get ready for bed, my parents' voices carry through the door, slowly growing louder.

"I didn't say that. Please stop putting words in my mouth," my dad yells and a door slams. I stand there staring at myself in the mirror. I'm so sick of my parents arguing, especially when it involves me. I quickly brush my teeth, rinse my face, and then head to my room.

As I told my mother, I'm not tired. Crawling into bed, I rub my hands slowly down my pudgy midsection, like I had one too many cookies for dessert. I know women have said that one day they just…pop. I wonder when that is going to happen. Until then, I hate every piece of clothing in my closet. Nothing fits correctly.

I grab my iPad and pull up the sketch I was working on earlier. *How would this work?* Grabbing my throw blanket, I get up, testing the idea out in the mirror. As I work out details in my head, I add pieces to the sketch that would make the design functional. Before I realize it, it's a quarter to eleven. I set my iPad aside and lie down, hoping my brain will quiet so I can sleep.

Since agreeing we were not ready to be parents, I began researching different adoption agencies. I'm looking at one while sitting at lunch. I slide my phone over to Kyle. "What do you think about this one?"

Kyle picks up the phone, chuckling at the name, before he scrolls through the home page.

"Hey, what we looking at?" Andi asks, sitting down.

I begin to bite my nail.

"It's worth making an appointment." Kyle pushes my phone back toward me.

"Appointment for what?" Andi's eyes flick down to my belly and then back to my face.

"When do you think you're going to call Mother Goose Adoption?" Kyle asks, a grin on his face.

Andi breathes a sigh of relief. "Sounds like something straight out of a nursey rhyme. That cannot be a real place."

I nudge my phone toward her. She peruses the site before handing it back. "I can't believe it actually seems legit."

"What's a good time for you?" I look at Kyle. Andi turns her attention to her lunch.

Kyle gives me his schedule and I tell him I will make an appointment after school.

It's silent as Andi and I walk to class. Andi inhales deep before asking, "How is everything at home?"

"Tense."

"What do they think about you giving the baby up?"

I bite my nail again. "Just more ammo for them to use against each other," I mumble.

Andi stops us outside the classroom. "What does that mean?"

"*Jim, she has no idea what she's getting into. Also, if she is going to give the baby up, she needs to be taking better care of herself.*" I pitch my voice lower to mimic my dad. "*Considering the circumstances, I think she has a handle on this and I think we need to trust her.*" I adjust my voice once more. "*I've been through this. She hasn't. You make it sound like I don't know or trust my daughter at all. Well, sorry to burst your bubble, but you are not the perfect parent around here. You're barely here to be a parent.*" I shrug. "That's what that means."

Andi frowns. "Mac, that's rough. How are you?"

My lip trembles. I shrug again. The bell rings and I turn toward the door. Andi loops her arm around my shoulders and pulls me close to her side. I lean my head on her, and as we approach our row, I stop and give her a quick hug before releasing her and heading for my desk.

The following week, Kyle and I visit the Mother Goose Adoption Agency. Surprisingly, the only goose I spot in the little lobby is on the door above the name. When I walk inside there is an assortment of nice chairs and a couple of couches. The walls are detailed with nursery rhymes in beautiful script, amazing artwork accompanying

each one. I make a little circle, taking it all in. I check in at
the front desk and then Kyle and I take a seat in a set of plush leather
chairs.

I run my hands down my skirt, clearing the nonexistent wrinkles.

"How ya doing?" Kyle asks.

"Um, okay. Nervous. You?"

"Good." I glance over at him, and he clenches and unclenches
his hands before resting them on his knees, his foot tapping furiously.
He is anything but good.

A woman who looks to be in her mid-forties, with salt and
pepper hair and wearing her glasses like a necklace, walks out and
calls our names. We both stand and make our way to her. She holds
out her hand. "I'm Mrs. Vale. Shall we?"

I nod.

She leads us to her office. There's a picture frame on the back
wall of interracial hands cupping letters that spell out FAMILY. I
take a seat on the couch facing a wall of bookshelves. Some shelves
are full of books, while others hold picture frames of families. The
lower shelves house kids' books and toys.

"Let's start by telling me about yourselves. You're both
seniors?"

I nod.

"What are you looking forward to after high school?" Mrs. Vale
asks, looking at Kyle.

"Well, I have a scholarship for baseball to the University of
Iowa. I also play club baseball and participate in camps throughout
the year."

Mrs. Vale nods and then turns her attention to me.

I shrug. "I don't really have plans."

Kyle turns, keeping his voice low. "That's not exactly true."

Mrs. Vale shifts in her chair. Her eyes bounce between us.

Kyle lifts his eyebrows, prompting me to speak up, but when I don't he says, "She is constantly drawing. She made the skirt she's wearing. She did want to go to school for design."

"That's wonderful," Mrs. Vale prompts.

"Not practical," I mumble. My mom has told me time and time again I need to focus my attention on a practical career. Fashion design may be a fun hobby, but it's a harsh business and difficult to break into.

"I think everyone has a different perspective on what practical is. If design is something you love, why not go for it?" Mrs. Vale asks.

I don't have an answer.

"Now, how is the baby going to fit into this future? I know you are looking into adoption, but why? What is the driving factor?"

"We're not ready to be parents," Kyle says.

"Just because you aren't ready doesn't mean you can't become ready," she counters.

I stare at her. Is she trying to convince us to keep the baby? She's an adoption agent. Her whole job is to convince families adoption is the best thing in the world. "Um…"

She chuckles. "I hear that reason often, but I believe there is something deeper. You are not ready, and…?"

"I know women who would kill to be in my position. They are so ready to be moms, but they can't get pregnant or can't keep a pregnancy. I figured if I could do this"—I rest a hand on my belly—"then why not help someone become a mom?" My voice catches at the end, and I clear my throat. Kyle reaches over and grasps my hand.

Mrs. Vale smiles. "I love that. I want you to keep that in mind through this. You are helping someone become a mom, because one thing I know is that adoption is not easy. This is going to be one of

the hardest things you will ever do in life. It is also one of the most rewarding."

I wipe tears from my eyes and squeeze Kyle's hand. Mrs. Vale speaks with us a bit longer, explaining the different types of adoption. Once we agree on whether we want a closed, semi-open, or open adoption, Mrs. Vale sends us home with some adoptive parent packets to review. If no one looks like they will be a good fit, she can send us some more on our next visit. I hug the packets to my chest on the way out.

When we get to the car, Kyle looks at me from across the roof. "Here we go."

Six

After many discussions and several arguments, it was decided I would move in with my dad. The house has been tense since the decision was finalized, so I've been hiding in my room. I take a break from packing boxes and grab the packets of adoptive families. Even though I'm thoroughly annoyed at my mom for her constant worry and nagging, I want to make sure I'm taking care of myself. I flip the cover of one and stare at the profile picture of the couple inside.

Kyle peeks over. "I think they look like a good pick," he says before going back to packing a box.

I flip through their information and shrug, sliding another packet in front of me and scanning through it. I then pile all the packets in front of me and begin sorting them by potential, placing the packet Kyle commented on in the yes pile. When I'm done, I lean back, sighing.

"Everything okay?" Kyle joins me on my bed. I pick up the yes pile, which only contains three packets.

"I need your opinion on these."

He looks over at me, trying to read my face. His scrutinizing gaze makes me bite my nail and the tears start to pour over.

"Mac, are you sure about this?"

I heave a stuttering breath, not answering his question. I squeeze my eyes shut. His arm wraps around my shoulders and he pulls me into his side.

A knock sounds on my doorframe. "Am I interrupting?" Andi asks, her voice strained. I glance up and see her jaw is clenched.

I shake my head and pat the bed on my other side. She comes over, kicking her shoes off before crawling up next to me. She reaches up, wiping the tears from my face.

"Um…we were looking at adoptive parents. Maybe you could give some advice?"

Her eyebrows shoot up in surprise. Kyle gives my shoulder a little squeeze. I look up at him and he nods.

"Are you serious?" Her eyes flick to the packets in front of us.

"I don't know how to pick. I figured you know both of us really well. Maybe you could give us your opinion. If that's…" I trail off. The quiet is deafening. Fresh tears begin to fall. "Oh my gosh. Andi, you don't have to. I'll figure it out. I'm so sorry."

Andi slides a packet in front of her. She opens it, studying the couple's picture. Her eyes scan the text. She then grabs another one.

"Wait, who am I looking at? Are these ones you like?"

I shake my head and grab the pile in the center. She pushes the other pile aside and begins to study the packets. Kyle pipes up with the different things that he thought were interesting or that he liked about each couple. Andi nods.

"Which one do you like?" Her focus comes back to me.

"I can't…" I breathe.

"Maclaren, I can give you my opinion, but you have to like them. You have to trust them enough to be this little one's parents." She rests her hand on my belly. "I can't make this decision for you."

"I'm not asking you to," I manage to say.

She cocks her head to the side and gives me a sad smile. "You want me too though." She inhales deeply, spreading the three packets out in front of her, opening them so we can see each couple's picture. "Which one?" she asks Kyle. He points to the packet on the left. "And you?" She turns to me. I stare at the picture of the couple, scan their bio, and then point to the one on the left.

"There you go." She closes all the packets, stacking them in a neat little pile, the couple we chose at the top. She climbs off the bed and begins assembling boxes.

"When does your dad get the keys?" she asks. I watch her reach up and swipe a tear from her cheek.

"Andi, I'm—"

"Keys, Mac," she bites out.

"Friday."

Kyle gives my shoulder another squeeze and then walks over to Andi. Her focus remains on the boxes. Kyle reaches over and squeezes her hand, whispering something in her ear as he does so. She shakes her head. I stay sitting on my bed, not really sure what I should do.

My mom kicks the two of them out when she deems it's time for me to go to bed. I walk them out. Kyle gives a wave and climbs into his car. I stay with Andi by her car, turning to apologize for the millionth time.

"Are you even tired?" she asks.

I roll my eyes. "Not even a little bit."

She gives me a sympathetic frown. I open my mouth but Andi shakes her head. "But…"

"I think you guys made a good choice," she blurts out. "And I'll be here for opinions and anything else you need. This has to be you two first though."

"I don't want this to hurt you though."

She shrugs. "It already does."

A tear slides down my cheek.

"I can't do this. You are not the one who cries. That's my role." She wraps her arms around me. I hold her tight. "Mac, you're okay." She strokes my hair, only releasing me when the front porch light flickers. "They're summoning you."

I throw my head back and let out a huff of frustration.

"Go before she comes out here. I'll see you later." She opens her car door and I head back toward my house.

"Mac," Andi calls. I turn and she blows me a kiss. "Love you!"

"Love you more," I answer.

Bright and early Saturday morning, my dad and I head to the apartment. I make it up the three flights of stairs without any issues, but still find my hands drifting to my belly. I've definitely popped. My dad studies me as he sticks the key in the lock. "You're going to have to do that quite often."

"I'm aware," I say and nod toward the door. He unlocks it, opening it to a decent-sized living room to the right and then a small kitchen to the left. Straight ahead is a small hallway with three doors.

"The door to the left is your room. The master is straight back, and then your bathroom is the door on the right."

I take in the apartment with its bare white walls and faux hardwood floors.

"I'm going to start unloading boxes. Martin and Doug will be here soon to help with the furniture."

"I'll be down in a moment."

Even though my dad is exponentially better than my mom, he gives me a concerned glance. As he opens his mouth to protest, I interject. "I promise, no heavy boxes, and I'll limit my trips. Plus,

I'm headed down because Andi is picking me up so we can grab donuts." I give him a smile.

At the mention of donuts, my dad grins. "Bring back a maple," he says as he heads downstairs.

I walk to the door on the left, take a deep breath, and then step into my empty new room. The walls are a sandy tan color and the carpet is cream; it looks plush. I open the closet door, surprised that it's a walk-in. It looks big enough to be its own little room. I begin to think of how I want to arrange everything as I make my way downstairs.

Once our donut run is complete, Andi stays to help unload boxes. Kyle joins us about an hour later. I stay in the truck for a bit, arranging boxes into what rooms they will go in. The weather is warmer, but still nice. When I finally decide to head up and see what progress looks like upstairs, my eyes catch on a box I can definitely bring along.

I make it to the sidewalk before I hear, "What do you think you're doing?" Footsteps pound on the stairs and then Andi uses the rail to whip herself around the corner, jogging toward me. "Give me the box," she demands.

I pull the box away from her awaiting arms. "I got this."

"Three flights of stairs with a baby on board. You don't 'got this.' Give it."

I roll my eyes. "Fine." I drop the box into her open arms. She braces for the weight of it.

"Woah." She lifts the box a few times. I take the box and turn it so she can see the label. Pillows.

"Didn't know I was incapable of carrying such a box." I sidestep her and head up the stairs.

"Don't be mad. We're just looking out for you," she calls out.

I pass Kyle on the way up. Whatever look he glimpses on my face, he's wise enough not to say anything and just continues down the stairs.

When I get to our landing, my dad's standing in the doorway guzzling a bottle of water. "Hey, peanut. How ya doing?"

"Peachy," I snap. "I'm gonna see if I can set up anything in my room."

My dad frowns.

"Nothing heavy, I promise." I'm about to step inside when I hear Kyle's phone ring from downstairs. I walk over to the railing and watch as he sets a box down and slides his phone from his pocket. On the call, he begins to pace, and I see him nod. He looks up and catches my eye. His face is serious, and a shiver runs down my spine. He hangs up and then goes and taps Andi on the shoulder. They stand there for a moment, Kyle filling her in on his phone conversation. Andi glances up and spots me, her face full of worry. My heart begins to race.

I meet them at the stairs. "What's going on?"

"Let's go inside," Kyle suggests.

"Why don't you just tell me? It's bad, isn't it?"

"It's not great," Andi affirms. Kyle shoots her a warning look.

I turn and head inside, going straight to my room. I take a seat on my mattress and wait for Kyle to explain. Andi plops down next to me and takes my hand.

"My mom just called, and I guess my grandpa isn't doing well."

"Oh, I'm so sorry."

Kyle shrugs. "He's been sick for a while." Kyle clenches and unclenches his fists and then wipes his hands down the side of his shorts. "The thing is, my parents want the family out there after graduation, to help my grandma."

"Okay, for how long?"

"That's the problem," Kyle says and Andi squeezes my hand.

"They want to stay out there as long as possible, and since both my parents are able to work remotely, they're thinking of staying for the summer. And then there's baseball camp too."

"The whole summer?" I ask. I'll be almost twenty-seven weeks by graduation. That means if Kyle is gone the whole summer, he will miss the last trimester.

"Look, I'll figure it out. I'll see if I can come back for doctor's appointments and all the adoption appointments. We'll work it out."

I sit frozen. That's a lot of flying, and him being in town for a few days here and there is very different than him being here twenty-four-seven.

"I'll talk to my parents. Maybe there's something else we can arrange. I'm not bailing on you."

"I-I know," I stammer. "It's…" I sigh. "It's fine." I stand and head for the door.

"Maclaren?"

"My dad needs help. I'll see you guys down there."

Seven

It's been a week since I started living with my dad, and Kyle and I still haven't talked about his move in detail. I'm still trying to process the fact that I might be alone for the last third of my pregnancy. Maybe not completely alone—I'm sure Andi will be here—but our relationship is still strained. I don't want her to feel like she has to step in. My phone buzzes, interrupting my thoughts.

My mom's number flashes on my screen. Groaning, I answer. "Hi, Mom."

"Hi, how are you?"

"Fine."

"How've you been feeling, especially with school and everything? That has to take up some energy."

I roll my eyes. "Fine."

"Maclaren, I'm just asking a simple question. I want to make sure you're taking care of yourself."

"Thanks for the concern. I'm good. I have to get ready for work."

"You're going to work? Are you sure that's not too much? I really think you should consider stepping back and taking it easy."

I hold the phone away from my ear, letting out a big sigh. When I bring it back, I plaster a smile on my face. "Everything's right on track."

"Look, I'm going to propose an idea and I really want you to keep an open mind." She pauses. "I've been thinking I could step in and help you financially for a bit. At least until—"

"You want me to quit my job?" I clench my hand into a fist. "I'm not doing that."

"Hon, I know how taxing pregnancy can be and I just want to make sure you are being extremely careful. I just thought if you cut out some of the stresses in your life, it would make things a bit easier. Then once you've had the baby, you can go back to normal."

Does she really think that after all this, I'll go back to normal? "I appreciate the concern, but my doctor says I'm doing fine and to continue with my normal routine." I've checked with Dr. Huff every step of the way. She knows my concerns about my pregnancy and continues to affirm that I am doing splendidly. "Look, I have to go."

"Maclaren, please listen to me. I've had experience with high-risk pregnancies. I took every precaution with you, and I think you should too."

"Thanks. I'll talk to you later." I hang up before she can say anything more. I know she's worried. I'm sure this pregnancy has brought up quite a few feelings for her, but shoving all her worries onto me isn't helping me any.

I walk behind the order counter, shove my purse underneath, and let out a small huff. Everything about the last few hours is causing my brain to short circuit. Chris glances over at me. "What's up?"

"Nothing," I snap.

"Well, I see those hormones are coming in strong today. If you need me, I'll be in back." He turns and makes his way toward the kitchen. I narrow my gaze at his retreating figure just as Mr. Cruz rounds the corner.

"Hello, Mac." He glances behind him. "Is everything okay?"

"I don't know." I slide the flattened stack of cardboard in front of me and start aggressively folding boxes for our wing orders.

Mr. Cruz stands there silently for a moment. "If you need something, I'll be in my office."

I give him a curt nod.

After my shift, I pull up a text from Andi. It's an address to a party, along with a plea. *Need my wing woman.* She also attached a fuzzy picture of some guy's profile. I squint to see if I can identify him. I send a quick text to my dad and head for the party. I find Andi twirling her hair, giggling at something the guy beside her just said. I tap her on the shoulder.

"Hey, you made it." She beams, quickly wrapping me in a hug.

I lean in close to her ear. "Yeah, wing woman at your service."

She turns her head, whispering, "Actually, I may not need you." Then she gestures to the guy. "Mac, this is Travis. Travis, this is Mac."

Travis gives me a once-over, his gaze pausing on my midsection before returning to my face. "Hey." He nods.

"Nice to meet you."

"You guys can chat more later." She waves me off, her attention focusing back on Travis. "You were saying?"

I leave Andi, on my way toward the kitchen when I feel a trickle down my upper lip. I dab at it and when I remove my finger, there's blood. I grab a paper towel and then step out onto the back patio.

"Who decked ya?"

I turn to see a guy with dirty blond hair, lounging in a wicker chair, legs kicked up on the coffee table. His storm cloud blue eyes are staring at me. He takes a drag of his cigarette. "Hopefully the other guy looks worse."

I walk over and take a seat on the couch. I lean forward as much as I can, holding the paper towel to my nose.

"You look familiar." I glance up, his eyes still tracing my figure.

I narrow my eyes. "I must have one of those faces."

The back door slides open. "There you are." I recognize John's voice immediately. "Hey, Mac."

"That's it!" Chair Lounger snaps his fingers. "You're Clinic Girl."

"Well, that's a lovely nickname." I sit up and check to see if the bleeding has subsided.

"Everything all right?" John asks, taking a seat on the other end of the couch.

"I asked who looked worse. You interrupted," Chair Lounger comments.

A sudden flutter sends my hand to my abdomen.

"I wasn't asking her," John says, focusing on the guy in the chair.

"Oh, I'm great." Chair Lounger takes another drag of his cigarette. The wind shifts and the smoke drifts over to the couch.

"Wait, how did you know I was at the clinic?" I keep my hand on my belly, feeling nothing.

"I was there," the guy says matter-of-factly, stubbing out his cigarette. I'm not sure if it's because he's done or if he's being polite. "Name's Dustin." He holds out his hand.

"John was—" I feel another little pulse. I drop the tissue as both hands fly to my stomach.

"Mac?" John slides closer to me.

"Can someone—" I try to take a breath. "Can someone please get Kyle?"

"I'll go." Dustin drops his feet and heads inside.

"Hey, what's going on?" John asks.

"I don't know." I glide one hand down my belly and then back up, waiting for something to happen. What could be wrong? What did I do? If I end up in the hospital, my mom is just going to say that she told me so. What if this is the start of a miscarriage? Did I really push myself too hard today? My breaths come out in rapid bursts. Little black dots cloud my vision.

"Mac, hey. I'm right here. You're okay." John rests a hand on the middle of my back.

I feel so far from okay and if I don't get oxygen I'm going to pass out. I sway forward. John places his other hand on my shoulder, keeping me upright.

"I don't know"—I gasp—"what I did." I try to suck in another gulp of air.

"Mac, I need you to take a nice slow breath in through your nose and hold it." I do as he instructs. "One," he counts. "Two." Pause. "Let it out *slowly*. Good. Now do that again."

John rubs gently between my shoulder blades and I focus on the rhythm of his hand and on breathing slowly.

"There you go." He sighs in relief, dropping his hand from my shoulder. "How are you feeling?"

I don't answer, I just keep breathing. I run my hand up and down my belly again. I feel another slight flutter, and my hand pauses. John reaches over, giving my knee a slight squeeze. "You're doing great," he affirms.

I'm breathing in through my nose when Kyle steps out onto the patio. "What happened?"

John drops his hand from my back but stays sitting right beside me.

"Something's wrong," I squeak out. "There was this fluttering sensation and…and…" Realization hits me.

"And what? Mac?" Kyle sits on the coffee table, staring at me. He places a hand on each of my shoulders. "Mac, talk to me."

"It's the baby," I breathe.

"Something's wrong with the baby?" Kyle's grip tightens on my shoulders. "Um, can someone call—"

"No, the baby's moving." I reach up and take Kyle's hand and rest it on my stomach. I feel the quick fluttering again. "Do you feel that?"

Kyle shakes his head. My panic turns into excitement and then back to panic.

"Oh my gosh, there's a baby in here!" It's not like I wasn't aware, but feeling movement makes it more concrete. I'm growing a human being in my body, a human being that's now beginning to wiggle and kick and punch.

A chuckle comes from someone. Kyle fights a smile.

"I'm going to have a baby." My eyes are firmly fixed on Kyle's face.

Kyle leaves his hand resting on my belly and moves the other one to brush a stray strand of hair off my face. "You're going to have a baby."

Kyle and I don't move for twenty minutes. His hand remains resting on my belly. John has shifted to the other end of the couch and Dustin has taken his original seat in the chair. I feel another little pulse. "What about that?"

"Mac, the only reason I know the baby's moving is because you keep asking."

I frown.

"He probably won't be able to feel anything for a little while," John interjects. We both whip our heads toward him.

"I'm the oldest of five. My mom's been pregnant a lot. I've picked up some things." John shrugs.

"Five?" Kyle's eyebrows shoot up.

John nods.

"No girls either," Dustin chimes in.

"That sounds chaotic," I say.

The back door slides open. "Hey, hey!" Andi calls out. She tenses a little when she catches Kyle's hand resting on my belly. "What's going on?" She hesitantly makes her way over. I catch a tiny tick of her jaw as she sits beside me. "Is everything okay?"

"She felt the baby move," Kyle says.

"Oh." She glances up at me. "May I?"

I nod.

Kyle leans back and Andi's hands replace his. She sits there for a moment before looking back at me. "What am I supposed to feel?"

I roll my eyes.

Since Friday night, it's hard to ignore the sporadic flutters. Sunday evening, I'm sitting on the couch with piles of jeans surrounding me, my sewing kit and elastic on the coffee table. I reach for my scissors when a little flutter sends my hand to my belly, and I let out a little gasp.

"Maclaren, peanut?"

"Hm?" I sit, waiting for more movement.

"What's the matter?"

I glance up. My dad has both hands braced on the arm rests, looking like he's about to bolt out of the chair.

"Nothing?" I tilt my head. "Oh, it still catches me off guard."

"What does?"

"The baby moving."

"Oh." He sighs in relief. The tension in his arms releases and he sinks back into his chair.

I grab a pair of pants and cut out the pockets and then measure out some elastic to add. I'm hoping this trick works, saving me some money and giving me more wardrobe options.

On my third pair of pants, I reach for my iPad, pulling up the sketch of the skirt I made a few months ago.

"Oh, she has an idea," my dad remarks.

"I'm not sure it will work."

He gets up, stopping by the couch and peeking at my iPad. "Doesn't hurt to try." He pats my leg. "Do you want anything?"

"Can I get a lemonade?"

He chuckles. "You and your lemonade."

He brings back a large glass of lemonade, setting it on the coffee table, before returning to his recliner.

"Dad?"

"Yeah, peanut?"

"Do you think I could become a fashion designer?" I ask tentatively.

"Do you?" he counters. When I don't answer, he inhales. "You, young lady, are very talented. I think you can do anything you put your mind to. If you want to pursue design, I will support you."

"It's not impractical?"

"Impractical, no. Everyone wears clothes, right?"

I nod.

"The fashion industry is tough. I wouldn't let that stop you from pursuing your dream though."

"Okay."

I take some time to sketch out my idea for adjustable pants before pulling up design programs. Most have deadlines that are quickly approaching, if not already past. I put in a request for information for a couple schools. I'm not sure I'll be enrolling in college right after I graduate, but it wouldn't hurt to have information for next year.

At lunch on Monday, Kyle is the only one at our table. I set my tray down across from him and glance around the cafeteria.

"Where's Andi?"

Kyle shrugs. "I tried texting her. Haven't gotten a response." He glances up at me. "How are you?"

"I'm good." I slide my phone out of the side pocket of my backpack, pulling up the text thread I have with Andi. Now that he mentions it, she was pretty quiet this weekend.

Kyle clears his throat. "How's it been living with your dad?"

"Pretty good, I guess."

It's different for sure. My dad works for a large corporation as the vice president for the Western region. He wasn't home much already, but now that it's just him and me, it's hard not to notice how much he is actually gone. He's been good at communicating, texting when he's going to be late, or letting me know he has an early morning meeting. When he is home, he checks up on me and makes sure I'm doing okay.

There have been a few times I've wondered what it would have been like to live with my mom. She would be around more often. From the few phone calls I've had with her, it's become less hard to imagine. She is constantly letting me know how my schedule is affecting me and is continuously encouraging me to take it easier. If I were living with her, I'd have very little freedom.

After lunch, I find Andi waiting outside our English class. I tentatively approach her.

"I can't believe those pants still fit." She nods to the little heart she drew on them months ago.

I lift my shirt, revealing my handiwork from the weekend.

"Nice." She gives a nod of approval.

"So, where were you today?" I ask as we make our way into class.

"Being a saint." She plops down into her seat, dropping her backpack onto the floor.

I scrunch up my nose in confusion.

"Jace Miller will not flunk out of high school."

I raise my eyebrows. "I thought he was a pile of crap? Mound of garbage? Something completely horrid."

She sighs. "He is, but he's also friends with Luke, who hangs out with Travis. So, hoping they talk me up."

I shake my head, internally grateful she missed lunch for a boy.

The next weekend Andi drags me to another party, laying on the guilt a little heavy beforehand.

"We had planned on hitting up all the major parties until you and Kyle…" she trailed off, eyes flicking toward my belly as we made our way toward the parking lot.

"Ugh, fine. Text me the address."

Now walking into the crowded living room, Andi veers to the left when she spots Travis. I wander a bit, even stepping out on the back patio, hoping Dustin might be here. If Dustin's here, maybe John is too. With the back patio empty, I head to the kitchen to grab a drink. As I do, a guy bumps into me. His eyes fall directly to my midsection.

"So sorry." He gives me a wide berth. Several more people step out of my way, giving me curious glances. I grab a water bottle and head back to the living room. Andi is still there. She tucks her hair behind her ear, releasing a flirty giggle. Travis is soaking it up. Out of all the guys Andi has been with, he doesn't seem like a complete slime ball from the looks of him. I'm going to have to actually talk with him to find out if my initial assessment is accurate.

When I'm sick of the glances and hushed whispers, and with no sign of John in the crowd, I find a spare bedroom and slide to the

floor, leaning against the bed. I'm scrolling on Instagram when Andi finds me.

"You okay?" She plops down next to me.

"Yeah." I realize what skirt she's wearing. "I was wondering where this went. I searched for it all afternoon." I brush my fingers along the hem. "If you like it, I might have some pants for you to try."

Andi claps her hands. "Goodie. I love that you're a designer. So, what's up?"

I shrug.

She studies my face. "Awe, you're bummed."

"What? No," I scoff.

Kyle peeks in. "What's going on?"

"She's sad because John isn't here."

I shake my head as Kyle sits on my other side. Andi grabs my chin and scrutinizes my face, turning it toward Kyle. "Look at her. It's the same face she had when she fell for Kody Miles in seventh grade."

Kyle looks me over. "Man, she has it bad."

I pry Andi's hand off my face. "You two are ridiculous."

"I can't believe you have feelings for someone else. I mean, after all, you're carrying my baby," Kyle comments, his tone light.

I frown and feel tears well in my eyes. I push myself to my feet.

Kyle swears. "I'm sorry. That was a joke."

I wipe my eyes. "It's fine. I'm going to get a drink."

"Maclaren." Kyle catches my wrist. Andi is standing behind him. Her shoulders are tense and the light joking manner she had moments ago has vanished. She glances at Kyle then back at me.

"Just a water?" she asks. I nod. She inhales deep as she passes. I catch her clenching and unclenching her fists as she exits the room.

"Sorry. I didn't mean to upset you," Kyle whispers.

"You didn't." I shrug, staring at the floor.

Kyle releases me and I quickly swipe away the tears. His eyes are sad when I finally look up at him again. "Sorry. It's really fine if you like him. He seems like a cool guy."

I nod.

Andi walks back in, handing me a water bottle. "Wanna get out of here?"

I nod.

"Good. I need fries. Also, Travis will be joining."

Eight

Prom and graduation are quickly approaching. Banners announcing our prom theme, When in Rome, line the school hallways. Unfortunately, I've waited until the last minute to design dresses for Andi and me. We're perusing the aisles of JOANN, searching for fabric.

"Oh my gosh! I found it. I found it," Andi exclaims. I heave myself up off the floor, annoyed that all the fabrics I like are on the bottom shelves.

"Marco," I call out.

"Over here," Andi answers. I turn the corner two aisles down from where I was to see Andi unraveling an electric blue silk. Of course, it's on the top shelf and easily accessible.

"What do you think? And then some tulle to make the skirt fluffy?"

I walk over, running my hand along the smooth, cool fabric. Andi wants her prom dress to be a cocktail dress with a halter top and a full skirt. Being Andi, she selects one of the brightest colors out there, totally matching her outgoing personality.

"Let's do it. Grab that, and then I need your opinion." I head back over to the fabrics I was looking at before she called out. I squat down and run my hands over a periwinkle sateen. "What do you think?" I look up at her.

"I think you're going to get stuck down there."

I roll my eyes and pull at the fabric. She squats down beside me to examine it. "I think it's perfect." A mischievous glint lights her eye. "Now race you up." She instantly pops up, while I grab the shelf above and pull myself up slowly. I flash her a look before making my way to the cutting station, Andi cackling behind me.

EEEKKK!!!! I FRICKIN' LOVE YOU!!!
  SATURDAY BABY!!!
After several weeks of work, I added the final touches to Andi's prom dress and sent her a picture. I quickly read Andi's response and then look back up at myself in the full-length mirror with my dress. I debate taking a picture and sending it over to Andi, but instead I throw my phone on the bed. I reach for the zipper, sucking in my stomach a little as I zip up the dress. Once it's up, I let out my breath. I tried to leave a little room in the midsection for my growing belly.

I turn to the other side then face the front. Turning again, I frown. When I first envisioned this dress, I knew exactly how I wanted it to look and the fabric I wanted to use. Silk was unforgiving and didn't provide any sort of stretch, though, so sateen it was. Looking at myself again, tears swell in my eyes.

"Knock, knock." My dad peeks his head in.

I quickly swipe at my face and turn to face my dad.

"Wow. You look gorgeous. That is some fine craftsmanship."

I roll my eyes. "Thanks," I mumble.

His face grows serious. "You don't like it."

"No, it's just… I mean…" I shake my head.

"It's not what you wanted," he finishes. "For what it's worth, I think it looks spectacular. You adapted your vision really well."

I grab Andi's dress and slip it onto a hanger before heading over to my closet. When I step back into my room my dad is still standing at the doorway.

"Peanut—"

"Dad, I don't want to talk, okay? I'm going to get ready for bed."

He nods solemnly. "Of course. I'm going to turn in myself. I'll see you in the morning."

It didn't surprise me when Andi announced that Travis would be joining us at prom. What does surprise me is the electric blue bow tie he's wearing to match Andi. At every complement Andi receives, she's not hesitant to point out her dress is custom-made, doing a twirl which flairs the cocktail skirt. The shock of blue looks amazing on her warm ivory skin and makes her blue eyes pop. I've caught Travis admiring her several times this evening.

As we enter the hotel, Kyle nudges my shoulder. "You've created a monster."

I give him a half-hearted grin.

"What's wrong?"

I shake my head, keeping my focus on the ticket table up ahead.

We enter the ballroom, where several large columns lead to a pointed ceiling. Everything mimics the Pantheon, from the miniature Fontana del Pantheon in the middle to the marble statues and even down to the replica of the Colosseum in the corner.

Once we find an empty table, Andi leaves us, dragging Travis to the dance floor. When Andi returns, her face is glistening with sweat. "Why are you sitting here? Do you hear this DJ? Let's go." She tugs Kyle up and out of his chair and pulls him away.

"I'll meet you out there," I call, giving them a little wave.

Kyle gives me a withering stare over his shoulder. On the floor, he remains aloof until Andi imitates Jess from *New Girl* doing the slow chicken dance and he cracks. Two songs in and they are still going, laughing with each other. I kick my feet up and watch the two of them enjoy each other's company, no tension between them. Travis returns to the table with two glasses of water. He takes a sip and sets the other one aside.

With the music blaring it's hard to have a conversation, so I lean closer to Travis. "Having fun?" I yell.

Travis nods. He looks over. "You?"

I shrug. "Sure."

He gives me a little nod and turns his attention back to Andi.

I sneer at the back of his head. He seems nice enough but he's also friends with Jace, who is scum. I'm not sure about Luke because I haven't hung out with him enough to get a good read on him. I've seen them in the halls sometimes, and they're always causing trouble. If Travis is friends with them, how good can he be?

When the song wraps up, Kyle and Andi make their way back to our table. Travis holds up the second cup of water to Andi. She grins, chugging the water before planting a kiss on his cheek. She then looks over at me.

"Okay, your turn."

"One dance," I say, getting to my feet. She leads me out to the dance floor but stays closer to the edge, so we are farther from those who are throwing all their energy into their dancing. When the next song starts, Andi and I glance at each other and burst out laughing. When we were ten or eleven, we were rifling through her mom's playlists and found "Whenever, Wherever" by Shakira. We choreographed a whole little dance to it. She gives me a little wink and we break out our rusty moves. By the end, we are both giggling. I pull her to me and hug her tight, swallowing the sudden knot in my throat.

"Whenever, wherever," she whispers.

I give her a kiss on the cheek. "You da best."

The next week, floodlights illuminate the football field. I
shift in my seat for the hundredth time. The tiny plastic chair is
wildly uncomfortable, and I would give anything for our
valedictorian to hurry his speech along. It seems to take an eternity to
get to the names. I watch as Kyle stands and heads toward the stage. I
glance over my shoulder to spot Andi a few rows back. We grin at
each other, and when Kyle's name is called, we both scream. I sigh
in relief when our row is summoned and I can finally stand and
move. Kyle and Andi cheer equally loud for me. I also hear some
cheers from the stands. Both my parents are here tonight, along with
many extended family members. Kyle whistles loudly when they call
Andi's name, and my screams accompany him. A few names later,
Jace Miller is called. Andi, on her way back to her seat, catches my
eye and takes a little bow.

Sweat drips down my back as the ceremony wraps up. Caps are
tossed and then it's over. I quickly unzip the polyester gown,
thankful it's not one hundred degrees or pouring rain like the past
couple years. The cool breeze is refreshing.

"There's my girl! Congratulations, peanut!" My dad wraps me in
a bear hug.

"Hon, maybe you should remove your gown. It might make you
feel better," my mom says as she approaches.

It takes effort not to roll my eyes. "I'm good." Wearing the
gown is the biggest indicator that I graduated tonight. If I remove it,
I'm just another attendee.

"Your cheeks look flushed. Do you have any water?"

My dad casts a scowl her way. "Shel—"

"Jim, I'm just looking out for my daughter." She crosses her
arms. "Something you should be doing as well."

Their bickering is why I insisted on two graduation parties. Who
knows what could happen if we stick both my parents in the same

room together. The party with my mom will be tomorrow evening and then we will celebrate with my dad's family, poolside, on Saturday.

Thankfully, we are interrupted by family. I receive a lot of hugs and a few disapproving looks as well. I smile, trying not to be bothered.

I hear a squeal right before Andi rams into me. "We did it!" She grasps my shoulders, jumping up and down. I smile widely.

"Andi, that's enough," my mom snaps.

Andi freezes, her face falling.

"Yo, yo! We graduated…" Kyle throws an arm around both of us but his enthusiasm dies quickly.

I glare at my mother. This is supposed to be a time for celebration, and I should be able to do that however I choose. If Andi wants to scream and jump up and down, awesome. I'd be jumping up and down right along with her if I could. She deserves to celebrate, as does Kyle. And here we are, silent. Our whole little circle is quiet while boisterous noise surrounds us.

"Where are your parents?" I ask Andi.

"Gone. Had to go pick up the grandparents." During graduation practice Andi had informed us several flights had been rescheduled due to storms and both sets of grandparents would end up missing her graduation.

I turn to Kyle. "Yours?"

"I told them I had to find you two and ditched them. I'm sure they will eventually find me."

They do. I spot Mr. and Mrs. Hart and wave.

"I'm so proud of all of you!" Mrs. Hart says as she draws near. She gives each of us a hug. I catch her frown a little when she spots my flushed cheeks but doesn't say a word. She reaches for the tote bag Mr. Hart is holding and then fishes out a few bottles of water. "Here you go. You three must be parched after sitting through that."

I smile appreciatively. No fuss. No drawing attention to me, even though I know I'm the reason she grabbed us water.

I down half the bottle in a single gulp, not realizing how thirsty I really was. When our group shuffles toward the parking lot, I polish off the rest of the bottle. Kyle holds out his to me and I shake my head.

"Take it." He pushes it into my hand. I go to argue, but he nods to someone behind me. "Maybe it will make her chill a little." I don't have to look over my shoulder to know who he's talking about. I roll my eyes but take the bottle.

Our trio stops at my car. "So, whose house are we hitting up first?"

"Not tonight," my mom answers for me.

"It's my graduation night. I think I have the right to do what I want," I bite out.

She narrows her eyes. "Yes, but you also have someone else to consider. I believe it would be in your best interest to rest."

"Well, it's not like the baby has been that considerate." Lately, late nights are for dance parties or karate lessons.

"Maclaren, please don't argue with me."

"I'm not. I'm simply stating a fact."

"Mrs. Young, with all due respect, Mac prepped for tonight. She made sure to take a nap and rest most of the afternoon. That way, she could enjoy tonight. She'll be good. Plus, she's got us." Andi flashes a smile at my mom.

My mom shakes her head as she climbs into her car just down the row. She probably thinks I'm extremely irresponsible and not prioritizing my health or the baby.

"You okay?" Kyle whispers.

I shake my head and climb into the driver's seat. Andi plops down in the passenger seat and Kyle takes the back middle seat.

"Where are we going?" Andi asks, then shifts to look at Kyle. "How much time do you have?"

"Um, I got a couple hours. You guys don't have to take me though." Kyle catches my gaze in the rearview mirror.

"Yeah, we do. You'll be gone all summer."

Kyle rolls his eyes. "I'll be back in a few weeks."

"Yes, of course." Andi turns back around and stares out the windshield.

Kyle will be back for our appointment to meet the adoptive family. He'll miss a doctor's appointment and the anatomy scan. I should have scheduled the scan sooner, but with my schedule and the doctors and just being nervous overall, it kept getting delayed. The last time we spoke to Mrs. Vale, she had asked if we wanted to know the sex of the baby and if it would be okay for the adoptive parents to know the sex. After several minutes I glanced at Kyle, who shrugged. "I kind of want to know." I just nodded. Now, I will be attending that appointment alone and Kyle will be a few hundred miles away at his grandparents' house. I told him I would try to FaceTime him, but it won't be the same.

Tension fills the car as the weird balance between the three of us remains strained. Prom must have been a weird fluke. "I think we should hit up Sander's party first and then see what time it is," I suggest. The other two nod in agreement.

Pulling up to the airport terminal, I put the car in park. Kyle climbs out and goes to the trunk to retrieve his bags. Andi stumbles out of my car, having had a few more drinks than she said she would. She had wanted to be sober to say goodbye.

I stand on the sidewalk, waiting.

"You shouldn't sit here too long; you'll get in trouble," Kyle says.

I shrug. "I'm not worried."

"Okay, I'll see you in a few weeks." He pulls me in for a hug and squeezes tight. I wrap my arms around him, willing myself not to cry.

Kyle releases me and makes his way to Andi. They whisper to each other and then he gives her a hug. She says something in his ear and his eyes widen a little. He leans back and studies her. I didn't catch what she said, but it looks like Kyle tells her thanks.

Andi and I stand on the curb and watch Kyle walk to the double doors. He pauses, turning back, and we wave just as a security guard begins to head our way. I tap Andi on the shoulder and we make our escape.

Nine

The following weekend, I'm trying to escort a drunk Andi to my car. We're halfway down the driveway when she stumbles, losing her balance and falling to the grassy lawn. I let out a sigh. "All right, come on." I reach out my hand. She takes it and I try to pull her up. "You're gonna have to help me out here." I tighten my grip. Andi reaches up, grabbing my arm and causing me to lose my balance. I quickly let her go before joining her in the grass.

She plops back down. "Hey," she moans. I let out a short growl.

"Want help?" a voice says from behind me.

"Jeez." I put my hand over my heart. "I think I just peed a little." John walks up beside me. "Sorry."

"I'm getting wet," Andi whines from the ground. John bends down, wraps her arm around his shoulder, and then hoists her up.

"Thanks, handsome," she breathes in his face. He leans away.

"I know, she smells like half the liquor cabinet."

I lead the way to my car. Once Andi is securely in the back seat, John turns to me. "Need help getting her home?"

My only goal was getting her to the car. I didn't think about how to get her to her house.

"I'm free, I can help." He opens the passenger door.

"Oh, no, I'm good. I can totally…"

John cocks his head and stares at me.

"Fine, get in."

We're on the road when Andi leans forward. "You know what sounds *amazing*?" She waits for an answer, but when one doesn't come, she finishes with, "Tacos."

"Not tonight," I answer, casting a quick glance at her.

"You are such a party pooper. C'mon, John could go for some tacos." Andi punches his shoulder. I peek over at John, his expression unreadable.

"Next time," I say.

"Suck." Andi throws herself back against the seat and proceeds to pout.

When we are five minutes from Andi's house, light snoring begins drifting from the back, but ever since tacos were mentioned, they are all that consume my thoughts.

"Wasn't that…?" John asks as he looks back toward Andi's street.

"Yes, but I now need tacos."

"You *need* tacos?"

"Yep." I glance over at him. "Is that all right?" I hesitate at a stop sign. I can turn left and take Andi home or I can go straight and get superb tacos from a twenty-four-hour taco stand. John's doing me a favor, though, and I don't want to keep him.

"There's actually a great taco stand up here," John says.

"Roberto's Tacos," I state.

"Ycah, you been?"

"All the time."

At one in the morning, John and I lie out on the grass by a small park in Andi's neighborhood, tacos between us. My car is in front of us, the back door left open so I can keep an eye on Andi, who's still sound asleep. I'm on my third taco when I catch John staring.

"What?"

"There was a point when you couldn't eat anything," he says, taking a bite of his taco.

"Oh, yeah. Now I eat all the time."

"So, the pregnancy's going good?"

"Everything's right on track." I smile. I stare down at my half-eaten taco. "Um, I actually never said thank you for, um, your assistance a few weeks ago."

"No problem. Glad I could help."

A small pick-up pulls in behind my car and Dustin climbs out. I catch him flick something, presumably a cigarette, out in front of him, stubbing it out with his toe as he heads our way.

"Yo," John calls out.

"What up?" He nods at John. "Hi, Clinic Girl," he says, taking a seat.

I groan. "That nickname can't stick."

"Why not?"

"Then that would make you Clinic Boy. Perfect. I'll start calling you that."

Dustin grimaces. "Yeah, no. We're not doing that."

John hands Dustin a taco.

A moan comes from the back seat and I look up as Andi stirs, pushing herself into a sitting position.

"I saved you a taco," I yell.

"*Ithinklamgonnahurl*," comes Andi's response, before she slumps forward.

"Not in my car," I squeak. I try to get up but it's too late.

"Well, I'm done," John comments.

"I didn't even start," Dustin pouts.

"I have to clean that," I groan.

"Come on, let's get her home." John stands, extending his hand when he notices me struggling to get up. The sudden movement makes the world spin. I latch on to John's arm and close my eyes. His other hand reaches up to steady me.

When I open my eyes, everything is as it should be. "Thanks." I release my grip on his arm and take a step away.

Dustin stands. "I guess that is something you're going to have to get used to."

"What is?" I ask.

"Puke, pee, spit-up, et cetera, et cetera."

"Oh, I'm not keeping it." Out of the corner of my eye, I see John's eyebrows shoot up in surprise.

"Sorry, I just assumed," Dustin says.

I shrug. "No worries."

"Mac, I don't feel good," Andi whimpers from the back seat.

"I know. I'm coming," I call out. "I gotta go."

"Can you follow us?" John asks Dustin. He nods.

Andi groans from the back seat and I hope she can hold it for a few more seconds. I park in her driveway and a car, one I don't recognize, pulls in behind us.

John makes his way around the trunk to help me with Andi when I hear, "Surprise!" Andi stumbles out of the car, trying to stand on wobbly legs. "Oh, oh shoot." Travis is at her side in an instant. He wraps an arm around her waist, steadying her. "I take it someone had fun."

She burps in response and then lurches toward the lawn where she proceeds to puke. Travis hurries over, holding back her hair as she heaves again. When she straightens, a smile lights up her face. "Hey," she rasps. "Thought you couldn't come out."

"I snuck out. Let's get you to bed."

They turn and Travis catches my eye. "I got it from here."

I just stare at him, eyes narrowing.

He pauses, Andi leaning into him. "She's good. I promise." Annoyance laces his tone.

"Okay," I retort. I give him a small nod and he proceeds to lead Andi into her house.

I turn to see John standing at the rear of my car, his eyes following Travis. "Um, thanks for the help."

He glances at me. "No prob. What are you going to do?"

I peek over my shoulder back at the house, wondering if I should stay or if I should head home. "Um…" I bite my nail. "Uh, you can go. I'll—yeah, you can go."

"You sure?" John's eyebrows lift in question.

I nod slowly. From behind me, I hear a loud squeak. I turn to see Dustin has lowered the tailgate of his truck. He hops up, feet dangling over the side. He takes out a cigarette and lights it.

"What are you doing?" I call.

"Waiting." Dustin takes a long drag of his cigarette and then exhales a puff of smoke.

John nods toward the truck. "Come on."

The three of us camp out on Dustin's tailgate for twenty minutes before the front door opens and Travis walks back to his car, stopping when he spots us.

"She okay?" I ask.

"She'll probably have one hell of a hangover in the morning. I left a trash can by her bed and made sure she was on her side."

"Thanks."

"Yep," he snaps. His lips purse and he shakes his head before he climbs into his car. I see him study his phone before his car starts. My phone chimes as he drives away.

I pull up my messages, seeing an unknown number. *This isn't the first time I've helped Andi home from a party. You're going to have to trust me at some point. Stole this # from Andi's phone. It's*

Travis. Now you have my contact info. I type a quick thank
you, wondering when on earth I'm ever going to need his contact
information.

Ten

I'm too lazy to make anything for lunch, so I stop at Freddy's on my way into work. Standing in line, I hear two children behind me arguing over whose turn it is to use the iPad. I try to tune them out when their arguing becomes physical, until one of them careens into my back. I take a step forward to catch myself from the impact. I then turn to glare at the little troublemakers. The mother quickly grabs each of them and pulls them apart. She snatches the iPad away and slips it in her purse. She looks up and apologizes but I just turn around, not saying anything.

"Excuse me." I feel a tap on my shoulder. I glance back. "I couldn't help but notice you're expecting." The lady's eyes drift to my bulging midsection. This is all anyone notices anymore. "There is a cute boutique downtown with an adorable maternity section," she adds.

As politely as I can, I smile. "Thanks, I'll keep that in mind."

"I know this may seem forward, but if you need any parenting advice or a great support group, I know of several resources. Motherhood can seem daunting, especially for someone your age."

My age? What the heck does that mean? I square my shoulders. "I'm good."

She continues, "I don't mean to offend. When they say it takes a village, they mean it. Here, let me give you my card."

"Look, that's a nice gesture, but really, I'm good. I have support."

"You can never have too much. I work with a wonderful organization and there are so many options out there for mothers."

I don't want to tell this stranger I'm not going to be the mother, I'm just temporary housing. I feel the familiar sting of tears in my eyes and look away. Turning, I see the counter is free and, to my surprise, Dustin is standing at the register, glowering at the woman. I step up to the counter, ignoring the woman. "Sorry," I whisper, my voice cracking.

"The nerve of some people." Dustin shakes his head.

"You heard?" A tear slips down my cheek.

"Um, our fries are excellent and our shakes are amazing." Dustin slides a napkin across the counter. "Our chicken tenders are super crispy. Oh, our California burger is my favorite."

Dustin continues to detail all the items on the menu while I collect myself. Every once in a while, he shifts his focus to something under the counter.

"So, really, just peruse the menu. Take all the time you need. And when you're ready for dessert, a lovely concrete will satisfy your sweet tooth. Or I guess you could mix salty and sweet with fries and a vanilla custard." He shrugs.

"That's actually delicious. Wait, have you never done that?" I ask.

"I can't say I have."

"Well, you should."

He gives me a doubtful look. "Seriously? It's not, like, a pregnancy thing?"

"Not a pregnancy thing," I confirm. "It's so good."

A loud sigh comes from behind me. Dustin narrows his gaze at the woman.

I wince. "You should probably let me order," I whisper.

Dustin glances down and then slides what's presumably his phone back into his apron pocket. "Only if you're ready."

"Hey, what's going on?" John appears at my side. I catch his phone screen still illuminated on a text conversation, Dustin's name at the top. Dustin fills in the gaps I assume he didn't have time to type out in the text. John balls his hands into fists when Dustin repeats the age comment. Hearing the interaction again brings fresh tears to my eyes. John gives me a sympathetic look.

"Excuse me, but people are waiting to order." The woman is standing with her arms crossed, tapping her foot.

John slides his arm around my shoulder. He turns slightly. "You must know how it is," he says and looks to the two kids standing beside her. "Pregnancy and cravings. Sometimes she can't decide what she wants. However, with all the raging hormones, I don't dare rush her." He takes his free hand and places it over his chest. "I value my life. And let's be honest, it's not her who's deciding here." He places his hand on my belly. The baby decides at that moment to do a roundhouse kick. John tries to maintain his composure, but I see shock flit across his face. "So, she will order when they are good and ready. She's going through so much and from what I can tell, pregnancy's a witch."

I know he altered the last word for the sake of little ears but the bite behind the delivery made his point.

The lady draws back. John just turns, keeping his arm around my shoulders.

"Can I have chicken tenders, fries, a drink, and a vanilla custard?" I say, a smile on my lips. John begins to order, but Dustin stops him.

"Already got it. Anything else?" They both look at me.
I shake my head. Dustin hands us our cups and John leads us to the
drink fountain.

"Holy cow, that was quite strong," John says as he fills his cup.

I nod. "Yeah, and he's growing stronger every day."

"He?"

"Yep."

"When did you find out you were having a boy?"

I clear my throat. "The anatomy scan was a few weeks ago. We
asked the Challinors if they wanted to know. I mean, they could have
found out without us knowing, but I was a little curious. So was
Kyle. Plus, this way, they don't have to worry about slipping up."

We find a table and I slide in across from John. I stare at the
laminate surface and fiddle with my cup.

"Does knowing make it harder?" John's words are soft. I glance
up and catch him looking at me. "Sorry, we don't have to talk about
this."

"No, it's fine. At least we can stop referring to the baby as 'the
baby' or 'it.'" It's not an answer to his question but I don't really
have an answer for him. In some ways it's easier, but in other ways it
has made it harder. I now know I'm carrying a little boy. In a matter
of months, I will be handing him over to a couple who seems
wonderful, and will love him unconditionally. At least, I hope. They
will be the ones to name him, the ones to dress him, the ones to
watch him grow up and experience all his firsts. I only have this short
period in his life. Ever since finding out, I've tried to stop thinking
up names, avoided the baby section in any store, and basically have
been repeating, *He's not mine* over and over in my head.

John's fingers brush my hand. "You're okay. You'll survive
this."

I take a deep breath, swiping at the tears that have formed. I'm about to ask John what he was doing earlier when Dustin plops a tray of food down on the table and slides in next to me.

"Dude, your face earlier," Dustin says and laughs. "It looked like you wanted to rip your hand away from her belly so bad, like it shocked you."

"The baby moved. It's a creepy sensation," John says.

Dustin turns to me. "Can I feel?"

"He's quiet right now and I'm not waking him up." Dustin's eyes widen at the pronoun. He seems to digest this information but doesn't say anything. I slip a fry through the vanilla custard and pop it in my mouth.

"And?" Dustin looks at me expectantly. I take the custard and angle it toward him. He takes a fry and dips it in the custard. He examines it thoroughly before placing it in his mouth. "Well, that's delicious."

"Told you."

Dustin plucks up another fry, dipping it in the custard and popping it in his mouth. He grabs a napkin and wipes his hands before pulling out his earbuds. He slips one into my ear and then searches for something on his phone. It takes a moment before a song floods my left eardrum. I glance over at him.

"Wait for it." He raises his eyebrows, a wicked look on his face.

When the song reaches the chorus, my mouth drops open. "Dustin. Oh my gosh, that is so mean."

He shrugs. "It sums up the feeling someone may have about certain people though." He nods across the restaurant to where the woman sits with her two kids.

I try to keep a smile from forming but fail miserably.

"You're welcome." He smiles, giving me a little nudge with his shoulder.

"You're amazing," I say, chowing down on another fry with custard.

John and I finish and are on our way out when the baby stirs. "Give me a second." I turn and head back toward the counter.

"Dustin." I stand by the little door that leads behind the counter. When Dustin reaches me, I take his hand and place it on my belly.

"What's supposed to happen?" Dustin whispers, looking back toward the register.

"Give him a minute."

Finally, the baby kicks. Dustin pulls his hand back; his face looks slightly repulsed.

John chuckles behind me. "Told ya."

"Creepy doesn't even begin to describe that. Ew, just ew." Dustin waves his hand, shaking off the feeling.

I just roll my eyes and place a hand where I feel the most movement.

"Does it hurt?" Dustin asks, reaching over and placing his hand next to mine.

I shrug. "Sometimes. He's landed a few good kicks to my ribs today."

"This is so weird."

"And you only feel it from outside," I say, to which Dustin scrunches his face.

I've been at work an hour and I cannot get the song Dustin played out of my head. I pace at the counter because standing still is killing my back, but stop when customers come in. As soon as the family takes their cups and heads toward the dining area, I pull out my phone to text Dustin, only to realize I don't have his number. I contemplate texting John, but then Mr. Cruz steps around the corner and I quickly slide my phone in my pocket. I rest my hands on my back, rubbing slightly.

"How's it going up here?"

"Seems slow." I shift my weight, wincing.

"Have you had a break?"

"It's a little early for a break. I'm good." I flash a smile.

Mr. Cruz gives me a look of disbelief. I think he's going to return to his office but he lingers near the register. I shift again, trying to hide my discomfort. "Is there something else?"

"Well, Sarah called and…"

I roll my eyes. "You need me to stay."

"No, well, maybe just an hour. I'm going to call Caleb and see if he can come in."

I let out a small laugh. "You know he won't."

Mr. Cruz sighs in frustration.

"It's fine. I can stay."

Mr. Cruz studies me. I narrow my eyes. "I'll be fine." *I hope.*

Coming back from my first break, I find a stool near the register with a small little pillow propped up against the back. I pull it toward the register and slide into the seat. I adjust the pillow and lean back, my back instantly feeling better.

Later when I'm in the middle of taking an order, Mr. Cruz comes into view after making a lap around the dining room. I catch his attention and mouth a thank you. He nods and heads toward the back.

During my last break, I message my dad and let him know I'll be working late. He just sends a thumbs-up in response. Since I no longer live with my mother, I don't bother messaging her. I hear my phone buzz in my purse as I fold pizza boxes. After the third phone call in a row, I check to see if there is an emergency. I've missed three calls from my mother and see a string of text messages. I

quickly type a reply, letting her know I have the late shift at
work but leave out that I'm covering for someone. She calls again, so
I message her that I can't talk. Then my work phone rings. I say the
scripted greeting.

"Maclaren, honey, it's your mother." I roll my eyes.

"What can I get you?"

"I don't want a pizza. I want to make sure you are being wise
with your decisions. Mr. Cruz is a reasonable gentleman. Maybe you
could talk to him about your shifts."

"What about my shifts?" I ask innocently.

"It's almost ten o'clock."

"And?"

I hear her frustration building. I grind my teeth together. She has
no idea how late I'm up on a normal night. Not only that, but it's also
summer. I can sleep as long as I want during the day.

"Maclaren, I didn't call to argue with you."

"Great, then don't. It's one shift. I have to go. Thank you for
your call. Have a pleasant evening." I hang up before she can say any
more, growling at the phone as I do.

I've been craving fries and custard ever since I stopped at Freddy's. I
have tried to ignore it, but I cave after a week. Walking up to the
entrance, I spot Dustin outside smoking. "Hey," I call out, Taylor
Swift playing loudly through the speakers. "Have you heard the
cover by We Came As Romans?"

Dustin's eyebrows lift in surprise. "I wish we could play that
version. I've heard this one too many times." He wrinkles his nose.

The wind shifts and smoke drifts my way. "Sorry." Dustin takes
one more drag of the cigarette and then puts it out.

"You don't have to do that, you know."

"Isn't secondhand smoke bad for babies?"

"Secondhand smoke is bad for everyone. Firsthand smoke is also bad." I give him a wink. Dustin's face turns hard.

"Unbelievable." He shakes his head and heads toward the door.

"Wait, Dustin. That was a joke. Don't leave." My voice cracks.

"I have to get back to work." He whips the door open and steps in. I don't follow. I stand there for a minute replaying the conversation. I have no idea why Dustin is mad, but I have a feeling he won't be happy if I stay. I turn and head back to my car.

As I'm clocking out for the evening, I receive a text from John asking if I want to see a movie. I glance at the time. I'm not sure if I'll be able to stay awake, but the baby has been super active during the night, keeping me up, so I text back and ask him what theater.

As I walk to the front, I see John and Dustin standing near the ticket kiosks. Dustin looks my way and then walks off. I pause and ponder going back to my car. John will understand if I text back and say I'm tired. I pull out my phone ready to do just that when he spots me. He waves and I wave back.

"Hey, glad you made it," John says.

"Yep." I give a little half-smile.

John gives me a questioning look. "Everything all right?"

I nod but I can feel tears in my eyes.

"What's wrong?"

I shake my head. "Just stupid pregnancy hormones," I lie. John hands me a ticket and we head toward the ticket taker, who looks utterly bored.

John and I meet Dustin in the concession line. Fresh tears prick my eyes as we step up next to him. I'm waiting for the same hard look on his face. When Dustin turns to greet us, his smile instantly falls.

"Woah, what's wrong with you?"

"I don't know what I did," I blurt out.

John's brows furrow.

Dustin sighs. "You didn't do anything. Have you been stuck on that all day?"

I nod.

"Mac, it had nothing to do with you. I got halfway to the counter then turned around to come talk to you, but you were gone. I don't have your number, so I wasn't sure how to get ahold of you."

"You were really mad."

"Not with you. You just hit a nerve."

I wipe my eyes. John stares at us, completely lost.

"I may have overreacted earlier," Dustin admits.

"About what?"

"I made a quip about smoking," I explain.

John looks disapprovingly at Dustin.

Dustin grows defensive instantly. "Dude, don't. I feel horrible."

"For what exactly? For snapping at Mac or for smoking?"

Dustin narrows his eyes, getting ready to lash out, but I interrupt before he can. "Wait, I didn't mean to make this a thing. Please, don't fight." My voice cracks. I'm so sick of people arguing, especially since I seem to be the one who puts people at odds with each other. I don't want to be blamed for a friendship ending. I turn and start heading toward the exit.

"Mac, hey. Wait." Dustin catches up and moves in front of me. "Don't leave." I try to step around him, but he blocks my path. "Look, I kind of suck to be around right now. The lack of nicotine leaves me cranky. I've been trying to quit and it's…well…"

"Going spectacularly," I quip.

"I've had some things come up. I just needed a fix, okay?"

I shrug. "Whatever you say."

Dustin huffs in frustration.

"How many weeks?"

Dustin startles. "What?"

"How many weeks has it been since you had a cigarette?" I cross my arms.

"It was three and a half, then four days, and now I'm back to square one." Dustin hangs his head.

"Why are you quitting?"

"Firsthand smoke is bad for you," he responds, flexing his jaw.

"If you don't want to tell me, fine. I'm feeling tired. I think I'm going to head home."

"Mac, please." His voice turns pleading. "I really don't want you to. I have a better reason, I just…" He glances at the floor and then up at me. "Just don't leave, okay?"

I'm a little taken aback. "Okay," I whisper.

"Do you want popcorn? John and I usually split one."

I nod.

We turn back toward the concession stand, Dustin peeking over his shoulder at me to make sure I'm following. The people behind grumble when we jump into the line. John leans close to Dustin and Dustin shakes his head, answering whatever question I can't hear. John glances at me and then back at Dustin. I smirk when Dustin lifts up on his tiptoes to whisper something to John. John nods.

"Care to share?" My gaze bounces between them.

"We were trying to determine if you are a chocolate girl or more of a sour worms girl when it comes to candy. I bet five dollars you are all about the gummies." Dustin winks.

I tilt my head. Whatever transpired between them, they don't want me to know. I try not to dwell on what I'm missing. "Um…pregnant or not?"

"Does that make a difference?"

I shrug. If he's not up for offering answers, neither am I.

Dustin glares at me. "Well played."

The guests at the counter move and we step up. I order a pack of Cookie Dough Bites and a pack of sour gummy worms. John chuckles as I do.

Since I'm sitting in the middle, I'm in charge of the popcorn bucket. The movie is a quarter of the way through when Dustin reaches over for another handful of popcorn at the same time I shift my position, moving the popcorn out of reach.

"Um, rude," Dustin whispers.

"Sorry." I hand the popcorn over. "Do you want some gummy worms?"

Dustin leans close to me. "Is there any chocolate left?"

I shrug, knowing the chocolate was gone ten minutes into the movie.

Dustin holds out his hand and I give him a few sour worms.

After the movie as we're heading to the parking lot, I ask Dustin for his phone. He gives me a quizzical look but unlocks his phone, handing it to me. I enter my number into his contacts and then quickly text myself, so I can save his number. Handing his phone back, I say, "Now you don't have to wait to apologize."

Dustin smiles. "Thanks."

Eleven

Andi glances at her phone and then out the window. "Shouldn't he be here by now?"

I scan the crowd, hoping to spot any sign of Kyle. We've circled the airport three times now. I'm about to pull into traffic and begin our fourth lap when Andi yells to stop. I quickly pull over, causing several cars behind me to honk. Andi is immediately out of the car. I check my side mirror to see Kyle drop his bag as she throws her arms around him. I grin as they make their way back to the car.

I pop the trunk. Kyle throws his bag in and then climbs into the front passenger seat while Andi climbs in back, taking the middle seat. She leans forward. "So, did you miss us?"

Kyle smiles. "Of course I did."

"So, how's Michigan?"

"Not too bad actually."

"How's your grandpa?" I ask.

"Hanging in there." Kyle glances over at me and then down at my belly. "How have you been? How's the little man doing?"

I rest a hand on my always expanding midsection. "We're good. I swear he's training for his blackbelt or something. He's constantly moving."

"She's a bottomless pit," Andi pipes in. "I swear she's always snacking."

I roll my eyes even though she's not wrong.

Kyle laughs. "What else is going on?" Andi and I tell him everything while we drive away.

Kyle stayed the night with Andi, so both of them are waiting outside as I pull up. I roll down the passenger window and say hello. Andi waves, still looking half asleep.

"You ready for this?" Kyle asks as I pull away from the curb.

"I think so?" I barely slept last night because I knew today was the day we meet the adoptive parents in the flesh. In less than an hour, they become people and not just a file in a folder.

When we arrive at the agency, Mrs. Vale guides us back to her office. She goes over what we can expect from this first meeting and then excuses herself.

"Here we go," Kyle whispers. He wipes his hands down the side of his shorts. His foot is tapping a mile a minute.

The door creaks and in steps Mrs. Vale, followed by a couple. They look to be in their early thirties. The woman has auburn hair, a fair complexion, and round hazel eyes. She's wearing jeans and a floral blouse. The man has mousy brown hair with a gray streak right up the front. His eyes are more narrow and deep brown. He's wearing jeans and a nice button-down shirt. I turn to Kyle and examine his cargo shorts and plain gray T-shirt, then glance down at my own navy cotton dress and flip-flops. Maybe I should have dressed up more. Maybe I should have told Kyle to bring more than a carry-on.

"Maclaren Young, Kyle Hart, I would like to introduce Tanya and Joel Challinor."

I stand. Joel steps forward first and extends his hand. Kyle and I each shake his hand. Joel turns to his wife, who's still standing by the door, tears glistening in her eyes. She clears her throat. "Sorry, this is just a bit overwhelming."

The baby chooses this time to catapult off my ribcage and backflip. I inhale sharply. All eyes flash to me. I rub the top right of my belly. "Sorry, the baby is super active right now."

"May I feel?" Mrs. Challinor asks. I nod. She reaches out her hand tentatively, and I gently take it and place it where I feel the most movement. Tears begin to spill over. I bite my lip to keep from crying myself. Her husband comes up beside her and loops his arm around her waist.

"You have to feel this." Mrs. Challinor looks at her husband. She moves her hand, allowing her husband to feel.

"That kid has some moves," Mr. Challinor comments, his voice rough. He blinks a few times and then drops his hand.

"How about we all have a seat and get acquainted?" Mrs. Vale says.

The Challinors take the love seat across from Kyle and me.

"I like to have each couple share a little bit of their story. Maclaren, Kyle, would you like to go first?"

"Um, well, I'm Maclaren, but my friends call me Mac. This is Kyle. We met in sixth grade and have been friends ever since. We weren't dating or anything when this"—I look down—"happened."

It's silent for a bit. I'm not really sure of what else to say and Kyle doesn't elaborate. Mrs. Vale turns to the Challinors.

"I'm Tanya. This is my husband, Joel. We met when we were freshmen in high school. I couldn't stand him at first, but he eventually won me over. We started dating junior year. We did long distance for the first year of college, which was torture."

"Yes, when I told my parents I was moving back for a girl, I thought they were going to drop dead." Joel chuckles.

"They were quite shocked. However, he moved back, and we finished school and were married within two months of graduating. We waited a couple years before we started trying for kids and after

two miscarriages, I went in for tests and found out the
reason. I ended up having a hysterectomy three years ago and…here
we are." Mrs. Challinor shrugs.

"Okay, at this time I would like to open up the conversation to
questions. I find that conversation flows more naturally this way,"
Mrs. Vale states.

The room is silent.

"So, do you actually use your degree in your profession?" Kyle
asks finally. "Also, what is your profession?"

"She does, I don't," Joel answers. "I thought it would be smart to
get a degree in business. You know, start making money straight out
of college. I currently work as a general manager for a major grocery
chain."

"But," Tanya adds, resting a hand on Joel's knee, "he recently
went back to school for architecture. He has a year and a half left."

"What do you do?" Kyle nods toward Tanya.

"I freelance as a graphic designer."

"She is spoiled and works from home." Joel winks.

"How will a baby work into your life?" I ask.

"Since most of my work is freelance, I can choose which jobs I
take. In the beginning I will probably focus on small jobs, just so we
have supplemental income, and then take on more projects once he's
in school."

"Right now, my schedule fluctuates. Hopefully in the next
couple years that will change," Joels adds.

"Do you guys talk about life changes?" I ask.

"Yes," Joel answers.

"Have you ever had a major fight?" I whisper.

"We've had some doozies," Joel answers, glancing over at
Tanya.

"Did you ever think about calling it quits?" My voice cracks.

Kyle slips his hand in mine and squeezes.

"Never. We have always been able to work out our differences. Communication is extremely important to us."

"What happens when or if you can't?" A tear slides down my cheek. I think of my parents once upon a time saying I do and having me, only to end up separated.

"That is never going to happen," Joel says adamantly.

Tanya focuses solely on me. "Speaking as one who came from a broken home, it seems that at any moment a couple could fall apart. Parents always say they will be together forever, so when they fight, you think they will make up. When that doesn't happen, trust in all relationships is broken. I was terrified to marry Joel. I was so afraid that we wouldn't last. We have had some knockdown, drag-out fights. Once, I made him sleep on the couch for a week. I never once kicked him out of the house though. We have always found a way to communicate. If we couldn't do it by ourselves, we got a mediator involved. We've done counseling. We have worked extremely hard to maintain a healthy relationship. We will do it until the day we die. So, when Joel says that is never going to happen, he means it. I know I can't sit here and promise forever, but I promise to do everything to keep my marriage and family together, which for me is going to be forever."

I nod.

"We are also very fortunate to have wonderful examples of what healthy, godly relationships look like," Joel tacks on.

"Godly?" Kyle asks.

"Yes, we attend church regularly and are part of one of our church's life groups, made up of about six couples. We meet a couple times a month to study the Word and fellowship with one another."

"Huh." Kyle nods, taking this in.

"Do either of you attend church?" Tanya asks, eyes bouncing between Kyle and me.

I shake my head. "Is that a problem?"

"Oh my goodness, no, absolutely not. No, it isn't. It was just a question. We really don't care." Tanya's voice jumps an octave.

Joel reaches over, lacing his fingers through hers. "It's not a problem whatsoever. However, since we do attend church, this little boy will be raised in church. Is that something you two are comfortable with?"

I peek over at Kyle who is also staring at me.

"The most important thing is that he's loved. If you guys can give him that, then that's all that matters." My voice catches.

"We can do that," Tanya affirms.

We chat for a little longer and then Mrs. Vale escorts the Challinors out.

The door clicks shut. "I think this is going to be good," Kyle says.

I sit, staring at my belly. I don't know if it was because he could sense I was nervous, but he would not stop moving. Sitting here talking to the Challinors, he settled. Maybe it's because he found their voices soothing or maybe it's because I could feel myself relax. Either way, he's now content. I rub my belly.

"Mac?"

"This isn't going to be good; it's going to be great," I whisper.

Mrs. Vale steps back in. "So, what did you two think?"

"I think they're perfect." A smile spreads across my face.

After dropping Kyle off at the airport and Andi off at Travis's, I'm ready to put some comfortable clothes on and watch television or doodle, maybe both. I'm halfway up the stairs to my apartment when my phone begins to ring. I dig it out of my pocket. "Hey."

"How fast can you get here?" John asks. A bloodcurdling scream pierces through the phone. I pull it away from my ear, wincing. "Mac, if I send you my address, how soon can you get here?" The urgency in his voice reminds me of all the 911 texts Kyle, Andi, and I have sent. I might have to teach him that.

"Um…" My phone buzzes and I click on John's message containing the address. Calculating the drive time and factoring in traffic lights, I answer, "About twenty minutes or so. What's going on?"

"Great. See you soon." The line goes dead. I stare at my home screen for a moment and then make my way back down the stairs.

I climb in my car and bring up the address again, using Google to start the navigation. When I arrive, commotion comes from inside as I raise my hand to knock on the front door. A little boy about four or five answers. "It's a girl," he announces and then goes running. I step inside and close the door.

"John?" I call out.

"Kitchen," John yells over wailing. I follow the sound until I see a little boy sitting on the counter, John holding a blood-soaked towel to his chin.

"Woah, what happened?" I step up beside John. The little boy has tears streaming down his face. He takes a deep breath and lets out another wail.

"I know, buddy," John consoles him. He eases up on the towel and a stream of blood pours out. John quickly presses the towel back, eliciting a high shriek.

"Hey, Jackson, wrap your arms and legs around me, like a monkey." Jackson obeys and John slips his other arm under his bottom. He starts toward the front door. "Can you just make sure everyone stays alive? They've all had dinner, and you don't have to

worry about bedtime. Eric and Jonah will crash on their own, but Eli will stay up as long as possible."

Following John to the door, I realize he expects me to stay here with his three siblings. I look back inside the house. "Okay…"

John smiles and then seems to pause. His eyes trail down my figure, toward my hand pressed on my lower back and stopping at my swollen ankles. His eyes return to mine, and a frown appears. "I'll try and see if Dustin can come over after his shift. I'm not sure how long we'll be, and I know my parents will be out late."

"John, I'll be fine. Just go."

"You sure?"

"Bye," I say, closing the front door. Taking a few steadying breaths, I turn and head toward the sounds of the television. There is a little playpen in the corner with a toddler standing against it. When he sees me, he reaches his hands up and clasps his little fingers together.

"He wants out," the boy who answered the door informs me. There's also an older boy sitting on the couch with red-rimmed eyes.

I leave the toddler in the playpen since he isn't fussing and sit down on the couch next to the boy. "Hi, I'm Mac. Who are you?"

"Eli," he sniffles.

"What's wrong?"

"It was an accident. I didn't do it on purpose," Eli cries.

"I'm sure it was. I'm sure John knows that too." I try to sound comforting but I'm out of my element. I have no idea what to do here. "Can you tell me what happened?"

"He wasn't playing right, and I took the controller from him. He was the one who started it," Eli says defensively.

"How did he get hurt?"

"I moved out of the way and he hit his chin on the table." Eli points to the end table at the other side of the couch. I see a red stain on the carpet near the table. The corner is sharp and could easily slice open a chin.

"I'm gonna be grounded and Jackson probably won't even be in trouble." Eli crosses his arms and pouts.

"That's probably not true," I say, but I have absolutely zero idea if it's true or not. I look up at the television. "What were you playing?"

"Mario."

I nod. I hear a little cry from the playpen, so I walk over and pick up the youngest one.

"That's Jonah," Eli says. "He's supposed to be sleeping. Eric should be too."

"Nuh-uh." Eric shakes his head.

"All right, well, maybe I can get Jonah to sleep and then you can teach me how to play," I suggest.

"Sure, I'm really good. I bet I can beat you a lot."

I sit in the recliner, hoping it rocks. It does. Jonah falls asleep quickly and I lay him back in his playpen. My brain begins to think of what it would be like to rock a small infant. Before my thoughts go too far, I look over at Eric to see if he wants to play, but he's passed out on the floor.

"Okay, teach me how to play."

Eli hands me a controller, briefly tells me what buttons to push, and then asks me to pick a course. I choose Rainbow Road, because it sounds pretty. It's also one of the hardest tracks to race, apparently.

Eli's right. He beats me a lot. We are racing through the Donkey Kong track when Jonah starts to fuss. I'm hoping if I ignore him, he will go back to sleep. By the time I finish the race, Jonah is wailing.

I pick him up and sit in the recliner, rocking slowly. Jonah's head is resting on my shoulder, his legs straddling my belly. As I rock, I feel Jonah relax and he becomes heavy. The baby settles as

well. I quickly blink back tears. This was probably a
mistake. Eli switches from the game to a movie. I'm still rocking
Jonah when the front door opens and John walks in, followed by a
woman in a formal gown carrying Jackson. A man follows dressed
up in a suit. He spots Eli still awake.

"Hey buddy, time for bed."

Eli groans but stops the movie and follows his mom up the
stairs.

John walks over to me. "Here, I can take him."

As I pass Jonah over, my lip begins to tremble. I'm going to lose
it right here in front of a room full of strangers. Concern passes
across John's face. His dad comes over, taking Jonah from him, and
then heads upstairs. The room falls silent.

"Are you okay?" John's voice is gentle.

I nod as a tear slips down my cheek. Standing, I begin to search
for my purse. As I head toward the kitchen, John's footsteps follow. I
grab my purse off the kitchen counter and when I turn John is right in
front of me. I advert my gaze.

"What's wrong?"

A few more tears slip out. I cradle my belly. "The rocking was
too much," I whisper.

John swears under his breath. "I didn't even think about that."

Neither did I, I think. The night was supposed to be simple.
Shrugging, I say, "It's not a big deal." I take a deep breath before
looking at John. "How's Jackson?"

"He ended up with five stitches."

"Ouch."

"Yeah, well, he's hoping he gets a cool scar."

I crack a small smile. "It's not worth it if you don't get an
awesome scar."

"I guess. How did everything go here?"

"Okay. Eli schooled me in *Mario Kart*," I say.

John rolls his eyes, but smiles. "I seriously owe you for tonight. You were a lifesaver."

"Psh." I wave him off.

"Maybe we could grab lunch sometime? You can come practice *Mario Kart*, maybe challenge Eli. He'd hate losing to a girl."

I hesitate before saying, "Okay, text me."

Twelve

John is finally able to repay me for watching his siblings two weeks later. We pull up behind a beat-up sedan in the Freddy's drive-thru. They must be placing the longest order known to man because after a couple minutes they still haven't moved. John rolls down his window and I recognize Dustin's voice over the intercom. "Hello?" Silence. "Hello!" There's still no answer, until Dustin begins speaking in a horrendous British accent. John and I turn to each other and snicker. The accent does the trick and the car finally pulls forward. Once we reach the intercom John adopts an impressive Australian accent.

"Good 'ay, sir. I'll have your number one and a number eight." He glances over and asks in his regular voice if I want a custard. I just nod because I'm laughing too hard. He turns and orders the custard in his Australian accent.

Dustin repeats our order in an exaggerated British accent and then requests that we move to the next window. I try to catch my breath when the baby shifts, pressing on my bladder.

I grab John's arm. "I'm gonna pee my pants," I say, trying to control the fit of giggles. "Oh crap." I cross my legs and look around. The drive-thru is positioned next to the outside patio and I spot a side entrance. "I'll be back."

John chuckles. "Okay, I'll meet you out front."

I climb out and immediately bend over. I pray I make it to the bathroom, but it doesn't look good. As I pass behind John's truck the passenger in the car behind us gives me a perplexed look. I give a little wave.

"Did you make it?" John asks once I finish and climb back in.

I smile. "Barely."

For the rest of the afternoon, John and I camp out on his living room couch. The boys are out for a summer play day at one of the local museums. I've just lost for the fifth time in a row on the same track. John's theory is that if I can get really good at a few tracks, then I can challenge Eli on them and smoke him. So far, it's a failed theory.

"You just gotta keep practicing. Again?"

I shift my position and wince.

"You okay?" John asks.

"Everything hurts," I complain.

"Can I do anything? Can you take something? I think we have some Tylenol."

I lean back but the movement sends a radiating pain down my right leg. I whimper and sit back up. "Actually, would it be okay if lie down?"

"Absolutely." John stands and gives me more room.

"Thanks." I lie down on my left side and try to rest my head on my arms.

"I'll be right back." John heads up the stairs and returns with a couple pillows. He hands them over. I place one between my legs and one under my head. "Better?"

"A little. Hey, can I ask you a question?"

"You just did." He winks at me.

"Haha." I roll my eyes.

"What's your question?"

"I've noticed the décor in your house has a theme." I nod toward the plaque hanging on the wall. *Faith, Hope, Love*. It's not the only item, just the one most visible. There are little platitudes down the hallway and a scripture verse hanging in the kitchen.

"That's not a question," John says.

"Do you go to church?" My heart starts to beat faster, waiting for his answer.

He shrugs. "I used to."

I bite my nail. "Do your parents?"

"Almost every Sunday. They usually cart my brothers with them."

"But you don't?" I clarify.

"Why are you asking?" John asks cautiously.

I sit and think of our meeting with the Challinors. They go to church, and they plan on raising their child in church. I didn't really stop to picture this. Now, the only people I can think of are the people who show up on your doorstep, pushing pamphlets at you and telling you Jesus is the only way, or the occasional lunatic on the street yelling at people that they are all going to hell for their sins. I glance down at my stomach. I guess I'm lumped in with the people going to hell. If I recall, premarital sex is a big no-no.

"Mac?"

"Hm?" I jump when I look up to see John sitting on the floor, right in front of me.

"Church?"

"If you don't want to talk about it, it's fine."

He leans back on his palms. "It's hard to explain." He takes a deep breath.

"If you don't go to church, do you believe in God?"

"Yes," he says without hesitation. "I believe God exists and I think church is good. I just…I don't know. I've been going to church my whole life. The older I got, the more I started questioning things. Once I was able to drive myself, my parents let me decide if I wanted to go or not. I still join them on holidays. I just don't attend regularly."

I nod, like this makes total sense to me. I'm about to ask another question when Jackson comes rushing in, bandage on his chin. "John, John, come look what we made!" He tackles John and then begins pulling on his arm.

"Ouch, okay. I'll be there in a minute."

"John," his mom calls out. "Do you have plans this afternoon?"

"I have to take Mac home at some point," he yells back.

His mom comes around the corner. "Hello, I didn't get a chance to introduce myself last time. I'm Marie. Thank you for watching these terrors. I truly appreciate it."

"No problem," I say.

She turns to John. "Eli was invited to a pool party and I have to do a couple things for the Gilman wedding. Do you think you could keep the others entertained for a couple hours? I bought all the ingredients to make slime."

John grimaces.

"I know, it's messy, but it will keep them entertained and I just need a moment to concentrate and get the material over to Bre by four. Then you will be free the rest of the day. Promise. Mac is welcome to stay."

John looks over at me and then up at his mom. "What if I take her home and then entertain the hoodlums?"

"I can hang out for a bit," I offer.

"Are you sure?" John asks.

"Yep."

I take a seat at the table. Marie gets Jonah strapped into the high chair as John grabs a mixing bowl and measuring cups. Jackson and Eric pull out their chairs.

"Be good," Marie says as she leaves. John puts a measuring cup in front of Jackson and Eric and then hands Jonah a little one, which he proceeds to bang on the table.

"Okay, it looks like we need one cup of glue and then half a cup of starch. Jackson, you want to measure the glue?" John slides the bottle over.

"Hey, I want to do it," Eric whines.

"No, John said I'm doing it." Jackson snatches the bottle up and unscrews the cap.

"Eric, you can pour the starch," John says. Eric crosses his arms as John reaches for his measuring cup.

"You're not helping Jackson," Eric mumbles.

"Fine. Be very careful though." John hands Eric the jug of liquid starch, keeping one hand close in case Eric faulters.

They pour the glue and starch into the mixing bowl. "I'm mixing!" Eric announces, grabbing the spatula. He immediately splashes liquid everywhere.

"Slowly," John instructs.

Jonah looks up. "I do it. I do it." He chucks his tiny measuring cup and reaches for the mixing bowl.

John takes a deep breath. "In a minute."

I sit watching, resting my hands on my belly. John looks up at me. I give him a smile. "Did you need any help from me?"

He smiles back. "Do you want to pick the color?"

Both boys protest at this suggestion. I shake my head too.

"Please do," he insists. "Otherwise, we will have a fight."

"Um…" All of a sudden, my belly tightens. I scrunch my face and hope it looks like I'm contemplating a color. "Green?"

John tilts his head, studying me for a second. "Perfect," he says and grabs the bottle of food coloring.

"No," Eric and Jackson moan.

John adds a few drops to the still liquid mixture and slides the bowl over to Jonah. He holds the spoon and guides his hands. After a few stirs, John hands the bowl over to Eric. "Mix it a little and then pass it to Jacks. I'll be back in just a moment."

John stands and leaves the kitchen while Eric continues to stir. Jackson drums his fingers on the table and then reaches for the spatula. "My turn!"

"Not yet. I'm still stirring." Eric wraps a protective arm around the bowl.

"Hey, Eric. Let's let Jackson take his turn," I say.

"Yeah!" Jackson nods at me. He grabs the bowl and yanks. It flies out of Eric's arms, spraying green everywhere. Cold liquid slides down my belly, into my lap. The bowl lands with a clang on the table.

John, staring at his phone, rounds the corner.

"That's not my fault!" Jackson yells.

"Well, it's not mine," Eric retorts.

John looks up, eyes widening. Jonah reaches over and splashes in the liquid that still hasn't solidified into anything resembling slime. When he moves to put his fingers in his mouth, I grab his arm and he begins to cry. Eric and Jackson continue to argue.

"Enough! Go wash up. Now," John erupts. Eric begins to protest, but he cuts him off. "*Now!*" John points to the sink, face turning red.

Eric's little lip trembles, but he gets up and goes over to the sink.

John is silent as he unbuckles and pulls Jonah from the high chair. "You too." He lightly punches Jackson.

Eric leaves the sink and heads toward the living room, water still running. John washes Jonah's hands and arms and then disappears. When Jackson is cleaned up, he too is gone. I sit there in the empty kitchen, not really sure what to do. The liquid is still slowly dripping from the table onto my lap. I do my best to push the liquid away from the edge.

John comes back in and grabs the paper towels off the counter. He unwraps a few and piles them on the giant puddle. He blows out a hot breath and then looks over at me. He shakes his head. "I'm so sorry."

"No biggie. Can I get a few of those?" I point to the paper towels. John hands me the whole roll. I rip off a few and begin to pat my lap.

"Oh dear," Marie says, entering the disaster zone.

"So much for your quiet afternoon. Sorry."

"You tried." She pats John on the back. John takes the soiled paper towels to the trash.

"Hey, I'll go grab you a change of clothes. I'll be right back," he says to me.

"Thanks."

Marie grabs a washcloth from one of the drawers, wets it, and comes over to the table to finish cleaning.

"Um…I promise to clean up but I really need to use the bathroom. But…" I gesture to my clothes, covered in slime.

"Don't worry about the mess. Go, go."

As I'm washing my hands, I hear a knock. "I brought you some clothes." I open the door and John hands me a T-shirt and denim shorts. "The shorts were my mom's. If they don't work, let me know."

I nod. Surprisingly, they fit well. I meet John back in the kitchen when I'm done. "I'm so sorry. That did not go how I planned," he says, handing me a plastic bag for my soiled clothes.

"We never actually made slime." I frown.

"When it works, it's pretty cool. The boys would have sat here forever. Granted, after ten or fifteen minutes, all they would've done is make fart noises. Whatever keeps them entertained."

"I guess." My belly tightens again worryingly, but I fight to keep any reaction off my face.

John gives me a concerned look. "I think we're just going to chill in the living room. Are you sure you're okay?"

"Yep." I flash a smile, trying not to overreact.

John opens his mouth and then closes it. "Come on." He nods toward the living room.

After thirty minutes watching the boys entertain themselves on different devices, John catches me grimacing. He disappears upstairs and ten minutes later, his mom comes downstairs with her laptop. John gathers his keys and says we are free to go.

In the truck, I feel the same tightening sensation and slowly massage my belly. I take slow purposeful breaths because I can feel myself starting to panic.

"What's wrong?" John asks. He looks over once he comes to a complete stop at a light.

"Nothing, I hope." I leave one hand on my stomach and bite down on my thumb nail.

"What are you feeling?"

"Like, cramps, kind of. My belly gets really hard, but then everything relaxes," I explain.

"Hmm."

"Hmm? What? This is probably bad, right?" I squeak.

The light turns green. He hits the phone button on his steering wheel and scrolls through his calls until he lands on his mom's number. The cab of his truck fills with the phone ringing.

"Hey, miss me already?" she answers.

"Yeah. Hey Mom, how can you tell when you're really having contractions and not the fake ones? What are they called?"

"Braxton Hicks?"

"Yeah, those."

"It can be hard to tell at first. Why? Is Maclaren having contractions?"

John reaches up and pulls my hand away from my mouth. "She's not sure."

"Okay. What is she feeling?"

John looks at me and nods.

I try to explain exactly what I'm feeling in as much detail as possible. I reach to bite my nail again, but John stops me. I clench my fists together.

"Does that feeling last a long time?"

"No, maybe a minute or so."

"When did you notice this?"

We pull into a parking spot outside my apartment complex. What if this is the start of labor? What if contractions get worse? Are these even contractions? It's way too early to go into labor, but it happens. I've been trying to do everything by the book, trying to ignore all the fears other people have about this pregnancy, including my own, and focus on what he needs. Every doctor's appointment I've had so far shows a perfectly healthy baby, but what if what I've been doing isn't enough? What did I do wrong?

"Mac, hey, it's okay," John whispers. "Breathe."

I shake my head. This is not okay.

"Did I lose you?" his mom asks.

John takes my hand and squeezes. "Nope. Still here. Mac's nervous."

Nervous is an understatement. I'm full-blown panicking, I think.

John looks right at me and takes a deep breath in through his nose. He holds it then releases all the air through his mouth. I nod and imitate him. He interlaces his fingers through mine, his thumb slowly rubbing back and forth. "Mom, what should she really be paying attention to?"

"I think the most important thing right now is how long they last and the intensity. Honey, do they hurt?"

I shake my head. "No," John answers for me.

"I would suggest putting your feet up, making sure you are hydrated, and doing something relaxing. Hopefully they will subside. If they become consistent, more painful, or there are any other symptoms that are concerning, call your doctor immediately or go to the hospital. That's my motherly advice."

"Mom, I'm gonna stay with Mac until we're sure everything's good," John says.

"Perfect. Call me if you need anything. Mac, hang in there. Pregnancy is the worst sometimes."

I chuckle despite the situation. "It kind of is."

"Here, do you want to sit down? Do you need anything?" John asks as we walk into the apartment.

"I think I'm just going to grab some"—I scrunch up my nose in discomfort as another wave passes—"pillows."

"I can go grab them. Unless that's too weird," John offers.

Thinking of the state of my room with piles of dirty laundry on the floor, a bra hanging from my bedframe, and scraps of fabric littering my desk, I shake my head. "I'm good. Do you mind grabbing a couple water bottles from the fridge though?" I call as I walk to my room. I message my doctor's office, hoping these are Braxton Hicks like John's mom said and I don't have to go in.

John is waiting in the living room, two water bottles in hand, when I come back. I plop the pillows onto the couch and then start arranging them. Once I lie down, I fiddle with the configuration until I'm somewhat comfortable.

John sets the water on the end table within reach and then sits down on the floor in front of me. I close my eyes, resting my hands on my belly, waiting for another contraction. When I blink them open again, John's ocean-blue eyes are focused on me.

"Are you sure you don't want to go in?" John asks, brows furrowed.

My phone chimes with a message from my doctor, and I breathe a sigh of relief. "Yeah, I was able to message my doctor, and she gave me the same advice as your mom. It's just a little scary," I admit.

"That's understandable. Let me know if something changes, okay?"

I nod. John turns toward the television and we pick something to watch. Eventually, I don't feel any contractions and my eyelids grow heavy.

"John?"

"Hm?" He turns.

"I think I'm okay. You can leave whenever." My words slur with sleep. If John responds to me, I don't hear it.

I'm woken by commotion coming from the dining area. I sit up and see John's back and Dustin's profile. Their attention is fixed on something on the table. I walk over and see a Nintendo Switch setup.

"No! What? That move is supposed to kill you," Dustin protests.

"Apparently not," John quips.

On the screen, Mario runs across a bridge over to another floating island. Yoshi is quick to follow, launching a shell at Mario. Mario dodges it and then attacks Yoshi.

"Who's who?" I ask. Dustin jumps. He must not have noticed me. John just laughs and then looks up at me.

"How was your nap?" he asks, turning his attention back to the screen.

"Okay. How long was I out?"

"A couple hours."

I glance at the microwave and realize it's a quarter past six. I wander over to the fridge and look to see what I have for dinner, then move to the pantry. "You guys hungry?" I peek around the pantry door.

"Sure," Dustin answers, frowning. He sneers at the screen.

"Okay. I have spaghetti or…" I walk back over to the fridge. "Quesadillas." I glance back at the boys but they are too focused on the game.

"Ha! Suck it." John throws his hands up in victory.

"No way. Rematch, now."

John looks over at me. "Quesadillas sounds good. Do you want help? I can make them if you're not feeling up to it."

I roll my eyes. "I'm fine." I spot a bag of tortilla chips and then have a brilliant idea. "We can do dessert nachos afterward."

"What are dessert nachos?" Dustin asks.

"Okay, stick with me here. Tortilla chips covered in Reese's Pieces or M&M's, or both, and then mini chocolate chips and marshmallows, drizzled in caramel sauce, dipped in ice cream." I mime a mic drop.

Neither of the boys say anything. I stand there a moment longer. "No? Just me then."

"Do you have everything to make that?" Dustin asks.

I look back at the pantry. "I'd have to go to the store. I only have chips. But, man, that sounds so bomb." Even if the boys think this idea is crazy, my mouth is watering just thinking about it.

"What all did you list?" John whips his phone out. I start repeating all the toppings and he types everything in his phone. "I can run to the store really quick."

"Are you serious?" I clap my hands excitedly. "You're the best."

"I'll be back."

"Perfect. I'll get dinner going."

Dustin stays behind, partly because I don't think John wants to leave me alone. I'm slightly annoyed, but at the same time, I think it's really sweet. I start warming up the skillet, playing music in the background.

"Is that John's shirt?" Dustin pipes in.

"Mm-hmm."

I turn and Dustin raises his eyebrows.

"Slime experiment gone wrong." I shrug. The song changes to Arrows in Action.

"Oh, did you see them when they were here?"

"I wanted to." I lay a tortilla on the skillet, add some chicken, and sprinkle a handful of cheese on. I lean against the counter and wait for the cheese to melt.

"Why didn't you? The show was great. Maybe we could have met there and then you would have a much cooler nickname."

"That was when I found out." I pat my belly.

"And? All of a sudden you couldn't do anything fun?"

"No. I just didn't want to spend the whole show in the bathroom puking my guts out, which I was currently doing at the time."

"Yuck."

I nod. I fold the quesadilla and make sure the tortilla has a nice crisp shell. I move the completed quesadilla to a plate and start the next one.

"Have you heard of You've Got Mail?" Dustin asks.

I shake my head.

"They're this great local band, very similar vibe to Arrows in Action or Heroes Like Villains mixed with The Cab."

I grab my phone and search for them on Spotify. I hit play and listen as I finish the quesadillas.

John arrives with all the ingredients to make dessert nachos. We sit and eat our quesadillas and then I get up to start the nacho assembly. I have a brilliant idea to broil the marshmallows so they get all gooey. I spread out a layer of tortilla chips on a cookie sheet and then sprinkle marshmallows on top. I set the oven on broil and wait for it to heat up. When I bend to put the pan in the oven, the same tightness as earlier returns. "Ouch."

"Everything okay?" John walks up behind me. He rests his hand on the small of my back for a nanosecond and then removes it.

I straighten, catching Dustin watching us intently. John only looks at me in concern.

"Sorry, all good," I answer.

John's brows furrow. I give him a smile and open the bags of the other toppings. I leave the pan in for less than a minute and then pull it out, letting it cool before transferring the chips onto a large platter and adding all the chocolate. I scoop some ice cream into a bowl and take it all into the living room.

Once I've eased myself down to the floor, I lean over and pull a tortilla chip out of the pile. I pop it in my mouth while both boys stare. "If neither of you move, these will be gone in seconds," I proclaim, grabbing another chip, this time dipping it in the ice cream. "Oh. My. Gosh."

Dustin plops down next to the coffee table and tentatively grabs a chip. He examines it and then dips it in the ice cream, crunching down. His eyes immediately light up. "Woah."

"So good, right?" I scoop some mini chocolate chips up with a chip, dip it in ice cream, and take a bite. I glance up at John. "You're missing out."

Dustin nods enthusiastically, grabbing another chip. "On second thought, this is horrible, and I think Mac and I should spare you." Dustin winks.

John comes over, taking a seat beside me. He snatches one up and eats it, chewing slowly. "You're right, this is horrible." John reaches over and slides the plate away from Dustin. He lunges, swiping another chip.

We turn on Hulu and binge a few episodes of *Schitt's Creek*. The nachos are, unfortunately, consumed in minutes, but they'll be easy to make again. Halfway through an episode, I move to the couch. I'm situating the pillows when the front door opens and my dad walks in.

"Hi there," he says, taking in the two boys sitting in our living room.

"Oh, sorry. I guess I should have messaged you. Dad, this is John and Dustin." My dad nods to each of them. "I made quesadillas. Do you want anything?"

"I'll scrounge up something." He heads to the kitchen and makes a quick bite for himself. "All right, I'm going to let you guys enjoy your evening."

A small contraction makes me flinch and I can't help it—a gasp escapes me.

"Maclaren," my dad snaps. "How long has that been going on?" Shattering glass accompanies the end of his question.

"Not long." I shrug, glancing up at my dad. His hand is frozen like he's still holding the cup. The plate remains in his other hand.

He stares at me, eyes wide, and his free hand curls into a fist. "I need an actual length of time, young lady."

"It started this afternoon—"

"Have you been ignoring this?" My dad's anger flares. "Maclaren Fay, this is serious."

My lip trembles and a tear slides down my cheek. Out of the corner of my eye I notice Dustin tense and John shifts closer to me.

My dad lets out a sigh. He sets down his plate and sits in front of me on the coffee table. John scootches out of his way.

"Peanut, I'm sorry. Let's try that again." His voice is calm. "It looked like you had a contraction. Is that what that was?"

I nod.

"This has been going on since this afternoon?"

"Yes, but I didn't ignore it." I explain all the steps I took.

"Okay." He nods. "That's good."

"I'm really sorry." My voice breaks.

"Don't be sorry. Just scared me is all." He smooths back my hair then leans over and kisses my forehead. "I didn't mean to snap. I apologize."

I nod.

"I'm going to let you watch your show and hang out with your friends. You'll come get me if you need anything?"

"Yep," I whisper.

He gives me another kiss on the forehead before grabbing the broom. The room is silent except for the clinking of glass. Once the floor is clean my dad leaves. John slides over to the couch. "Do you want to talk?"

I shake my head and push play. I desperately want to reach down and lace my fingers through John's. The feeling of his hand in mine earlier was comforting and that's all I want right now. As if he can sense me staring, John looks back. I give him a small smile and then divert my attention toward the television.

Once the episode ends, John and Dustin take off. Heading for bed, I peek my head into the hallway and say goodnight to my dad.

"Peanut, can we talk?" I enter his room and sit on the edge of his bed. "Look, I'm sorry for lashing out earlier."

"You already apologized."

"I know. I just felt like I should explain." He takes a deep breath. "When your mom was pregnant with you, she took *every* precaution. She was determined to have a healthy, successful pregnancy, and she did. But we were in the emergency room or labor and delivery quite a bit. The first time she ever experienced contractions, I rushed home from work and took her in. Of course, it was just a normal part of pregnancy, but for her it was terrifying. When you announced you were pregnant, it scared the crap out of me. I didn't want you to walk through what your mother did. I didn't want you to have to deal with the heartbreak of a miscarriage at such a young age. Not that I wanted you to deal with a pregnancy at this age either..." He raises his eyebrow. "When I saw you tonight, I panicked."

"I'm not her," I whisper.

"I know."

"Dad—"

"Maclaren, you're going to have to go easy on me. I'm trying to be the cool, relaxed dad. I'm trying to let you do you. Stress is not good for the mom or the baby, so I've been trying to create a stress-free environment here."

"And you're doing great."

He smiles. "Hopefully that can continue. If I lose my cool, just know it's because I love you and I'm worried about you."

I nod, grateful he told me why he reacted so strongly. "Love you too."

Thirteen

"Hi," I greet John, winded from the stairs. He and Dustin have come to pick me up for a day out.

"Hey." He furrows his brow but doesn't say anything.

He turns and I follow him to his truck. Dustin is sitting on the running board, his fingers tapping against his leg. It seems ever since quitting, he's more fidgety. He lets out a little cat call and I roll my eyes. "You look way too good to be hanging out with us. What's the occasion? Or is this one of those dress-for-how-you-want-to-feel moments?"

"Had to meet with my adoption agent."

"Oh."

"You're right though. I look *way* too good to be seen with the two of you." I wink.

John parks in front of Jolt. Outside, there are a few metal tables and then what looks like inflatable couches and chairs in neon colors.

"What is this place?"

"Where the best coffee lives," John says. I scrunch my nose. "Not a coffee drinker?" I shake my head. "Don't worry, they have tea and lemonade too."

As we step to the door, I catch John watching Dustin. A slight frown pulls the corners of his mouth and his brows are furrowed. I've

seen that look aimed at me several times—he's worried. I
look back at Dustin, who seems perfectly fine.

Walking in, it takes a moment for my eyes to absorb everything.
In the left corner, there is a living room set up with carpet, a couch,
and chairs. There are shelves against the wall and in the corner full of
video tapes and CDs. The other side has plenty of tables, all of them
covered in bright neon geometric shapes. The menu looks extensive.
I step up behind John and Dustin. They both order and then step
aside for me.

"How's the special?" I ask. I've never heard of blueberry
lemonade, but it sounds appealing.

The girl behind the counter peeks back at the special board.
"Um, its good." Her response does not convince me, but my brain is
stuck on the lemonade.

"You're sure?"

She nods. "I was really surprised. If you end up not liking it, we
can make you something different. We have a ton of flavors. Another
surprising one is the guava lemonade."

"Guava? Huh. I think I'll stick with the blueberry, but I'll keep
that in mind."

She types the order into her computer while John steps to my
side and taps his card. "Thanks." He nods to the girl. She gives him a
shy smile and then moves down the counter to make our drinks.

"She must be new. I haven't seen her before," Dustin remarks as
we take our seats at one of the tables. After shifting in my seat
several times, Dustin asks if I'd like to move to the couch. That little
frown appears on John's face but is quickly erased.

The girl at the counter calls our order and I get up. I grab two of
the three cups. John is behind me to grab the last one. "Let's try over
there." He nods toward the fake living room.

"I'm really fine," I say.

"Maybe it's me. Maybe I want a nice plush pillow to lean against."

Dustin meets us over there. I notice Dustin wince as he sits down and I realize maybe there's a reason John's worried about him and why he suggested sitting somewhere with a little more cushion. John's not looking out just for me.

John and Dustin escort me back to my apartment. I make it to the second landing and have to stop and catch my breath. "Sorry," I wheeze. With my free hand I push down on the top of my belly, hoping the little man will get the gist and move away from my ribcage. He shifts a little but then settles, now feeling even higher than before.

"All good. Take your time." John leans on the railing.

I hear voices coming from the floor above, clearly in a heated argument.

"Of course I'm thinking about her," my dad yells. I glance up, listening more intently.

John follows my gaze. "What's up?"

"Tonight's complex drama, brought to you by my parents."

The voices grow louder. I sigh and begin up the stairs again when Dustin darts in front of me. "Maybe you should wait." There's a hint of worry in Dustin's voice.

"It's fine. They fight frequently." I roll my eyes.

Dustin still blocks my path. "Maclaren, are you sure it's safe?"

"They yell all the time. I should see if I can defuse this." I go to take a step, but Dustin doesn't move.

"It's just yelling?" Dustin asks. I nod, a little perplexed. Dustin hesitates and then slowly moves aside. When I pass him, he mutters, "Sometimes it can become more than just yelling."

I glance over at him, realizing what he means.

"I'll be okay. You guys can go. I'll talk to you later."

I make it two steps when my mom says, "You're letting her chase some unhinged dream."

That stops me cold. *What does that mean?*

Pressure on my back causes me to suck in a breath.

"Are you okay?" John whispers from right beside me. His fingers twitch, but he keeps his hand pressed in the center of my back.

Shaking my head, I look up at John. His beautiful blue eyes stare at me. Dustin stands on the stair behind us, steadfast, glowering up at the third story.

"I should go," I murmur.

"Maclaren, you don't have to. We'll bring you back later," Dustin offers. It strikes me that Dustin hasn't used his nickname for me once in the last few minutes. It's so unnerving to hear my full name from Dustin. The situation seems to have a more serious tone without it.

When I shift, John drops his hand. I lean over and give Dustin a quick hug. "I'm okay."

Straightening, I look over at John, reaching out and giving his hand a squeeze. "I'll see you later."

I leave the boys on the stairs. When I reach the third floor landing my dad is standing in the doorway, my mom outside, her arms crossed.

"Hi," I say breathlessly.

"This is what I mean." My mom gestures to me. "It's too much."

"Mom, everything is fine. I'm fine."

"Honey, I know you think that, but—"

"But what? The doctor said physical exercise is good for me. There haven't been any complications so far. Stop worrying." I head inside while my dad steps out, closing the door behind him. Taking a seat on the couch, I see a crumpled paper on the floor. I lean forward and retrieve the paper to flatten it out. All the wind is knocked out of me when I read Otis College of Art and Design at the top of the advertisement. I requested information a few months ago. How did my mom know?

I flip the paper over to see our home address printed in the corner. It must have autofilled the information when I completed the form. There is no way I would have entered my mom's address. I crumple it back up and toss it in the trash. When my dad walks in, he looks tired.

"That was my fault," I blurt out.

My dad shakes his head.

"Dad, I'm really—"

"Maclaren, stop. It was supposed to be a civil discussion." My dad sighs, taking a seat in his recliner. "Before you react, I need you to really listen."

I sit up a little straighter.

"I know I've mentioned I have a conference in Atlanta next week, and I'm a little concerned about leaving you alone. I thought maybe staying at your mom's might be good. That was the only thing we were supposed to discuss," he mutters.

"No," I say adamantly.

"Just think about it."

"No. I don't want to. My stuff is here. I'm comfortable here. If I go over there…" I trail off. "Please don't make me go."

My dad gives me a look.

"Dad, she worries about everything. If it were up to her, I wouldn't do anything that whole week. I'd be in bed all day, every day, with her waiting on me. Yuck."

"If you don't go to your mom's, there will be rules. You will have to check in with me and you will have to be honest, especially now that contractions have started."

I try to rebut, but he holds up his hand. "I don't care if they are normal," he says, reading my mind. "Again, cool dad here. However, I am still your dad, and you are still my baby. This is one of those instances where you have to go a little easy on me."

"I promise to abide by all your rules." I smile.

"We will discuss this. I'm not making promises." He pats my knee before making his way to his room.

My phone pings with a text from Kyle saying he will be able to fly in for the meeting with the Challinors next week.

"I won't be by myself now." I smile as I share this news with my dad.

"Kyle will not be staying here," he says sternly.

"What do think will happen?" I ask innocently. My dad cocks his head, scowling. "Kyle won't be staying, but Andi might spend a night or two here. I promise to check in constantly, but this way you don't have to worry, and you don't have to tell Mom."

My dad frowns. He knows I don't want to tell my mom, but he's worried if we don't, and she finds out, it will turn into a fight. I concede. "I'll let her know you will be out of town but that I'll be staying here."

He crosses his arms. "Fine."

"Great." I head toward my room.

"So, when were you going to mention Otis?"

I freeze, turning slowly.

"Do you know when classes start? When was the registration deadline? Is there a possibility for financial aid? When would you have to move in?"

"Dad, it was dumb, okay? Let's not talk about it."

"Who said it was dumb?"

It's what I've heard my whole life, I want to say. Instead, I stand in the hallway, silent.

"Honey, if the school is interesting, then maybe we should look into it. I'm not opposed to you going out of state for college."

I'm not even sure when I'll be attending college. As it is, my due date is a couple weeks before classes start. It's not unheard of for a pregnancy to go past the due date. Not that I think that will happen, but what if it does? Will I be ready for school weeks after having a baby? After giving up a baby? The information I requested wasn't for now, it was an option for later.

"Would you be disappointed if I didn't go to school?" I ask, staring at the floor. I run my hands down my protruding belly.

"Yes," he says, matter-of-factly.

My eyes snap to him.

"If you decided to never go to school, then yes, I would be mildly disappointed. However, I would understand if you needed some time, a gap year if you will, to reorient yourself before starting. Is that what you're thinking of doing?"

I shrug.

My dad stands and envelops me in a tight hug. I wrap my hands around his waist, leaning my head against his chest.

"Peanut, you have a lot going on right now. I trust that you will figure out exactly what you need to move forward. You know I'm always here for you."

"I know," I whisper.

Fourteen

It feels like my whole weekend has revolved around driving to the airport. Saturday morning, I drove my dad to the airport to drop him off for his conference. Then on Sunday, I'm back again to pick up Kyle before we meet up with Andi and the guys.

Kyle climbs into the passenger seat. "Wow, you're so…" He purses his lips. "You look good."

I check my mirrors and pull away from the curb. "Um, thanks. You need a haircut…and you were going to say big, weren't you?"

"No," he scoffs.

"I won't be offended. I feel ginormous."

"The baby is growing quite nicely." I glance over at him and he winks.

"He is." I smile. "So, you ready for tomorrow?"

Kyle rubs his hands down his legs, then interlaces his fingers together and tries to rest them in his lap. "I mean, I guess. It's crazy that we have this visit and then, what, you have one more, right?"

I nod.

Kyle swallows. "And this still feels right? This is still a good idea?" I put the car in park and then turn toward him. "I mean, I'm still in. I don't want to be a parent, but you've had time with him and, I mean, you feel him, so I just wondered if that was changing your mind." Kyle grows quieter at the end like he's afraid to say it out loud, like it could be a possibility.

"We're still on the same page," I reassure him. I catch his mouth fall into a slight frown, but he turns and opens his door.

I step out of the car. Kyle comes walking around and we meet at the hood. It surprises me when Kyle bursts into laughter. I glance around, wondering what I missed. I go to ask when Andi is suddenly there, tackling Kyle.

"Oh my gosh! I'm so happy you're back. I missed you!" She turns toward me. "Oh my gosh, your shoes." Andi bursts into giggles.

I look down but my belly obstructs my view. "What about them?"

Andi grimaces.

"They don't exactly match," Kyle responds.

"What?"

My phone buzzes. I pull it from my purse and see a picture of my feet, one in a black ballet flat and the other in a coral pink flat. I mutter a couple expletives as I turn and head toward the restaurant. I quickly swipe at a tear before it can make its way down my cheek. As I near the front, I see Dustin and John. John furrows his brow. "What's wrong?" Dustin also wears a slight look of concern, but I notice the instant he sees it. A smirk appears on his face, but he tries valiantly not to let it turn into a huge grin or laugh.

"I'm going to the bathroom," I announce.

"Is everything okay?" John asks, not taking his eyes off mine. I nod, walking past them.

I take some time to gather myself in the bathroom and find them at a table afterward. As I approach, John glances down at my feet and finally notices. A smile tugs on his lips. He looks up at me. *You okay?* he mouths.

I shrug and take a seat next to Kyle. Andi sits across from us, Dustin sandwiched between her and John.

"I wouldn't beat yourself up, I'm sure it happens all
time," Andi comments.

I don't respond, picking up my menu, trying to decide if I want a
waffle, pancakes, or maybe an omelet.

"Oh my gosh, it's shoes," she suddenly snaps.

"Andi," Kyle warns.

I glance up to find Andi glaring at Kyle. Very rarely does Andi
lose her temper about Kyle and I hooking up, but something about us
being together must have triggered her anger. There's more behind
her lashing out about shoes.

I clear my throat. "You're probably right. She's right, isn't she?"
I look to John for confirmation.

"Um, yes? I mean, yes. It does happen."

No one says a word, slowly diverting our attention to our menus.
I'm playing eenie meenie miney moe with my breakfast options
when I feel a contraction. I place one hand on my belly and exhale
slowly.

"What happened? What's wrong?" Kyle turns toward me.

"Dude, relax, it's a Braxton Hicks contraction," Dustin answers.
Kyle glances over at him. Dustin shrugs. "Happens."

"How on earth could you possibly know that?" Kyle asks.

"It's the contraction scrunch. If the baby is in her ribs, she
grimaces, and if he kicks her bladder, she'll flinch." All heads turn
toward Dustin. "What? I notice things. Like, how her shoulders"—he
nods toward Andi—"have been up to her ears since she got here. It
seems to have something to do with you two, and I have theories, but
I don't need to know. Or I notice when this guy"—he points his
thumb at John—"makes the little concerned furrow. It's been
directed at Mac more these days, which is nice. But it's not like I just
focus on Mac. I do not have the hots for her the way this one…"
Dustin tilts his head toward John, but then seems to catch himself. He

glances down at his menu. "Hey look, free stack of pancakes for all dads on Father's Day."

The table is silent.

"I wonder how you claim that," I murmur, unsure of what else to say.

"For starters, you have to be a guy," Dustin retorts. "You can come back and get your free pancakes on Moth—" Dustin clamps his mouth shut. I look up at him. *Sorry*, he mouths, which catches me off guard. I haven't really talked about people calling me Mom. When it does happen, I try to shrug it off. In conversations I don't call myself a biological mom or use any terminology referring to Mom. It's not like I don't understand how biology works. I will always be his birth mother, but I won't be his mom. Mom should be reserved for the person who raises you. The one who kisses your boo-boos and brings you soup when you're sick. Mom is the one who enforces curfew and grounds you when you break the rules. I will not be a mom, and if I call myself as such, I'm not sure how I will handle giving him up. He isn't meant to be mine.

I sniffle, immediately grabbing my napkin to blow my nose. I quickly swipe away the tear that starts to fall. Kyle places a hand on my knee and gives it a gentle squeeze. The gesture is comforting but it's not Kyle's comfort I want right now. I glance over at John, who's studying his menu.

Once we order our food, the conversation shifts to lighter topics. Kyle tells us about baseball camp that started up last week. I'm barely listening, too focused on the look on Kyle's face earlier. He seemed disappointed in the car, which is weird because we don't want to be parents. In the beginning, his first thought was to get an abortion. Boom. Easy peasy.

"Who is this?" I look at Andi, who is laser focused on Kyle. I tune back into their conversation. He must have been talking about a girl.

"She's Nate's sister. She's insanely knowledgeable about all things baseball. She can rattle off stats like a pro," Kyle says in awe.

"Uh-huh." Andi nods and I can see the wheels turning, trying to figure out how she can set them up from a couple hundred miles away. "What's her full name?"

"Megan Sharp." Kyle looks at Andi skeptically. "What are you doing?"

A mischievous grin appears on Andi's face. Kyle mutters a curse, and I chuckle. He should have known better than to open his mouth in front of Andi. He throws me a look for help.

"You're on your own," I say.

On the car ride to the adoption agency, we don't talk. Music fills the otherwise silence. Kyle idly drums his hands on his legs.

"How are you?" I finally ask.

"Fine." He glances over at me.

"Are you really though?"

He sighs. "I should know when you have a contraction or what your newest craving is or how many times you peed today."

"Woah, only I know how many times I use the restroom. That's not public knowledge, nor should it be."

"You know what I mean."

I nod.

"I'm missing it," he mumbles.

"You're not missing it. You FaceTime me and I send you videos and pictures. You still get to see him moving and how much I'm growing. Plus, you get to be here today which is exciting." I smile.

"Being a few hundred miles away is not the same. I mean, I'm the dad and yet two other guys know more about this pregnancy than I do. How messed up is that?" I'm shocked at his use of the word Dad. I open my mouth to answer when he states, "It's messed up."

I have no idea what to say to make this better. There are times when I miss Kyle not being here, like he is missing out, but I can't tell him that. We agreed we didn't want to be parents. We wanted to keep our dreams and goals, which was why adoption seemed like the best solution. Sure, heading to his grandparents for the summer was not part of our plan, but we were making it work. At least, I thought we were making it work. Sitting at the red light staring at Kyle, now I'm not so sure.

I park in front of the adoption agency. "Do you want to change anything? I mean, we could—well, I could—send more pictures or FaceTime you more. I could text you updates about the day so you know what's going on."

Kyle lets out a big sigh. "I wish I could just be here." He rubs his hand over his face. "I didn't think this would be so difficult."

"I don't know what to do." I start biting my thumb nail.

"You're doing plenty. I'm just being ridiculous." Kyle takes a deep breath.

"Kyle, this was the deal. We get to live our lives and in another eight-ish weeks, Joel and Tanya get a baby. And before you ask if I'm sure, I'm sure. This is still what you want, right?"

Kyle is silent and my heart starts racing. "Sometimes I've wondered what it would be like." Kyle shrugs. "I know we say we aren't ready, and I know Mrs. Vale told us to remember our why, but I don't know. She said people become ready…"

The wind feels like it's been knocked out of me. I stare out the windshield.

"Sorry."

I shake my head. "Don't be. If that's how you feel, I want you to be honest."

"Maclaren, I'm still on board one hundred percent with adoption. I need you to know that. I can think about being a dad and watching my—watching *him*—grow up, but then I think of everything that would mean giving up and I feel selfish for not wanting to. I know we're doing the right thing."

I peek at the dashboard and catch the time. "We have to go in," I say, my voice cracking.

Kyle swears under his breath. "I shouldn't have said anything."

I open my door, heading into the adoption agency. Kyle follows behind. When Mrs. Vale comes out, she has a huge smile on her face. She leads us back to her office where Joel and Tanya are already seated. Tanya stands when she sees us. "Oh my goodness, Mac. Look at you. You look beautiful."

I give her a smile, afraid any words will get stuck in my throat.

"May I?" She gestures toward my belly. I nod.

She places her hand on each side of my belly, leaning down. "Hi, baby boy. How are you today? It looks like you've grown since I last saw you." The baby kicks and then rolls. Tanya's eyes glisten with tears. She smiles up at me. "How are you doing?"

"Um, this is a lot. Can I just…can I have a minute?"

"Of course." Her smile falters.

"Mac?" Kyle's voice wavers.

"I promise I'll be right back." I leave the room and head down the hall. I pull out my phone and step outside as it starts ringing.

"Hey, Clinic Girl," Dustin greets cheerily.

"Hi. Are you busy?"

"I got a few. What's up?"

I want to ask him if he observed anything weird at breakfast. Maybe he picked up on a vibe. "Um…have you heard 'Tainted Love' by Marilyn Manson?"

"I don't think so."

"It's really good. You should definitely listen to it sometime."

"Okay…" He pauses. "What's going on?" There's a tinge of worry behind his words.

"Nothing, I just, um…" My phone buzzes with a text message but I ignore it. "It's, well…"

"Maclaren, I'm going to need a full sentence at some point."

"The original version was playing when we pulled up to the adoption agency and I kept thinking about the Manson version and then I thought about you because you're into music," I ramble.

"Seriously, Mac. What's wrong?"

"Nothing. I'm fine. You should probably get back to work and I need to get back inside. I'll talk to you later."

"Hold on. Don't hang up."

"No, really, I'm fine. I'll talk to you later." I hang up and head back inside. When I reach the door to Mrs. Vale's office I check my messages. The text from earlier was from Andi.

What the heck is happening? Are you okay? Kyle's panicking. Said you walked out.

I enter Mrs. Vale's office. "Sorry, emotions got the best of me." I take a seat next to Kyle.

"I may have told them what happened," Kyle whispers.

My head whips toward Joel and Tanya. Tanya bites her lower lip, her eyes red, tears streaking her cheeks. Joel clutches her hand. He clears his throat and addresses us. "We knew there would be a chance and we want you to know, if you need time to reevaluate some things—"

"We don't," I interrupt. I look at Kyle, who subtly shakes his head. I keep my focus on him. "This is a lot and it's scary and there are things we didn't realize we would miss"—my voice breaks—"but I really think we aren't meant to be his parents." There's a slight hesitation before Kyle nods. My heart aches but I turn toward Joel and Tanya, trying to sound confident. "You are. Please don't leave doubting that. I really, *really* need you to know that. I'm not changing my mind."

"We're not," Kyle adds. "I'm really sorry about this." Kyle's eyes well with tears and he quickly swipes them away. "This is hard."

Mrs. Vale's voice is soft. "Adoption is tough, but you two are tough as well. I want you to know it's natural to have reservations. Kyle, can you tell me why you decided this was the best route?"

Kyle slides his hands down his thighs. "Because we aren't ready to be parents and because I want a chance to play baseball and because Mac knew if this pregnancy went full-term she wanted to give someone the opportunity to be a mom." He leans close to my ear. "I didn't forget. I think about it twenty-four-seven."

Tears prick my eyes. I swallow. "That's our why." I shift and look at Mrs. Vale.

She nods. "That's your why." She inhales deep. "Before we go any further, I want to make sure both parties are comfortable moving forward. If you want to take some time, Joel, Tanya, I can escort you to a separate room where you two can discuss privately."

Tanya turns to Joel and a knot twists my stomach. I'm terrified they will change their minds all because Kyle expressed reservations. I try to think of something to say to fix this, but no words come to mind. Mrs. Vale leads them out.

"Maclaren, I am so sorry. I didn't mean to mess this up. You walked out and they asked what was wrong. It just came out and now I may have ruined everything. I didn't mean to."

I sit there, staring at the empty couch across from us. If Joel and Tanya decide the adoption process is too much, what does that mean for the baby? What does that mean for me? Do we try to find another couple? Would Kyle keep the baby? When we started looking at couples, it seemed daunting trying to pick someone. The Challinors seemed perfect, and we both agreed on them. Kyle seemed so on board at the beginning.

"What changed?" I whisper.

Kyle startles. "Nothing, I swear. I'm still in this."

"I'm not mad," I say. Kyle sniffles beside me. I reach over and grab the tissues, passing them to Kyle.

After what seems like a lifetime the Challinors walk back in and take their seats. I open my mouth to apologize, but Joel holds up his hand. "My wife and I had our own reservations about this process coming in. We want you two to know, if you're still in, so are we. However, if you are even remotely unsure, you need to be forthright with us."

"This is my fault," Kyle says.

"This is not your fault. You were honest, and that is all we've ever wanted," Tanya consoles.

"I want to move forward," Kyle states and then looks at me.

I agree. "You were meant to be a mom, Tanya. I can tell. I really want that for you, and I really want this little boy to have you as a mom."

Mrs. Vale smiles. "Okay, if we are all in agreement, let's continue and discuss the birthing plan and what will happen when this little guy decides to make an appearance."

Fifteen

I grab my phone. 2:47 AM. I turn over to my left side and try to get comfortable, but it's impossible shifting my thoughts from my meeting with the Challinors earlier to anything else. I scroll through Instagram for a bit. When I glance at the time it's only been ten minutes. I groan and send a message to John.

Are you at work?

You're up late. Or early, I guess, John answers.

Can't sleep. I lay there for a bit then open a new message thread.

Whatcha doing?

I was sleeping. What's up, Clinic Girl?

I roll my eyes and respond. Twenty minutes later, Dustin is outside my apartment complex and we head over to the grocery store.

Dustin frowns when I turn down the stereo. "That was a good song."

"It was. Um, I was actually wondering if I could talk to you."

Dustin's eyes flash to me and then back to the road. "What's up?"

"The other day at my apartment…um…you seemed very concerned about my safety. I was just wondering if everything was okay at your house."

His hands tighten on the steering wheel and he slowly nods. "I knew this conversation was coming." He's silent for a moment. "My parents fought a lot when I was little. I always thought it was just yelling too. That is, until my dad hit me. He immediately apologized and begged me not to say anything. He promised it would never happen again. Me being five, I believed him, so when my mom saw the bruise, I lied about where I got it. For the next couple years he'd knock me around a little, but one night he lost his temper and I ended up in the hospital. It was bad." His voice breaks and he takes a shaky breath. "I remember overhearing my grandmother tell my mom that she would fight her for custody if my mom didn't get me out of the house. She told her there was no acceptable reason my dad could give her to make her stay, especially considering the extent of my injuries."

"Dustin," I breathe.

He shrugs. "It was a long time ago. I lived with my grandmother for a little while but eventually moved in with my mom, and it's been the two of us ever since. I probably overreacted the other night." His eyes shift to me and then down to my belly. "I just don't want to see anything happen to you."

"I'm safe. It's *never* turned physical. At least that I'm aware of."

"Good." Dustin nods once. We grow silent again, tuning back into the music.

Do you get a break soon? I text John as we pull into the parking lot. I watch the three little dots blink as John types out his response.

Yeah, in about thirty mins.

Can you take it early?

Everything all right?

We're bored. And I'm hungry. Bring something chocolate.

We climb out of the truck and as soon as Dustin reaches me, I wrap him in a tight hug. His arms come around me. "It was a long time ago, Mac," he whispers.

"Still." I squeeze tighter before releasing him.

Dustin and I wait on a metal bench outside, still warm from the afternoon. When John finally comes out, he extends a Hershey's chocolate bar to me before taking a seat.

"Really? So basic," I comment.

John swipes the candy bar from my hand. He opens it, breaks off a little section, and then hands it back. "It's chocolate."

I pop one of the squares in my mouth before offering Dustin some. Dustin takes a section. "You know, chocolate is the worst right now." Dustin shoves the whole little strip in his mouth and then licks the melted chocolate off his fingers.

"This was not my choice," I point out.

"You asked for chocolate," John says, exasperated.

"Thank you." I nudge him with my shoulder.

"So, what are you guys doing here?"

"Ask her." Dustin pulls a cigarette from his pocket and moves to lean on the brick pillar.

"I thought you were quitting." The last time I saw him with a cigarette was at the night of the movies.

Dustin rolls the cigarette between his fingers. "I did."

I watch him, but he says nothing more. I turn to John. "How's work going?"

"It's work. I have the freezer section tonight, so it kinda sucks. Now, what's up?"

I rest my hands on my belly. "I told you, couldn't sleep." I try to stifle a yawn.

John studies my face for a moment. "Do you want to talk about anything? You and Kyle met with the adoptive parents, right?" I stare down at my stomach, not answering.

"Oh, I listened to the 'Tainted Love' cover," Dustin pipes up. "I like it."

I nod. Thinking about the cover leads to thinking about what transpired afterward. I close my eyes and force the tears back. John's knee nudges mine.

"Did you see You've Got Mail put out a new single?" Dustin asks. I shake my head and look up.

Dustin fishes his phone out of his pocket, swipes at the screen, and then music fills the night air.

"Not bad," I comment when the song begins to repeat.

"I'd love to see them live sometime. I haven't seen them list any shows recently."

"Let me know when they do play. I'd love to go." My voice trembles a little.

"Mac?" John starts.

"Hey, have either of you thought about just running away?" Dustin asks.

John looks over at Dustin with a mixture of confusion and annoyance.

"What? I mean, I thought about it when I was little, and one time I did. My dad had to come get me." Dustin winces. "I didn't do it again, but I've thought about it from time to time. You know, when life gets really difficult."

"Where would you go?" I ask.

"Somewhere with a beach."

I nod. Running away sounds appealing. I glance down at my midsection. "Some problems you can't run from," I whisper.

John reaches over and gives my knee a squeeze, drawing my attention to him. *You're surviving,* he mouths. I take a deep breath. It's silent for a bit. Dustin fiddles with his cigarette before dropping it to the ground and crushing it with his toe.

"You know, if you can't sleep tomorrow, feel free to come by," John offers.

"Sounds good." I yawn.

John looks over at Dustin. "Please take her home. I'll talk to you two later."

I get a few good hours of sleep in before I have to be up for my shift. As I'm getting ready, my mind replays the events in Mrs. Vale's office for the hundredth time. I quickly shut them down and go to work.

"Hello, earth to Mac." Mr. Cruz waves a hand in front of my face. I startle, realizing I must have zoned out at the register.

I look over. "Sorry. Did you need something?"

"How about calling it early tonight? Go home, relax."

"I'm fine. I can finish my shift." I sit up straighter on the stool, trying to look more alert.

"I know you can. However, you've been distracted for the past couple days. I figured you may appreciate the extra time off."

I glance at the time on the computer. I still have two more hours. "Umm…"

"How about this? I have to finish up some paperwork, should take me about ten, maybe fifteen minutes. You think it over and when I come back, you can let me know your decision."

I nod.

When Mr. Cruz comes back to the front, my purse is on the counter. I thank him for letting me off early and head to the apartment. I text Andi and let her know she can come over whenever she wants.

I'm curled up on the couch, sketching on my iPad when Andi walks in.

"Hey, hey." She plops down on the cushion next to me.

"Hi." I glance up, giving her a small smile.

She frowns. "Everything okay? You left work early."

"Mr. Cruz gave me the option to leave. I figured I'd take it." I shrug.

Andi's eyes examine my face and then look over the rest of me. "You're sure? There's nothing you want to talk about?"

"Yep. Hey, did you get everything figured out for next week?"

"Uh-huh." She scrunches her nose. She opens her mouth to say something but then seemingly bites her tongue, asking instead what we're doing for dinner.

We make chicken alfredo, and then I introduce Andi to the brilliant concept of dessert nachos.

"Holy cow! These are amazing." Andi scoops ice cream onto another chip, popping it in her mouth. "You are a genius." She reaches over and pats my belly. "Thanks, little dude."

I run my hands down my stomach. What if Kyle can't go through with adoption? Would he think of keeping the baby? Would he still go to college in Iowa or would he move back here? Where would he live? His parents are still out in Michigan with his grandparents and don't have plans of returning anytime soon. And then where does that leave me? Would I be involved? How much of the responsibilities would I take up? I wasn't planning on being a mom. I think of Tanya and the look on her face when she realized we could change our minds. My heart splintered. She wants to be a mom so bad and ever since meeting her, I knew she would be amazing.

I clear my throat and Andi peeks over at me. I give her a tentative smile and pop a chip in my mouth.

Andi and I get ready for bed. She is snoring softly when I climb out of bed and quickly change. This time, I don't message Dustin. He is too observant, and even though he stayed quiet last night, I felt like he could read my mind. I show up at John's work and text him that

I'm outside. I stretch out my legs and rest my hands on my belly. I chuckle as John approaches.

"What?" John takes a seat beside me.

"He's got the hiccups."

"I have to ask, how did you sneak out? I have a feeling your dad wouldn't be thrilled that you're out this late."

I shrug. "Easy, my dad isn't here."

"Where is he?"

"Had a business trip this week."

John gives me a once-over. "What?" I ask. "Oh my gosh. It's not like I'm incapable of taking care of myself."

He holds up his hands. "Woah, I didn't say anything."

"You have a look." I narrow my eyes at him. "Why is it when a woman is pregnant, everyone starts treating them differently?"

"Hey, I haven't been treating you differently," he says defensively.

"You're better than most," I concede. "By the way, I'm not by myself. Andi's there."

"She didn't notice?"

"She sleeps like a rock. The world could be ending and she wouldn't wake up."

I glide my hands down my stomach and feel a small contraction. I try to keep my face neutral, but John catches my flinch. He doesn't say anything, just sits back, stretching out his legs.

"So, what do you actually do?" I ask.

"This week I'm on tags." I give him a confused look. "The price tags don't magically hang themselves."

"Do you like it?" I ask. The heat is still stifling, even at 2 AM. Sweat slowly trickles down my back but the baby is now calm, and I feel my eyelids grow heavy.

"Sometimes. It's nice because I don't have to deal with customers." John slides closer, wrapping his arm around me.

"Yeah, customers are the worst," I mumble, leaning my head against his shoulder.

"They can be." I feel John shift and I think that I should sit up, but then John pulls me closer to him. "So, when does Kyle head back?"

I yawn. "Andi dropped him off this afternoon."

"How are you doing?"

I shrug. "I think he might be seeing someone, or at least is interested in someone, which is good." I inhale. "He should have someone. He's great." I glance down at my belly. My thoughts go back to the conversation before the disastrous appointment. Kyle has thought about being a dad. He never mentioned having second thoughts. I wonder how long he's been feeling this way. Has he been able to process his feelings with anyone? Is this new girl in his life aware of why he had to fly home? Has he talked to her? Has he talked to Andi? What if Andi knows something? If Andi knows something, she would tell me, right? Or make Kyle tell me.

As much as I tried to deny it, a piece of me is attached to this little guy, this boy growing inside of me. How could I not? It's been wild to slowly watch him grow, to feel him kick, to form little routines. However, for the past few months, I've been under the impression we would be giving him to the Challinors. Soon, they would be a family. I begin to sob.

"Maclaren?" John wraps his other arm around me. "Hey, what's wrong?"

"It's all falling apart. He said he was fine, but what happens if he's not? What do we do? We had a plan. I had a plan, and I still want to stick with the plan. I can't do this. I…" I sit up and wrap my arms around my belly, tears streaming down my cheeks. All the

emotions I've been holding in for the past couple days come flooding out.

"Mac, what happened?" John whispers, rubbing my back.

I shake my head, not wanting to rehash everything. I'm not sure I can say it out loud.

"Okay. It's…" He takes a breath. "You'll get through this."

I lean into him, my tears soaking his shoulder. As I bawl, John rubs his hand up and down my back comfortingly. At one point, he mutters, "Dude, answer me."

After several minutes, John asks where my phone is.

"In my purse," I blubber. I hear rustling.

"I need your passcode."

I hold out my thumb and he presses the screen to it. I wipe some of the tears from my cheeks, but fresh tears keep flowing, even as I close my eyes, willing them to stop. I'm slowly beginning to fade when a car pulls up to the curb. I open my eyes to see Travis's car parked in front of us.

"Why is he here?" I ask, sitting up.

"I didn't feel comfortable with you driving home by yourself and I have to get back to work."

Travis rolls down the passenger window. "I don't bite," he calls.

John stands and extends his hand to me. I hesitate but then let him pull me to my feet.

"I'll make sure I get your car back to you. Do you have to work tomorrow?"

I nod, swiping the remaining moisture from my face.

"Let me know what time and I'll make sure you have it back by then." John then turns and bends so he can see Travis through the window. "Thanks, man."

"Yep." Travis nods.

I stare at the car for a moment before climbing into the passenger seat. There is an awkward silence as we exit the parking lot.

"I didn't ask him to call you. I didn't ask him to call anyone," I mumble.

"Okay," Travis responds.

"I could have driven myself home," I bite out.

"Did you know driving while tired is actually worse than driving drunk? And driving when you're upset isn't good either."

"For one, it's not worse, and two, I'm fine," I argue.

"For one," he drawls, "they are at least the same and two, you're both. You were literally falling asleep when I pulled up and your eyes are red and puffy."

I open my mouth to continue arguing but I have no defense. I cross my arms and turn toward the window, awkward silence returning.

We're two blocks from my apartment when Travis sighs. I hear him drum his steering wheel and then clear his throat. "She knows something's up. She doesn't know what and she doesn't know how to approach it, but she knows."

I look over at him. His eyes are focused on the road ahead, but then he flicks them over to me. "You need to talk to her."

"With all due respect, this has nothing to do with you. If I were you, I'd stay out of it."

"With all due respect, Andi is important to me, and you are important to her, so like it or not, I'm now in it. I mean, it's a quarter to three and I'm driving you home."

"I didn't ask you to!" I shout, my voice breaking at the end.

Travis parks in front of my apartment building. He turns, his face serious. "You're right, you didn't. Someone who cares about you did and I showed up." Travis shakes his head, letting out a

humorless laugh. "The first few times I hung out with the
three of you, I knew something had happened, but I didn't know
what. I didn't even know Kyle was the father until we were out one
night and I finally pried it out of her. She's been trying so hard to
show up and be there. She is such a loyal friend, and you are so
incredibly lucky to have her. And I know—"

"Are you serious?" I yell. "I know I'm lucky to have Andi. She
is one of the best people on this entire planet. Don't you dare tell me
how lucky I am." I climb out of his car, slamming the door, and head
for the stairs.

After a moment, footsteps approach and then he's right beside
me. I curl my hands into fists. "Thanks for the interruption," he
quips. "I was going to say that I know you know that. You have to
stop tiptoeing around her. Try just having a normal conversation with
her, like how it was before."

He has no idea how it was before. I cast a glare at him as I reach
the steps. I start climbing, trying to go as fast as possible, hoping to
leave Travis behind, but of course he easily keeps up with me.
There's a brief moment where I think of pushing him down the stairs.
We're a quarter of the way up the second flight when he asks, "Do
you need a break?"

"Nope," I wheeze. I grip the handrail, using it to pull myself
along.

"For the love of—please stop."

I shake my head as I take another step.

"Maclaren!" Andi dashes down the stairs, stopping two steps
above me, halting my climb. I rest against the handrail, breathing
heavy. She reaches down to brush a sweaty lock of hair from my
face.

"I thought you were asleep," I pant.

"My phone woke me up and then I realized you weren't in bed. I waited because I know you're up a gazillion times a night, but then you didn't come back."

"You never hear your phone."

She joins me on my step. "Except when it's on full volume because your bestie's pregnant and you don't want to miss anything."

"But you're staying with me."

"Yeah, I figured no one would be calling me, so I just left it alone. Why were you out? Where were you?"

I don't answer, just turn and continue up to the apartment. Again, tears begin to stream down my cheeks.

"Maclaren, what's going on?" She stops me when we reach my landing, panic lacing her words. Travis steps up behind her, wrapping his arm around her waist. She leans into him and part of me wants to murder him. However, there is another miniscule part of me that wants to hug him and say thank you for being there for Andi and coming to rescue me tonight.

"It's really bad, Andi."

Andi turns and gives Travis a quick kiss. He leans in close and whispers something in her ear. She nods and then steps out of his arm, taking my hand and leading us inside. I sit on the couch and fill her in on what happened at the adoption agency and my thoughts ever since.

Sixteen

After I told Andi about Kyle's visit, I felt marginally better. Andi, on
the other hand, was livid. "I'm going to give Kyle a piece of my
mind," she proclaims as she throws a swimsuit in her suitcase.

I sit on her bed, watching her pack for her week out in Michigan
with Kyle. I'm slightly jealous she gets to go and I can't. Apparently,
it's not safe to fly around thirty-six weeks, but because I'm higher
risk, my doctor didn't even want me flying after twenty-five weeks.
"Please don't. Just leave it alone, okay?"

She turns, giving me a look.

"Maybe wait and see if he brings it up," I suggest.

"Fine, but at some point I will be talking to him about this. He
can't just throw a wrench in your plans. Ugh, I can't believe he
didn't say anything to me. Between the two of you, he at least kept
treating me semi-normal."

"Excuse me?"

Andi sighs. "You kept your pregnancy a secret." I open my
mouth to rebut but she holds up her hand. "Even after I knew, there
was still this weird dynamic between us."

"It wasn't that bad."

"It was. Kyle at least tried to keep talking to me like everything
was normal. And I'm not dumb, I know it wasn't. I was so angry
with the two of you and I still have my moments, but it was nice that
he didn't treat me differently."

"Andi—"

"We are not rehashing everything. I'm just saying, Kyle kept up like nothing was happening, but with the one major thing he should have definitely talked about, he left us both out. I might have to hurt him."

"It's really hard." My voice breaks.

She stops packing and comes to sit in front of me. She takes my hands and looks me right in the eye. "I can't even begin to fathom how this is. I'm not the one going through it. You and Kyle are in this together and I'm right here for both of you. Always. Even if I've dreamed of the few dozen ways I could have ended you two for hooking up." She winks. "We're still three peas in a pod."

"I love you."

"Back at ya." She bops my nose and then goes back to packing.

I get an irate text from Kyle the next evening. *A warning would have been nice.*

I told her to go easy. I watch the three little dots dance at the bottom of my screen as I type, *Actually I told her to not say anything.* I hit send just as another message from him appears.

This sucks. I wanted a weekend with my best friend.

I bite my nail, trying to figure out what I can do to make this better.

Kyle's pissed. I may have come on a bit too strong. I roll my eyes at Andi's message.

I click over to our group chat. *Take a breath. Try not to kill each other because I love you both!* I add a kissy face emoji and hit send.

The first few times I video chatted with them over the week, there was definitely still tension. Thankfully, during last night's chat, they seemed to be back to themselves.

It's early when I move to the couch, turning on the television and trying to find a comfortable position. The light from my dad's bedroom illuminates the hall for a second before everything is dark again. My dad's feet pad down the short hallway.

"Morning, peanut. You're up early."

He sits down in his recliner, slipping on his shoes. When he straightens, he glances at me. I return a small smile.

"Is everything okay?"

"I think so."

He moves, kneeling in front of the couch. "What's the matter?" Worry flashes across his face.

My nose scrunches as my belly tightens again. I blow out a slow breath. My dad smooths his hand over my hair.

"How long have you been up?"

"Not a long time. I'm sure they'll go away."

My dad pulls his phone from his pocket. He frowns at the screen, swearing. "I'll see if Charles can cover our meeting this afternoon, but this morning's meeting is going to be tough to cover. Let me make a phone call."

He goes to stand, but I stop him. "Dad, don't worry about it. There's no point missing an important meeting for no reason."

"That didn't look like 'no reason.'"

"I'm fine, really. Have a good day." I push myself up, giving him a quick kiss on the check.

There's a brief window where I think I'm in the clear, but then contractions come back, stronger than before. Grabbing my phone, I open my pregnancy app and begin timing them again. An hour goes by, and they haven't stopped. I find John's number and call. I sit, listening to the phone ring. It's on the last ring when John picks up. I hear a grunt and then rustling.

"Hey. How are you?" I ask.

"Hm?"

"John, were you sleeping?" I glance at the clock, noticing how early it is.

"Almost," he says, his voice rough.

I gasp. "Because you worked last night. Oh my gosh, I'm so sorry. Please go back to sleep or, well, lie back down. I wasn't—" I suck in a breath.

"Everything okay?" John asks, his voice still laced with sleep.

"Mm-hmm." I exhale slowly. "Sorry, get some rest. I'll talk to you later."

"Wait, hey—" I hang up before I hear the rest of the sentence.

I check my pregnancy app. Contractions are all over the place and there is no consistency which means it's not real labor—yet.

I situate my pillows and lie down on the couch, hoping the contractions will subside. When the next contraction hits about twenty minutes later I decide to video call Kyle. He picks up on the second ring.

"Hey, you're up early."

"Yep." A tear slips down my cheek, unbidden.

Kyle frowns. "What's going on?"

"I really need you here," I whimper.

"I was just there and I'll be there in a few weeks."

"What if we don't have weeks?"

He stops what he's doing. "Do we not? Where are you?" Andi appears in the background and smiles when she sees me.

"Look, they're not consistent, but they are starting to really hurt."

"Are you serious?" Kyle says.

Andi looks from him to the phone. "What's up?"

I hear a knock on the front door. I miss what Kyle says as I shuffle over, peeking through the peephole.

"Never hang up on me again," John says, slightly breathless when I open the door.

"Hello?" Kyle yells, making my phone speaker crackle.

"Sorry. What?" I feel another contraction and suck in a breath. I cradle my belly in my arms.

"Do you think this is it? Should I move my flight? Do you need to go to the hospital?" Kyle prattles off.

John pries the phone from my hand. "Hey, man."

"I need an explanation," Kyle demands. Andi leans in next to Kyle.

"I'm a hundred percent sure she is having a contraction right now. I just got here, so that is all I have."

"I'll start checking on flights."

"Wait," I wheeze. "What if this is a false alarm?"

"What if it's not?" Kyle counters. Andi lays a hand on his shoulder. He glances at her and then to the phone.

I turn and head for the couch. John follows.

"Do you think this is it?" Kyle asks again.

"How am I supposed to know?" My voice goes up an octave.

"John's there now. Go to the hospital," Kyle says matter-of-factly. Andi nods.

"I'm not making John take me to the hospital. I'm not even sure I should go. I'm just… I'm just… I'm really scared." Tears spring to my eyes.

"Maclaren, we had a plan. I'm looking at flights now, but everything is later this afternoon, meaning I won't get there until late tonight."

"I know we had a plan," I choke out. "This isn't what I wanted." I bury my face in my palms.

"Mac? How long has this been going on?" John whispers. I minimize Kyle's screen and pull up my pregnancy app. I extend my phone to him and watch as he scrolls through the record of the contractions.

"I tried to be as accurate as I could. Not sure if all of them count, but if I felt anything, I recorded it. I've tried everything to make them stop." My voice breaks.

He kneels down in front of me. "You're doing great."

"Sure, yeah, great job timing. Mac, you need to go the hospital," Kyle snaps. Andi, who is studying her phone, smacks his arm. He scowls at her.

"She's freaking out. Take a chill pill," Andi scolds.

My vision blurs with fresh tears. John angles the camera toward him.

"Hey man, why don't you make note of a couple flights and then if Mac has to go in, she'll text you."

"And then what? Be forty thousand feet in the air while she's delivering the baby? I don't think so."

"Kyle, if this is real labor, then she's in labor. There's a chance she could deliver at any time." My eyes widen and my breathing quickens. John takes my hand, giving it a squeeze, reassuring me. "However, if this is a false alarm, you'll fly out here for no reason. Let's just give Mac a little time and see what happens."

"Fine." The screen goes black. John glances at the phone and then sets it on the coffee table. It lights up with a text message, which I assume is from Andi. I ignore it.

"I'm not ready. This isn't supposed to be happening. Kyle's right, we had it all planned out. He should be here or be able to get here. Maybe he should book a flight. Also, my bag isn't ready. I haven't called the Challinors. They need to know and—" I take deep breath. "It's early."

John takes a seat on the couch next to me, my hand still in his. "You said you tried everything?"

I nod, realizing John has not let go of my hand. All barriers we've kept between us, forgotten.

"Have you called your doctor?"

I shake my head. "I was waiting to see if they became more consistent."

"Why don't we call and see if it would be worth going in?"

I shake my head.

"Why not?" His brow furrows.

"It's too soon. I need more time." I glance down at my belly. "I'm not ready to say goodbye," I whisper.

John squeezes my hand. I hear his phone buzz and he pulls it from his pocket. "Did you text Dustin?" he asks.

"As I waited for Kyle to answer," I say. He turns his phone toward me.

Don't panic. Mac sent me a text. On my way to check on her. Update soon.

There's a knock on the door a minute later. The knob turns and Dustin peeks in. "Mac?" He steps in and spots me and John on the couch. "I thought she couldn't reach you."

"I was in bed when she called," John explains.

"What's going on?" Dustin asks as he plops down in my dad's recliner.

"She's been having contractions," John answers, giving my hand a little squeeze.

I squeeze back and then stand. Both boys sit up straighter. "I guess I should go pack," I say. I head toward my room, footsteps following behind me. As I flip on my room light, I call my doctor. The phone rings as I head for my closet. I take down my small duffle bag, set it on my bed, and then head for my dresser. As I gather clothes, I notice Dustin leaning over my desk examining the drawings I have on my wall. He reaches out and runs his finger down one of them.

"Hello, you've reached the on-call service line for Haven Women Medical Center. Is this an emergency?"

"No," I answer. Dustin looks over at me then takes a step back.

"Hello, this is Nadeem. Can I get your name and date of birth?"

I give Nadeem all the information she requests and then she patches me through to the doctor on call, which happens to be my doctor. I breathe a sigh of relief. After explaining my morning, she gives me instructions and a few additional signs it's turning into real labor. She leaves me with a, "Maybe I'll see you soon." I hang up and bite my fingernail.

"What did she say?" Dustin asks.

"That if they don't quit, I need to go in." My voice cracks. I step out toward the bathroom and the boys part, letting me pass. I grab up all my toiletries. I'm looking for my toothbrush holder when another contraction hits. I lean on the counter and try to breathe. A hand presses on my lower back and slowly rubs side to side.

"Keep breathing," John whispers. "You're doing great."

I shake my head. I take a few deep breaths before resuming my search. John's hand slides from my back but he stands in the bathroom with me.

Once my bag is packed, I check my phone, viewing the message from Andi. She says her flight out is today and asks me to keep her updated about everything going on. She can meet me wherever I am or stay the night, if need be. I reply with a thumbs-up and continue to pace the living room floor, praying that I don't feel another contraction. I'm also starting to feel nauseous, which makes me worried.

"Mac, I know you don't want to, but I think you should go get checked out." John's tone is gentle.

I stop pacing and look over at him. "I'm not ready."

"I know," John says.

Both boys get up. Dustin heads out the door and John comes to stand in front of me. He places his hands on my shoulders, bending over so we're eye to eye. "I can't even imagine how scary this is, but I'll be with you the whole time, and if they say that you are for sure in labor, then I'll help you contact everyone you need to. I promise."

"John," I breathe. "It's too early. I can't be in labor."

"You might not be. Let's go find out." His eyes stay on me.

I take a step toward him and he straightens. I wrap my arms around his waist and lean my head against his chest. Large, hot tears roll down my cheeks, and his arms come to slide around me. I should have another six weeks until my due date. Six more weeks to spend with the little boy growing inside me. Six weeks to feel him kick, roll, hiccup, sleep, or even startle at the sound of my voice. Six more weeks to prepare for goodbye. If I'm in labor now, it's too early. I'm not prepared to let him go.

I tighten my grip as another contraction hits. John moves his hand to the same spot on my lower back and rubs slowly.

"Sorry," I manage.

"You're doing awesome. You breathing?"

I nod, feeling his soft cotton shirt shift beneath my cheek.

John helps me down the stairs, my bag slung across his shoulder. Dustin is waiting in John's truck for us. I open the back door and look up, contemplating how I'm going to get in. From the front seat I hear a mumbled string of profanities before, "Sorry. We can take my truck, it's just a tight fit."

"This is fine. Just give me a minute." I reach up and grab hold of the doorframe and then step onto the running board. John grips my hips and helps lift me. He does it once more as I step into the truck. I slide over to the middle and pat the seat next to me. John obliges and climbs in next to me.

It takes some time to get checked in. By the time I'm in a room and hooked up to a monitor, the contractions seem to be settling. John is sitting near the bed, hand in mine, while Dustin lounges in the skinny recliner shoved in the corner.

A nurse in pink scrubs and a cute little top knot enters. She goes over to the sink and washes her hands. "So, Momma, how are we doing?" She smiles at me as she grabs gloves from the box.

I burst into tears. John squeezes my hand.

"Oh, sweetheart. It's always scary when it's your first, but trust me, once the baby is here—"

"Get *out*!" I scream.

The nurse halts her approach, taken aback by my outburst. I pull my hand from John's and begin to climb off the bed.

"Mac?" Concern seeps through John's tone.

Dustin launches out of the recliner and extends a hand to help me up. Once I'm standing, he takes both my hands in his. *I got you*, he mouths. I focus on Dustin and his beautiful thundercloud-colored irises.

"Sweetheart, calm down. Let's have you—"

"Get her out." My breaths feel shallow, like I can't get enough oxygen.

"Mac. Take a deep, slow breath for me." John's hand slides across my back and then he pulls me close to him. I twist, wrap my arms around him, and bury my face in his chest. I breathe in through my nose and out through my mouth like he instructed me to that night on the patio. I cry out and John holds me tighter.

"With all due respect, I need—"

"You need to leave," Dustin snarls. There is a beat of silence. "I will not say it again." After a moment, the door clicks shut.

"She's gone," John whispers. "Keep taking deep breaths. I'm not going anywhere."

The sound of Dustin's ringtone fills the room. "Hey, man. Huh?" There's a pause. "We're at the hospital, but there's a situation." The door opens and closes and I wonder who Dustin is on the phone with.

"I want to go home. The contractions aren't that bad. I want to leave," I plead. I don't want her or any other nurse to come back in and greet me with "Momma." *He's not mine. He's not mine. He's not mine.* "He's not mine," I say out loud. John's arms tense around me. "I'm not going to be a mom."

John doesn't say anything, just holds me. His arms loosen when I take a step back. I ease myself back onto the bed. John sits next to me and I rest my head on his shoulder. I lace my fingers through his and hold tight.

I thought all the details were supposed to be in my chart. We had a plan. Kyle knows the plan, that's why Kyle should be here. I haven't discussed it with anyone else. A tear slides down my cheek and I quickly swipe it away.

Dustin walks back in and looks right at me. "Someone will be in shortly."

"I want to go home." My voice cracks.

I try to keep my features blank as I feel a contraction but my grip tightens just a little, letting John know. "You can go home soon," he whispers.

A new nurse enters, greets me by name, and makes polite conversation with me about how my summer has been. The boys leave so she can perform an exam. When she's finished, she tells me I am doing great, and everything seems to be okay. She types up a few notes on the computer.

"We'll monitor a bit longer, but you should be able to go home."

I'm fading in and out on the bed, John next to me in the chair and Dustin back in the recliner, when Dr. Huff walks in, smiling. "I have good news. You, sweetheart, are not in labor. Yet."

"Okay…" I stare at her.

"However, you are two centimeters dilated and ten percent effaced."

"What does that mean?" I ask.

"It means you could be back here tomorrow or a few days from now. Or it could still be a couple weeks." She shrugs. "You did the right thing coming in. If you begin to feel contractions again, I want you do exactly what you did this time, okay?

"Do you think it will be sooner rather than later?"

"Every woman is different. I can't say for sure. But I am putting you on light bed rest for the remainder of your pregnancy. You don't have to stay in bed twenty-four-seven. You can get up, take a walk, run small errands. Any time contractions begin, I want you to sit and relax. I'm going to draw up the discharge papers and we'll get you out of here as soon as possible." She gives me another smile and walks out of the room.

I bite my nail, pondering my next steps. I should message Kyle and let him know. I don't know if he can fly out here right now. He is right in the middle of baseball camp and he was supposed to go back to his grandmother's before he flies out here to be with me. If he does come out now, and I don't go into labor, he might not be able to return when I do actually go into labor. Why does this have to be so unpredictable? I bite down and the taste of metal slides onto my tongue. I draw my finger back and notice I bit right to the quick. Blood spurts from my nail. John reaches over and grabs a tissue from the box on the little table by the bed.

"That's quite a bit to process."

I wrap the tissue around my finger and nod. I send a quick text to my dad, letting him know where I am, and then call Kyle.

"What am I supposed to do?" Kyle asks, agitated. John tenses.

I glance at him before responding. "I don't know. I'm just letting you know what the doctor said. I can call you tomorrow and we'll work something out."

"Maclaren," Kyle sighs heavily.

"Dude, seriously? She has no control over this!" John explodes, shoving himself out of the chair. He shakes his head and walks out of the room. Dustin looks at me and then points to the door. I nod and watch Dustin leave.

"Maclaren? Are you still there?"

"Yeah."

"Sorry, I'm not mad at you."

I inhale a shaky breath. "I know."

"I want to be there with you. I want to see our son being born. I want a chance to see him before we let him go."

That breaks me. Tears stream down my cheeks. I can't seem to catch my breath. If Kyle doesn't make it, then he misses his opportunity to say goodbye and I can't do that to him. "I promise, you'll be here."

"Don't make that promise. We'll try, okay? How are you?"

There are no words to describe how I'm feeling.

"Mac, you're going to be fine. Whenever the time does come, the only thing I want you to be focused on is *you*. Don't worry about me, don't worry about anyone else. You won't be alone. I have a feeling John's going to be with you no matter what. That makes me the tiniest bit relieved." He chuckles. "So, take some deep breaths and we'll talk tomorrow."

"I miss you," I whisper.

"I miss you too."

The room is eerily quiet without the boys and without the nurses bustling in and out. I rest my hand on my belly and feel the baby roll. I wonder how many more times I'll get to feel this.

There's a knock on the door and then Dustin steps in.

"Is he okay?" I ask.

Dustin nods. "Are you?"

I shake my head. The door creaks again and then John walks over to the bed.

"Everything okay?" I ask.

"Sorry." John reaches for my hand but then pulls back. I reach out and take his hand, lacing my fingers through his. He tenses but doesn't pull away. I look up at him and think of what Kyle said. He might be relieved John is here, but I know he's also jealous John may get to experience this and he won't. I have to find a way to make sure Kyle can make it.

"Are you okay?" I ask again. His eyes meet mine and he nods once.

John rides up front on the way home. I sit in the middle, staring out the windshield. Dustin breaks the silence with his sudden realization.

"You made that dress you were wearing the other day." He glances up at me in the rearview mirror.

"Uh-huh."

"That is insane. Dude, did you know she could do that?"

John shakes his head.

Dustin drums his fingers on the steering wheel. "Have you made all the pieces that are on your wall?"

"No, just a few. Some people think it's a waste of time," I blurt. I quickly clamp my mouth shut.

"Who thinks that?" John asks, turning to face me.

I shrug. "People."

"Oh, I bet it's the same people who think learning about music recording and production is a huge waste of time. Especially because the industry is brutal, and it would be more sensible to get a steady paying job," Dustin spits.

"Those would be the people."

John frowns. "I hate those people."

John's eyes shift to Dustin for a second before returning to me. I shrug a shoulder, feeling a lump in my throat.

"You okay?" John asks.

I shake my head and I catch John's hand twitch, like he wants to reach back, but he doesn't.

John ensures I make it safely up to my apartment. My dad is waiting on the landing for us. "No baby?"

I shake my head and give him a hug. He leans down and kisses the top of my head.

"I'm going to lie down." I turn and catch John's eye. "Thanks for being there today." I notice the dark circles under his eyes and remember that when I called him this morning, he was just going to bed. He spent the whole day awake, making sure I was taken care of.

"You're welcome. I'm going to head out. Get some rest." His mouth curves up in a courteous half-smile. I frown a little.

"I'll talk to you later?" Suddenly, it feels like I won't.

He nods and gives a little wave before heading down the stairs. I turn and walk inside.

Seventeen

Later that night, I can't seem to sleep. I continue to stare at my ceiling as the time stretches well past four. Labor could start at any minute and now not only will Kyle not be here, but John will decide this situation is too much and he'll bail. That's what it seemed like when he left. I grab my phone and pull up our text conversation.

I know it's late…or early. I really am grateful you came over today. I hit send and then set my phone down. I'm surprised when my phone vibrates immediately.

I know. You okay?

No.

My phone begins ringing. The moment I pick up, John asks, "What's wrong?"

"You should be sleeping," I respond.

"So should you. You didn't answer my question."

We sit in silence for a moment. "What happened today?" I ask.

He takes a deep breath. "I'm sorry about that."

"What was *that*?" When I don't get an answer, I keep going. "Look, I understand. Today—well, yesterday—was a lot. If it was too much, I won't call you again. You were the first person I thought of. You've been a safe place, I guess. It's not really fair to you though."

"Maclaren, you're fine. I'm glad you called and I'm glad I could be there. It wasn't too much."

"Are you sure? I feel like something has been off between us ever since the hospital."

"I'm very sure. Are you biting your nail?" I immediately stop. There's a long pause before he whispers, "We're not a thing."

"Um…"

"You're not mine. Yet, I arrived at your apartment, and I didn't think, I just did, and I had no right to step in and yell at Kyle. I feel like I crossed a line today."

I sigh. "I hate Andi."

"What?"

"She's right. About you and me. She's right. We work. I would have been a mess if you hadn't been there, and I didn't want anyone else. You were the first person I called. You, not Kyle. Yes, Kyle deserves to be here. He's the dad and one of my best friends, but I wanted you. I wanted you because you make me feel safe. If you feel like you crossed a line, I didn't stop you. In fact, I'm glad you crossed it." I take a breath. The line remains silent. "John?"

"Yeah?"

"Did you get all that?"

"Uh-huh."

Well, if false labor didn't scare him off, maybe this conversation just did. I have no idea what to say next. Or how to take anything back. What if he crossed the line, but realized it was a mistake? And here I am, admitting I'm happy about it.

Finally, after what feels like an eternity, he says, "I don't hate Andi. I think she's a freakin' genius."

"Don't tell her that, you'll just inflate her ego."

John laughs.

"So, now what?" I ask.

"Now, you get some sleep, because you need it. I'll talk to you later."

"John—"

"Mac, seriously, we can discuss what the line looks like later. Get some rest."

"Okay. I'll talk to you later."

"You most certainly will." I hear his smile.

"Night."

He says goodnight and hangs up. I stare at my home screen and smile. I have no idea how this is going to work, but I'm giddy with the potential.

The first thing I do when I wake up is call Mr. Cruz and let him know that I won't be returning to work until further notice. After, I organize my hospital bag, adding things I forgot yesterday.

For a snack, I mix yogurt and crushed graham crackers together, then drizzle some chocolate on top. I place it in the freezer and waddle back over to the couch. A knock comes at the door as I pass by it. I peer through the peephole, a grin spreading across my face. I glance down at my shorts and oversized T-shirt, but it's too late to put on something cuter. I swing the door open. "Hi."

John smiles. "Hey. How are you feeling?"

I shrug, stepping aside to let him in. I sit on the couch and John takes a seat beside me.

"What have you done today?" he asks.

"This." I gesture to the couch. "What about you?"

"Took Eli and Jackson to swim lessons." He sighs heavily. "I don't know what it is with the two of them lately. They are at each other's throats all the time. I actually used the line, 'If you don't stop, I'm pulling the car over.'" He shakes his head. "They've been arguing all day. I needed out of my house."

"Well, welcome." I smile, glancing over at the clock. John looks toward the kitchen.

"What?" Concern flashes on his face.

"Oh, I made a snack right before you got here. I don't want it to freeze." I shift to get up.

"Here, I can get it for you." He stands and I direct him on where to find silverware. I ask him to grab the box of graham crackers too when there's a knock on the door. I push myself off the couch.

"I could have answered that," John remarks.

"It's okay. Feel free to grab something for yourself while you're in there," I say as I open the door. I immediately draw the door closer to me and angle my body in the opening, blocking the view of the apartment.

"Mom, what are you doing here?"

"Well, after what happened yesterday, I figured I'd come take care of my baby." She takes a step toward the door.

"I'm good." My tone is a bit sharp. She catches it immediately and hardens her glare.

"Maclaren, you need to be resting and taking care of yourself and the baby."

"Mom, I'm perfectly fine. Thanks for stopping by though."

"Young lady, I am not leaving." She crosses her arms.

"I have friends coming over in a few minutes, so I won't be alone much longer," I spit out.

"Good, then I can stay until they get here."

I grit my teeth. I don't want to admit I'm not alone. If she finds out I'm in the apartment alone with a boy, she will go ballistic, but I can't keep standing here blocking the door.

I take a breath and open the door wider. She steps around me. "Was that so hard?"

When I hesitantly turn, John is nowhere to be seen. I close the door and take another look around the room. My mom makes her way to the kitchen, spotting the yogurt and graham crackers sitting on the counter.

"Please tell me that wasn't dinner."

I shrug. "It wasn't dinner."

"Maclaren, you need something more substantial than that. Why don't I make us a nice home-cooked meal?"

"I'm really not that hungry." I glance around as my mom begins to rummage through our refrigerator. "Um, I'll be right back."

I tear down the hall as fast as I can. John's not in my room, or my dad's. I step into the bathroom and notice that my once wide-open shower curtain is drawn shut. When I pull back the curtain, John flinches before breathing a sigh of relief at the sight of me.

"The bathroom?" I whisper.

"I don't know. I just picked a door."

"Why?"

He shrugs. "It sounded like you didn't want her to know I was here."

"Well, it's going to get awkward if someone has to use the restroom."

He grimaces. "Very."

"Okay…um, do you think Dustin can stop by?"

John gives me a quizzical look.

"Maybe if friends actually come over, my mom will leave. I'll text Andi."

John nods. I reach over and flush the toilet and then turn on the sink and wash my hands.

"Mac?" he whispers before I leave. I turn. "Do you actually have to pee?"

"Don't worry about it." I lift one shoulder.

Sorry, he mouths as I open the door.

"This kitchen is a mess," my mom states as I join her. I grab my phone and send a quick text to Andi, then spot my now melting yogurt still on the counter. I reach over and take a bite before placing it back in the freezer.

The baby shifts, alerting me that I desperately need to pee and I know I won't be able to hold it. However, my mom thinks I just went and another trip will only make her worry and insist I go to urgent care or the emergency room. So, I do the next best thing: I pretend to take a phone call.

"Hey, Dad," I say loudly. My mom glances over at me. "Oh, yeah. I can go look. Hold on." I hurry down the hall to my dad's room. "In what drawer?" I call out while simultaneously beelining it for the bathroom. Halfway through, I realize I can't flush because that would be suspicious, but I find some hand sanitizer so I don't have to run the sink. I close the drawer hard to mimic that I'm looking for something. "Yeah, it's here." I take a convenient pause. "You're welcome. Love you too." I pretend to end the call as I round the corner.

"Maclaren, sweet pea. Why don't you sit down, put your feet up? You've been up this whole time."

I purse my lips and count to five in my head. "I'm all right."

"Have you had many contractions today?"

I shake my head. She gives me a skeptical look and frowns. She knows me too well to believe I answered honestly.

"Maclaren," she sighs. "Why do you make my life so difficult?"

I clench my fists. "I'm not trying to be difficult."

"Go sit down," she says, her voice stern. I cross my arms, but remain where I am.

"Hey, hey!" Dustin shouts, entering the apartment. He turns to see the stand-off in the kitchen. "I told you I was ordering pizza. What's this?"

My mom's eyes widen as Dustin walks up beside me. He extends a hand. "Name's Dustin."

My mom shakes his hand. "I'm Shelly, Maclaren's mom."

"Well, Shelly"—Dustin slings his arm around my shoulders—"I appreciate you looking after our girl here, but we've got her covered. Wanted her to have a relaxing, stress-free evening."

I look over, smiling. My mom's glare turns icy.

"Told you," I mumble.

"Fine. If that's how you want it." She turns the burner off, leaving the pot on the stove and the ingredients to make soup on the counter. She grabs her purse and yanks the front door open.

"Woah. Hey, Mrs. Young," Andi greets her.

"Andi." My mom's tone is clipped as she passes her.

Andi steps inside, followed by Travis, and closes the door. "What is going on?"

Dustin looks at me, waiting for an explanation. I wiggle out from under his arm and knock on my bathroom door, yelling out an all-clear before flushing the toilet in my dad's bathroom.

John joins the others in the living room. They all stand there like statues as I sit back down on the couch and prop my feet up. Andi is the first to move and takes a seat on the floor in front of me.

"So, was she the emergency?"

I nod. I look up at Dustin who moves to my dad's recliner. "Did you actually order pizza?"

"Sure did. Guess I should have checked with you first. Does something else sound better?"

I shake my head. I'm just grateful they showed up.

The next knock at the door is the pizza. John answers it. Before he comes back to the living room, I stop him and nod toward the fridge. He turns and grabs my frozen yogurt and a spoon.

"Ice cream?" Andi raises her eyebrows at me.

"Nope. Frozen yogurt."

John hands me the yogurt and then sets the pizza down on the coffee table. He flips one of the lids open and pulls a slice out. I turn on the television and find something to watch.

Halfway through the episode, I shift positions and sigh. John taps my leg.

Okay? he mouths.

I give a little shrug.

He pats his leg. I take his invitation and lie down, using his lap as a pillow. He absentmindedly tucks a stray hair behind my ear. I jump when I hear a gasp a few minutes later.

I look over at Andi, eyes wide as saucers. "Shut the front door! When did this…?" She lets out a tiny, excited shriek and gestures between the two of us. I catch Dustin shake his head, like he's not surprised. Travis looks completely lost.

"I'm gonna need details," Andi says, turning her back to the television.

"Later." I gesture with my index finger to turn around. She narrows her eyes but obliges.

When I get up to throw my yogurt cup away, I can feel Andi tracking my movement. When I come back to the couch with a bottle of water, she's practically bursting with the need to ask questions. She doesn't hold out much longer.

"Wait, what were the two of you doing earlier? Did your mom interrupt something?" She wiggles her eyebrows.

I roll my eyes and take a sip of water.

"What? You can still, you know, get busy."

Water comes shooting out of my mouth, dowsing the pizza box lid in water. "Andi," I shriek. I glance at John. He's staring at me, a bemused look on his face. "We weren't doing anything. We didn't have time to do anything."

Andi bursts out laughing. Dustin doubles over in the recliner. Travis smothers his laughter. My cheeks feel like they're on fire.

"That's not what I meant. He just got here. And, well…"

"Please stop." Andi holds her hand to her stomach, trying to catch her breath.

I flop back into the couch and bury my face in my hands.

"No funny business happened," John explains. "As Mac said, there just wasn't time." I separate my fingers to catch John wink.

"Oh man." Andi wipes away the tears running down her face. "It's been a while since I've laughed that hard. Thank you."

The laughter dies down and I uncover my face. John scoots over and tucks his arm around me. I lean into him, now self-conscious. My gaze keeps flicking back to Andi, waiting for her to make a face or say something.

After a few minutes, I have to change positions. I sit up and John uses the opportunity to run his hand up and down my spine. I lean into his touch and let out a sigh of relief. He increases the pressure just a bit and continues. I roll my neck and he pauses at my nape and massages.

"Can you do this forever?"

John chuckles before resuming the trail up and down my spine.

"Would you mind rubbing my lower back?" I ask John as the front door opens.

"Well, hello everyone," my dad says in greeting. He surveys the living room and then heads toward the kitchen. "Didn't expect a crowd."

"Sorry."

"How ya feeling, peanut?" my dad calls out.

"Lots of people have checked on me. Including Mom. How did she know?" Agitation seeps into my tone.

John's hand freezes on my lower back. My dad immediately looks away.

"If I wanted her to know, I would have told her. You didn't have the right to do that." My voice catches at the end.

John resumes rubbing, shifting a little closer to me.

"Peanut, she called earlier to ask how you were. I thought it was fair for her to know. I tried to reassure her that you were fine and well taken care of."

"Well, it didn't work," I snap.

"I've gathered," he says, his tone clipped. He takes a deep breath. "You all are welcome to stay as long as you want." He collects his dinner and heads toward his room.

"Do you want to talk?" Andi asks. She slides next to the couch and nudges my foot with hers.

I shake my head. "You know what, I'm not feeling great. I think I'm going to turn in."

John frowns. "I can stay. Keep you company."

I shrug. I walk into the kitchen and grab a Ziploc bag for the pizza. Andi takes the bag from me. "I'll clean up."

I nod and leave her to it, treading down the hallway and knocking on my dad's bedroom door. I enter when he calls out.

"I'm sorry," he says immediately. "I didn't think she would come over. I would have told you if I thought she would show up."

"It's fine."

"She's just looking out for you. She wants to make sure you're safe and healthy."

"I said it's fine," I snap. I take a deep breath, composing myself. "Is it okay if John stays?"

"That's fine."

"I'm going to lie down. I'll keep the door open." I turn and head out. I grab my pajamas and change in the bathroom. When I walk into my room John's standing just inside the doorway. I climb on my bed and arrange my pillows into a comfortable position. John stands near the edge of my bed, only sitting when I stop fussing. John slides next to me, leaning back against the headboard. I look up at him and smile.

"Are you really not feeling well?" He looks down, brushing a finger along the edge of my jaw.

I chew on my fingernail. "Contractions started," I whisper. "Plus, I feel completely exhausted all of a sudden."

"Kick me out at any time, okay?"

"I don't want to kick you out. I wanted to talk to you. I mean, I still do. Just don't hold it against me if I fall asleep."

"All right. What do you want to talk about?" He winks. "I know you have a question for me."

I scrunch my eyebrows in confusion. "Um…" *I have several questions.*

"Come on, you're not the least bit curious?" He raises his eyebrows and the interaction in the living room earlier comes flooding back.

I shake my head.

"I saw your face. Just ask."

"John, the great thing about being a guy is there are no visible signs you've had sex. So, unless you share, no one knows."

"Do you want to know?" he asks.

I sit for a moment, thinking. "I don't need to know. We're not there yet."

"There yet?"

"Yeah, at that point in our relationship." If this is even a relationship. We haven't asked those questions yet.

"I'd say it's fair." He shrugs. "I mean, I know your answer." His eyes shift to my belly.

"Yeah, it's obvious I've had sex. You don't have to tell me."

"I haven't," he affirms.

I shrug. "Okay."

"Been close though."

My eyes widen. He chuckles. "Surprised?"

"No."

"Liar."

I swallow. "Is that why you stopped going to church?"

John stares at his lap. "Not the whole reason, but part of it, I guess." He takes a deep breath. "I don't know. I just sat there thinking about what a bunch of hypocrites we were."

"How so?"

"I mean, we were supposed to be living this perfect little life, not giving into temptation, yet I was about to have sex. And I didn't feel bad about it; I wanted to. Then I started looking at how everyone else was living and it wasn't like they were doing much better. I just couldn't do it anymore."

I stare up at John. "So you've never actually…?"

"Nope."

"But you were close?"

"Last year. My girlfriend and I had some time alone at her house. She stopped it."

"Were you happy she did?"

"Yes." He stares down, fiddling with the corner of my bedsheet. "It wasn't right."

I try to swallow the lump in my throat as my eyes prickle with tears. I rub my hands over my belly.

"What's the matter?"

"I really messed up. I should have stopped it. I shouldn't have even started it. I was just so… I mean, I just wanted to… I don't know. I should have been smarter."

"Stop should-ing all over yourself." John smirks.

"What?"

"*I should have done this. I should have done that.* Stop should-ing. It doesn't help anything."

I giggle. "Where did you hear that?"

"My mom says it all the time. You can sit and focus on the should-haves and get nowhere, or you can face the situation, figure out the best solution, and move forward."

I nod. "Seems like sound advice."

"So, stop should-ing. Now, if we back up, you said 'at that point in our relationship.' Is this a relationship?"

I shrug. "You were the one who said you crossed a line."

He nods. "And you said you were happy about it."

"I am. It's just that—I mean—" I look up at John. He raises his eyebrows, waiting for me to complete my thought. "It's complicated," I finish.

"You do realize you didn't answer the question, right?"

"What would a relationship even look like?"

"Well, if we're in a relationship then I can definitely do this." He laces his fingers through mine and gives my hand a little squeeze.

"We've been doing that," I point out.

"Yeah, but we could do it in public."

"But what do we tell people? Do you even *want* to tell people? Do you want to wait? I mean, we can wait. I totally understand."

"Considering Andi's reaction and Dustin giving me a fist bump and uttering 'Dude, finally' before he left, I would say cat's out of the bag."

"What about your parents?"

"They like you."

"Yeah, but I'm just your friend."

He shrugs.

"What does"—I mimic his shrug—"mean?"

"Mac, they're not going to care. If I'm happy then they'll be happy. Do I have anything to worry about?"

"Young man, you have quite a few things to worry about," my dad replies, standing in my doorway.

John and I both jump.

"Oh my gosh. How long have you been listening?" I squeak out.

"Long enough to know I'm not a fan of what's happening in here," he says, though his tone stays light and joking. "Just came to check on you before calling it a night."

"I'll come get you if I need you. Night, Dad."

"Night, peanut." He taps the doorframe, but turns back. "And John, the second my daughter walks through the door crying over something you did, that is the moment I will no longer be her cool dad, but your worst nightmare. Understand?" All sense of teasing is gone.

"Yes, sir."

My dad nods and heads down the hall.

"Cat's definitely out of the bag." John winks.

"Shut up." I scrunch my nose, tightening my grip on John's hand. I place my free hand on my belly and breathe.

"Can I do anything?"

"No," I exhale. I fidget a little, trying to get comfortable. I look up to find John studying my wall. I give his hand a little squeeze. "Did something catch your attention?"

"They're all really good. How long have you been into fashion?"

"Since my parents got me this little coloring set with these plates that you could mix and match and make outfits. You'd color over it and copy the imprint on the paper. I slowly learned to add little things to the outfits and eventually started drawing my own."

"That's pretty awesome."

I shrug.

"What are you going to do with this talent of yours?"

"Nothing."

"What do you mean?"

"Just that. Nothing. It's not practical. It's a *fun hobby*," I imitate my mom.

"Mac, I don't think it's just a fun hobby. I think you could definitely make a career out of this. Is designing something you love to do?"

I yawn. "Kind of."

"I have a feeling it's more than 'kind of,'" John comments.

"Maybe." I lift my shoulder. My eyelids feel heavy and it's taking work to keep them open.

"I think I'm gonna let you get some sleep." He pulls our entwined hands up and gives the back of mine a kiss. "Sleep good." He lets go and climbs off the bed.

"You too," I mumble, my eyes closing.

"Mac?"

"Hmm?" I pry my eyes open. John stands in my doorway.

"Text me if you need me."

I give him a thumbs-up.

Eighteen

The next afternoon, my phone buzzes with a text from John.

Feel like joining us for a movie night?

I don't even inquire who "us" is and instantly reply yes. I'm sitting on the steps when John and Dustin pull up to my apartment. I use the rail to hoist myself up and make my way to John's truck. Dustin hops out of the front seat, leaving the door open for me.

"We're really going to have to think of another form of transportation," he comments, extending his hand to help me up. "Maybe next time we can borrow the minivan," he calls out.

John rolls his eyes, grumbling, "I'm not driving the minivan."

"I hear they are all the rage right now," I say.

John gives me a side-eye. "Please do not encourage him."

"Have you been in the minivan?" Dustin asks me. "They have the one with the little screen that comes down from the roof so you can watch movies. It's awesome."

"Yeah, unless you're the driver and listening to *Moana* or *Mickey Mouse Clubhouse* for the thousandth time. In fact, it's not that fun when you're the passenger either. I hate the minivan," John grumbles.

I turn toward Dustin. *Wow*, I mouth. Dustin raises his eyebrows.

"So, Clinic Girl, what did you do today?"

"Not a whole lot. You?"

"Finished registering for classes. Which reminds me, what pre-recs are you taking?"

John glances in the rearview mirror, shrugging. "I'd have to check."

"We probably should have coordinated; we could have taken classes together. What about you?" Dustin taps my shoulder.

"What about me?"

"What classes are you taking? Actually, what school are you going to? Did you apply to any universities?"

"Um…" I bite my fingernail. Only the faint whisper of music fills the cab. John glances over at me quickly. I drop my hand. "I'm not going to school."

"Taking a gap year?"

I shrug.

"Huh. Interesting." Dustin leans back in his seat, not saying anything else.

I shift so I can look at him. "Why is that interesting?"

"Sorry. I pegged you as the type that would definitely go to school."

"Because?"

"I don't know." He sits there, thinking for a moment. "Honestly, I don't know. I guess I assumed it's what you do after high school."

"Okay." I turn and face the front.

John pulls into the grocery store parking lot. "We're on snack duty," he says as he parks.

He comes around and helps me down, interlacing his fingers with mine as we begin toward the entrance.

"Crap!" I startle as John draws us to an immediate halt. "I didn't even check. Are you up for this? Or would it be better to have Dustin run in?"

"I think I'll be okay. It's not going to take a long time."

Standing in the candy aisle, I shift my weight side to side while John studies the variety of gummies. He reaches over, eyes still on the candy, and rubs my back. "Sorry, I'm trying to make this quick." He turns to Dustin. "Worms or Kids?"

Farther down the aisle, Dustin grabs a bag of assorted chocolate and tosses them into the basket. "Kids."

John grabs a package of Sour Patch Kids and throws them to Dustin. Dustin skillfully catches them in the basket. John resumes studying the candy while an elderly lady rounds the corner. I glance over and see her frown in disapproval. I try to ignore her, focusing on the candy in front of me. The whole time, John continues to rub my back, oblivious. Or at least, I hope he is. As the lady draws nearer she clucks her tongue, shaking her head. At that, John glances up as Dustin saunters over.

"I know, right?" Dustin comments. "Kids these days with their public displays of affection. It's atrocious."

The woman looks taken aback. She quickly grabs her sugar-free Russel Stover chocolate and heads toward the other end of the aisle.

"Dustin," I hiss.

"People are the absolute worst."

"Yeah, well, it happens. Don't worry about it. It's not like we— I—can't handle it," I quickly correct. Suddenly, my checks grow hot. I'm used to the judgmental stares, but John sure isn't.

His hand moves to my side, resting just above my hip. He leans in close, whispering, "*We* can handle it. You ready?"

I nod.

While waiting in line, the woman from the candy aisle comes and stands right behind us. John releases my hand and I deflate a little. So much for we. I startle when his arms wrap around my midsection.

"Um, this is awkward." His hands pause on the sides of my belly. "Not sure where to go from here."

I take hold of both his wrists and gently guide his hands so they rest on the largest part of my ever-expanding midsection, then place my hands over his. I wish I could see the look on the woman's face behind us. From the chuckle coming from Dustin, I assume he can and I'm willing to bet it's priceless.

"Wow, he's moving," John whispers.

"Yep, I'm hoping he wears himself out soon. He's been kicking the crap out of me all afternoon and I'm over it." As soon as the words leave my mouth, I want to take them back. I'm not over it, not really. I need him to be content in there a little while longer. Maybe it will give me a little more time to build the fortress around my heart. That way, when the time comes, it won't hurt so much to say goodbye.

I tense as I feel the start of a contraction. John turns his hands, interlacing his fingers with mine. He shifts a little closer. "You okay?"

"Mm-hmm," I exhale.

"I knew we should have just—"

I cut him off with a shake of my head. "It's fine. They've been happening on and off all day." I bring our hands up to rest at the top of my belly. "They're just annoying."

A self-checkout opens and he releases me, but keeps our hands entwined and leads me to the kiosk.

On our way to the truck, Dustin turns, walking backward to talk to John and I since I move at a turtle's pace. He extends his phone to John. "Sometimes being the third wheel pays off."

John takes the phone and glances at the screen. He rolls his eyes and tilts it toward me. There's a picture of the woman behind us, eyes wide with a disapproving look plastered on her face.

"People." I shake my head, still examining the picture. John's head is down, whispering in my ear. My hands are blurred from movement. I reach over to zoom in on the woman's face but accidentally swipe to another picture. To my surprise, it's another picture of John and me. My head is tilted up, mouth angled toward his ear. John is bent over to hear me. The way John is looking at me makes my cheeks instantly heat. I grab Dustin's phone and send the picture to myself.

"Squeaky third wheels do pay off sometimes," I comment as I pass Dustin's phone back to him.

When we arrive back at John's house, I make a pitstop in the bathroom and then head toward the kitchen. John's pouring all the candy into bowls, Dustin is prepping drinks, and Maria is there dumping popcorn into a large metal bowl.

"Hello, sweetie. Nice to see a new face at movie night," Maria greets me.

"Thanks for letting me join," I say, easing myself into a dining room chair. I survey the wide array of snacks and notice tortilla chips are laid out.

"Dessert nachos?"

John nods. "Oh yeah, they're a hit over here. They've turned into a movie night staple." He tosses out the empty bags and then rounds the counter, resting a hand on my shoulder. "So, what speaks to you?"

"I'm actually not that hungry." John studies my face and a little frown appears.

"Can I get you water or anything?"

"They have lemonade. It's in the little boxes, and it's pink lemonade, but it's lemonade. I bet John will pour it into a cup for you, if you don't want to be five," Dustin says.

"Yes, there is lemonade too. And I would gladly pour it in a cup for you." John gives my shoulder a squeeze.

"Can I have the lemonade as is? Being a grown up is so overrated," I say.

"Of course. Why don't you go get comfortable and I'll be right in."

As I situate myself in the living room, Maria calls out that snacks are ready. Eli and Eric rush past me, nearly bumping into Dustin walking in. He spins to avoid them, and as he does, I notice a faded scar on the back of his arm peeking out beneath his sleeve. I briefly wonder if he got it from his dad. Before I can think on it more, John comes in carrying a plate of snacks and two small boxes of lemonade. Under his arm he has two water bottles.

"Catch." He opens his arm and lets the water bottles fall. I catch them and set them on the small end table. He hands me the lemonades and then takes a seat beside me. "Feel free to steal my snacks. All except the Kids. Those are mine."

I reach over and pluck a yellow Sour Patch Kid from the pile and pop it in my mouth. I instantly pucker from the tang of the sour lemon dusting.

John laughs.

Once everyone is settled in the living room, Maria dims the lights and *Encanto* begins. I sneak another Sour Patch Kid, receiving a disapproving glare from John. I wink and pop it in my mouth. He smiles. "It's a good thing you're cute."

Halfway through the movie, I have to get up for a bathroom break. As I come back and round the corner, I spot John mouthing along to the song. Laughter slips out, and several heads turn toward me. I take a seat, leaning close to him. He wraps an arm around me as I settle in, like it's the most natural thing in the world. "Can you sing along to the whole movie?"

John shrugs. Dustin peeks around him, nodding.

"I've only seen it a few dozen times. Are you telling me you can't?"

I nod. "This is the first time seeing it."

"Well, some of these songs are catchy. I won't say I told you so when you find yourself listening to them on repeat."

I give him an incredulous look.

The movie wraps up and John's dad stands, ushering the younger children to bed. He glances over at us and I freeze. John's arm is still wrapped around me and I'm not sure if his parents know. His dad gives us a little nod and tosses the remote to Dustin. "I'm headed upstairs."

Maria stands. "You two." She points toward John and my heart rate skyrockets, but then she turns her finger on Dustin. "You're both on clean-up duty." For me, she only smiles. "Mac, it was so nice of you to join us. I'm sure we'll be seeing you around more often."

I smile, feeling my cheeks heat instantly. "Maybe."

John slides his arm from around me and stands. Dustin follows suit. When I begin to stand, John shakes his head. "First-timers don't clean. It's a rule." I follow them into the kitchen anyway and prop my feet up on a chair.

John's phone rings halfway through cleaning. He answers and his eyes quickly flash to me. "Not right away," he tells the other person on the line.

I scrunch my nose, leaning a little to hear the conversation. Dustin taps John on the shoulder. They have a short conversation and then Dustin nods. John hangs up and slides his phone in his pocket.

"Who was that?" I ask.

"Work. They need a closing checker."

"Don't worry, your Uber drive just got way cooler." Dustin winks at me. "Gives us some good bonding time and an opportunity

to talk crap about you." He mock punches John's shoulder on the way
to put Ziploc bags of leftover candy in the pantry.

John rolls his eyes. "Thanks, man."

Dustin helps me into his cab, which still smells like cigarette smoke.
"Does that bug you?" I ask.

"Eh, doesn't help when I'm desperate for a light, but it's not the
worst."

I nod and look out the window, watching the neighborhood
streak by. After a few minutes, I glance over my shoulder. I open my
mouth to ask Dustin about the scar, then stop myself. He choked up
talking about what happened to him earlier and I'd hate to drag up
bad memories again. I'm quickly learning some experiences you
don't want to rehash. I let the question die at the tip of my tongue and
face the window. I begin to hum.

Dustin chuckles, grabbing his phone and switching the song. The
Encanto soundtrack starts.

"We will not tell John about this," Dustin says sternly.

"Absolutely not," I say with equal seriousness.

We're belting out "We Don't Talk About Bruno" as we pull up
to my complex. He parks and we bust up laughing.

As Dustin escorts me up to my apartment I catch him wince a
couple times. "Hey, are you okay?"

"Oh yeah." He waves me off. "I think I pulled something the
other day. No biggie."

Nineteen

Two days after movie day, I'm sitting in my apartment feeling completely exhausted but somewhat unsettled, and it's making me nervous. Grabbing my phone, I send John a text message to see what he's up to.

Video games with Dustin. What's up?

Part of me feels like I'm overreacting. I'm about to reply with my usual response, but instead I type back, *Can I join?*

Of course. He follows it up with the heart eye emoji, which makes me smile. Twenty minutes later, I pull up to his house and find them in John's room.

"Hey." John glances over as I enter. Whatever is happening in the game must be intense because both boys are super focused on the screen. I walk past Dustin, ruffling his hair on the way. He ducks out of the way and lets out a growl of frustration. I grab a pillow and lie down on John's bed. His eyes shift to me and then flash back to the screen quickly. "You feeling all right?"

I shrug and turn my attention to the screen. I slowly drift off but then wake up, feeling…wet. I stand and only take two steps before crossing my legs.

"You okay?" Dustin asks. "Kinda looks like you're going to pee your pants."

I roll my eyes, suddenly frustrated with his jokes. I all but fly to the bathroom, but stop to grab my phone. Out in the hallway, I dial my doctor.

When I step back to John's doorway, he peeks over. He must recognize what's on my face because he immediately tosses his controller on his bed and stands. Dustin turns in his chair toward me. "Woah, what happened?"

John is right in front of me. He cups his hand on my arm. I look up at him, his face blurred by my gathering tears. "What's going on?" he asks.

"My water b-broke." My voice cracks. A tear slides down my cheek.

"Isn't it supposed to be a big gush? Shouldn't I be staring at a huge puddle?" Dustin asks, glancing at where I was standing before.

I shake my head.

"What now?" John slides his hand down my arm and laces his fingers through mine.

"I have to go to the hospital," I say, voice trembling. "She said—" I clear my throat. "She said because I'm only thirty-five weeks I need to head in."

"Where are your keys?" Dustin asks.

"In my purse." A look of confusion crosses my face.

"Your car doesn't require you to climb and is roomier than my truck. I'll drive," Dustin explains. I grab my purse and toss my keys to Dustin.

We make it downstairs and are heading toward the front door when I feel a contraction. I don't stop, but I slow down. John's brow furrows. "Sorry," I breathe.

"It's fine." He squeezes my hand.

John crawls in the back seat with me. He rests his arm on my shoulders, and I lean into him, lacing my fingers through his. He idly rubs his thumb in little circles. Dustin hooks up his phone and then pulls up Spotify. Beyonce's "Run the World (Girls)" starts and Dustin turns it up.

"Figured you could use some girl power tunes," he yells over the music.

I call Kyle, praying he flagged a flight for today and that labor doesn't go super quick. As the phone rings my belly tightens again. I breathe in and out as best I can. Kyle doesn't answer. I try three more times and nothing. Letting out a huff of frustration, I try Andi. The call goes straight to voicemail. I call back immediately. Still nothing. Sending a 911 to Kyle and Andi as a last-ditch effort, I quickly search for the Challinors' contact. Tanya picks up on the first ring.

"Hello, Maclaren. How are you?"

I swallow. "Are you ready to have a baby?"

She gasps. "Where are you? Are you sure?" Her voice cracks, then I hear her call out for Joel. "Maclaren, sweetheart, where are you?"

"I'm on—my way—to—" I can't finish. I let out a little moan.

John interjects, "Hey, we're on our way to the hospital. I'd say another ten minutes out. Maclaren's water broke."

"Yep," I manage.

"Oh my, okay. We'll head that way. Gateway, right? Okay, yes. Oh my." I hear her inhale then let it out. "Maclaren, how are you?"

"Scared," I blurt out. John squeezes my hand and pulls me closer to him.

"You'll do great. We'll see you in a little bit, okay?"

"See you soon."

I send a text to my mom and dad and then call the only other person I can think of.

"Hey," Travis answers.

"Can you get ahold of Andi?" I blurt out.

"Maybe."

"I don't need a maybe. I need a yes. Are you going to see her tonight?"

"No. What's going on?"

"Ugh, can you go over to her house? This is important."

"Mac, she's not at home. She's down in Tucson for some new student orientation," Travis explains.

My jaw drops. I completely forgot about the orientation. I bite down hard on my thumb nail. The few times I imagined going into labor, Kyle and Andi were with me in every scenario. I never thought I would go through it without them. "I really need her," I whimper.

"I'll see what I can do. What do you want me to tell her?"

"That I need her here. I need her with me."

Travis sighs. "I'm aware, but why?"

"Because I'm scared and I can't reach Kyle and labor is already horrible and...and..."

Travis swears. "I'll see what I can do. Where are you?"

"Pulling into the hospital."

"I'll call you back." Travis ends the call.

Dustin offers to drop me off at the entrance, but I tell him I'll be okay to walk. Soon, I'll be confined to a bed. Might as well move around while I can.

"I changed my mind," I say, waddling toward the hospital.

"About what?" Dustin turns, walking backward.

"Maybe you should have—" I bend over, bracing my hands on my knees. Real contractions are very different from the Braxton Hicks contractions I've been experiencing for the past few weeks. The pain makes it difficult to breathe through them.

John places his hand on my lower back, massaging gently. When I'm able to stand up straight, I take his hand and continue.

"How do you know to do that?" I ask, thinking back to the first time I thought I was in labor.

John shrugs. "It's something I watched my dad do for my mom. If it's not helping, just say so."

"It helps a lot actually."

My phone buzzes in my pocket and I quickly answer it.

"I hate stupid icebreakers. They are so freaking annoying. We had to put our phones in a basket and we weren't able to check them until we were done with the exercise," Andi huffs. "Anyway, I'm on my way. Where are you? Are you at the hospital? All checked in?" There's a honk and a few choice expletives.

I squeeze John's hand. "Are you okay?"

"People are the worst," she tells me. "Learn to drive!" she yells at the other vehicle. She utters something I can't understand. "Jeez, okay, I'm on my way. Don't you dare have this baby before I can get there."

"I'll try not to. Be careful."

"I will. Love you."

"You too."

I end the call and immediately dial Travis. I pull John aside before we enter the sliding doors toward the nearest bench. Of course, a contraction starts. John massages my lower back while I try and breathe.

"Look, I've been trying, but I haven't gotten anywhere," Travis starts defensively.

"She called," I manage to get out.

"She did? Good. That's good." It's quiet. "Mac? Are you there?"

"Hold. On." It takes a minute to catch my breath. "You know how we agreed it's bad to drive when you're upset?"

"I'm pretty sure we never agreed."

"Travis, Andi called and she's freaking out. Can you please just, I don't know, call her and make sure she's okay?"

"I'll check on her."

"I don't need you to just 'check on her.' I need you to make sure she's safe," I snip.

"Got it," Travis replies, slightly annoyed.

"Dude, don't you even—"

"Mac, take a chill pill. I'll make sure she's fine. Did you make it to the hospital?"

A smile tugs my lips at his use of the phrase "chill pill." Andi is rubbing off on him. "Yes."

"Did you get ahold of Kyle?"

"I'm trying." My voice catches.

"How are you?" There's genuine concern in the question.

"Good."

Travis chuckles. "That's such a lie, but we're going to tell Andi you're doing great. Do you want Andi to come straight there?"

"No."

"No?" Travis asks, surprised. John and Dustin look over with equal shock.

"I need her well rested so she can go get Kyle when he arrives. One of us should get to sleep," I explain.

"I'll tell her, but…expect to see her in a few hours," he says. I know he's probably right but I can try.

Once we walk into the hospital, John squeezes my hand. "Go get checked in. I'll be right back."

"Wait, where are you going?" I grip his hand tightly.

John nods to the restroom sign.

"Oh." I release his hand and make my way to the check-in counter. The moment the counter comes into view, I freeze.

"What is it?" Dustin asks. When I don't answer, he shifts closer. "Clinic Girl?"

"Mom," I call out.

She turns, eyes widening when she sees me. "What are you doing?" She stands, hurrying toward us.

I meet her a quarter of the way but continue walking past her. The nurse gives me a smile as I approach.

"Hi, I'm Maclaren Young. I'm in labor," I explain.

The nurse greets me and begins to gather paperwork on a clipboard. I take a seat in one of the two plastic chairs they have there. My mom pulls the other one close to me.

"Now, she's high risk and is only thirty-five weeks. Is there any way we can get her back to a room now, and then worry about the paperwork?"

The nurse looks over at my mother, then at me. "Is this an emergency situation? Are you experiencing—"

"Nope. Just completely normal, very real contractions. I'm fine to fill out the paperwork," I say, reaching for the clipboard.

The nurse hesitates and then hands me a pen and the clipboard. As I begin to fill it out, a contraction comes.

"Honey, use your Lamaze breathing. It will help ease some of the discomfort," my mom says.

I keep my eyes fixed on the paper, hoping my grip doesn't break the pen. A strong hand clasps my shoulder and then John's breath tickles my ear. "You're doing good. I'm right here." I turn to him. His blue eyes and warm smile make me feel calmer. As soon as I'm able to breathe easier, I resume the pesky paperwork. John leaves his hand resting on my shoulder.

"Maclaren, what technique have you been using to prepare for labor?"

My mouth stays shut. I get to the bottom of the first page and flip it to see if there is anything on the back.

"Maclaren Fey, you have been to Lamaze classes, haven't you?"

I sign my name on the second page, ready to skim through the next, when she yanks the clipboard out of my hands.

"Do not ignore me, young lady."

John's fingers tense. He aims a glare at my mother.

"It's not a big deal. Now, can I please have that back? I really want a room."

My mother thrusts the clipboard back at me, eyes narrowed, face red. She's not going to push this. She wants me back where nurses and doctors can keep an eye on me.

Once I've completed all the forms, the nurse smiles. "Perfect. If you will follow me this way."

"We will need a wheelchair for her," my mom comments.

My teeth clench, holding in a growl. Standing, I reply, "That's not necessary. I'm perfectly capable of walking." I take John's hand, interlacing my fingers with his. My mom's eyes widen.

The nurse pauses at the large open door of a labor and delivery room. I'm trying to walk but with each step, I get slower and slower. John switches my hand from one to the other then rests his free hand on my lower back. I veer over to the wall, grab the rail, and squat down. My mom says something, but John's voice drowns her out.

"Try to breathe. Doesn't matter how, just breathe. Take all the time you need. I'm right here. You're doing amazing."

Once I've changed into a gown and convinced my mom that I'm fine and have plenty of support, she leaves. Dustin's girl power/labor playlist fills the room. I try Kyle again, leaving a voicemail, and then send him another text. He has to get this.

"I'll keep trying him," John reassures me.

I nod, bracing for another contraction.

The boys leave when a nurse enters to perform an exam. I expect them to come right back, but the nurse leaves and then it's just me. I close my eyes and try to catch my breath. I don't know how much time has passed when I feel John lace his fingers through mine.

"Is this the beginning of—"

I shake my head vigorously. "What took you so long?"

He squeezes my hand. "Kyle called. He said he was boarding."

A breath of relief whooshes through me, and my head falls back onto the pillow. "Oh, thank goodness." *He's on his way.*

Contractions have been coming steadily for the past couple hours, making me feel extremely nauseous. A nurse pops in to do another exam. Dustin excuses himself from the room. John goes to leave, but I grab his arm.

"Please don't."

He settles back on the bed. "You sure?"

I can't respond, but I hope the vice grip I have on his arm lets him know I'm very sure.

Once the exam is complete, the nurse informs me I'm four centimeters dilated and asks if I want an epidural.

"Yes, please," I tell her.

She heads out of the room. John leans close to my ear. "You're doing great."

I turn, resting my sweaty forehead against his. "I feel horrible."

The door creaks and we turn to see Dustin walking back in munching on a bag of chips. A wave of nausea passes over me, and bile rises in my throat.

"Dustin, hand me that pitcher," John says.

"What?"

"On the table. Now!"

Dustin grabs the pitcher and quickly hands it to John. Water splatters on the tile and he shoves the dusty pink pitcher in front of me just as I vomit.

Dustin heaves. "Dude, how did you know that was going to happen?"

"It was the same look she had the day at the clinic," John says with a shrug.

I smile weakly at him. "Thanks."

He tucks a loose strand of hair behind my ear. "Anytime."

Which he proves just a few minutes later, holding my hair back as I retch into the pitcher yet again. A knock sounds at the door and I expect a nurse to come walking in. Instead, a second knock follows.

"Come in," Dustin calls.

I sit up straighter, setting the pitcher aside and grabbing a tissue to wipe my mouth.

"Hi, peanut," my dad says, stepping into the room. My eyes instantly well with tears. He sets my duffle bag near the wall and comes to sit on the edge of the bed. John shifts from the bed to a chair.

"Hi, Daddy," I say, wrapping my arms around his neck. A sound of discomfort escapes him as I try not to strangle him during a contraction. Lying back on the bed, panting, I breathe out, "Sorry."

My dad pats my leg. "You're okay." He glances over at our other company. "I know why you're here." He points at John. "But what's your role?" he asks, looking at Dustin.

"Oh, um, the errand guy?"

"He also made one heck of a playlist." I throw Dustin a grateful smile.

"Sure did." Dustin winks at me.

Just then, the anesthesiologist comes in to prep everything for the epidural. My dad asks if I want him to stay and I shake my head, letting him know I have plenty of support and will talk to him later. He gives me a quick kiss on the forehead before leaving. Dustin gives John and I a nod and leaves the room.

The anesthesiologist has me sit up and slide to the edge of the bed. John angles his chair so he's sitting right in front of me. I grasp his hands as a nurse moves aside my gown. My phone starts to buzz and I glance over to see Kyle's name on the screen. John answers it, putting it on speaker.

"Did I miss it?" Kyle sounds winded. There's a rustle and some muffled voices and then more clearly, "Mac, did I miss it?"

"You didn't miss it," John responds.

From behind, the doctor explains that I'll feel a slight pinch. My eyes don't stray from John's ocean-blue irises. I grimace as I feel the needle, letting out a little moan as a contraction hits. The nurse said to stay still during the process. John winces as my grip crushes his fingers.

Sorry, I mouth.

"This is nothing," John murmurs.

"Maclaren, is everything okay?" Kyle asks.

John keeps his gaze fixed on me. "She's doing amazing, Kyle. She's getting her epidural now. I'm hoping she can rest after. Where are you?"

"I'm here. Well, my plane landed and I'm here in the airport. I'll be there soon. You know how fast Andi can drive."

"Be careful," I squeak out.

"I will."

Twenty

The epidural has definitely taken effect, except now not only do I still feel a little queasy, but I'm also shaky. At least the contractions aren't bothersome. I reach for my water and John pushes out of the chair, beating me to the cup.

He holds it for me while I take a long sip of water. "Thanks."

He sets the cup down and takes my hand. "Are you cold? Do you need another blanket?" There's a hint of worry in his voice.

I shake my head.

"I think I'm going to try and rest."

I close my eyes, hoping if I fall asleep the tremors will stop. Except, I hear the door creak. "Knock, knock. How we doing?" the nurse asks. "Oh sorry, I didn't realize," she whispers.

"Excuse me, she's been shaking pretty bad since her epidural. Is that something to be concerned about?" Any semblance of calm has vanished from John's voice. He's full-blown panicking. I squeeze his hand and peek my eyes open.

"It can happen sometimes; it should settle after a bit. Nothing to be too concerned with."

I wince at her choice of words. They don't seem to reassure him at all. I study John's face and realize not only is he freaking out, but he's also been up just as long as I have been, or longer, and hasn't left my side this whole time. I don't think he's eaten anything either. The nurse checks my vitals and the fetal monitor, records some notes, then leaves. "Sweets, would you like the lights turned down?" she asks before she goes.

"Yes, please."

The room lights dim and the door clicks shut.

"Hey, it doesn't hurt," I say, hoping it brings him some relief. "Why don't you go grab some food? Or a nap? You could probably use both."

"I'm good."

"John—"

"Mac, I'm not leaving," he snaps.

"I just thought a little break might—"

"I said no," he interrupts, eyes narrowing. "Believe it or not, it's not very fun watching you go through this. I'm staying."

"Maclaren." Dustin walks up behind John. It's rare he uses my full name. "You just worry about you and let him worry about you too. I'll worry about him. Deal?"

"Will you make sure he at least eats?" I ask, my eyelids feeling heavy. I blink a few times.

"Absolutely. Go to sleep."

"And let him have the couch if he wants to sleep." I close my eyes. I can feel myself slowly drifting off, but a loud thud on the door makes me jump. John grimaces. The door swings open and Kyle enters, doubling over, trying to catch his breath. Andi walks in behind him, laughing.

"Oh my gosh. Are you okay?" She gives Kyle a pat on the back.

"Did I"—inhale—"miss it?" Kyle asks.

"She still looks pretty pregnant to me," Andi says.

Kyle straightens and looks at me. I smile. "You made it." My words are slurred with sleep. I close my eyes, listening to Kyle's shoes squeak against the tile.

"Woah, is this normal?" Kyle asks, sounding far away.

I'm not sure how long I'm asleep, but I stir when I feel pressure. I glance over at the couch where Kyle sits with Tanya and Joel. I wonder how long they've been here. Andi has taken up one of the plastic chairs, feet propped up on the bed. John is on the right, arms crossed under his head, fast asleep. I reach over and run my still shaky hand through his hair. He bolts upright. "What? What's the matter? Are you okay?"

I nod. It's rather quiet in the room. I look around again. "Where's Dustin?"

"He had to go but told me to keep him updated."

A small wave of nausea hits but I try and breathe through it as I turn my head toward the couch. "Hi, Tanya. Hey, Joel."

Tanya gets up and stands beside John.

"Hi, how are you?"

I shrug. "I'm doing okay." Except I'm not okay. I feel like I'm going to throw up and the pressure is only intensifying.

I sit up, grabbing the little bowl they brought after the pitcher incident, my hands trembling. I'm surprised when Tanya reaches over and steadies it. I heave a couple times before throwing up mostly water. There's nothing else in my system. I lay my head back and close my eyes. Tanya slides the bowl out of my quivering hands. "Thanks. Sorry about that."

"Nothing to be sorry for." She gives my shoulder a gentle pat.

"John?" I whisper.

"Hm?" He laces his fingers through mine.

"I feel like I have to push." My admission comes out louder than I thought, and the room erupts into chaos.

Andi drops her feet. "Wait, seriously?"

Kyle jumps up and rushes over. "He's coming?"

Joel joins Tanya. Tanya has tears in her eyes, one escaping down her cheek.

John presses the call button on the bed and a voice crackles over the loud speaker. Several voices answer at once.

"One person, please. How can I help?"

I stutter as I answer, "Lots of p-pressure. Need to push."

"Don't push yet. Just breathe deeply; we'll be in momentarily."

Don't push yet? I feel like I'm going to burst. I try and breathe like the nurse suggested. Instinctively, I curl my shoulders, bringing my chin to my chest.

"Wait, you aren't supposed to do that!" I hear Kyle say, voice panicky. I lean my head back, grit my teeth, and let out a muted scream. John moves in closer and begins singing Destiny's Child "Survivor" in my ear. I turn and narrow my eyes at him.

"Not helping."

"Sorry."

"Nice try though," I say through gritted teeth. "Why that song?" Maybe focusing on something else will steer my thoughts away from the fact that I'm going to explode any minute.

John shrugs.

I blow out a slow breath. "There has to be a reason."

"It was one of the songs on Dustin's playlist. I heard it a few times today." He winks.

This conversation is not helping. "I really need to push," I proclaim to a room of non-medically trained individuals.

A nurse walks in at that moment. "Just a few more minutes, hon. Just breathe."

I'm sick of people telling me to breathe. Breathing is not helping. A second nurse comes in and lets out a low whistle. I'm so focused on not pushing I miss her question. I catch Kyle raise his hand.

"All right, everyone else out," the second nurse announces.

"Wait. No, she stays. Tanya stays."

"Kyle and Tanya, then. Everyone else not Kyle or Tanya, out. Now."

I look up into John's eyes, realizing he's included in the ones being kicked out. "No," I whimper.

John holds my gaze and for a second I forget about the insane pressure and the need to push. "You're going to do amazing." He leans down and plants a quick kiss on my forehead then turns. He gives Kyle a clap on the back before he heads for the door.

Kyle takes John's former position by my bed and grabs my hand. "I got you," he says.

Forty-three minutes later, there is a quiet cry and Dr. Huff exclaims, "Happy birthday, baby boy!"

"Would one of you like to cut the umbilical cord?" a nurse asks.

"Kyle?" Tanya offers.

"Um, sure." Kyle releases my hand and walks over to the end of the bed. He's handed a pair of funny-shaped scissors, and the nurse shows him where to cut. He blanches as the scissors sever the cord.

"Beautiful. Maclaren, would you like to hold him?"

I shake my head. "This time is all hers." I nod at Tanya.

"All right. We're going to get him cleaned up and get some vitals then."

Tanya follows the nurses over to the little bed. I hear him crying as they examine him and get him cleaned off.

"It's okay, baby boy," Tanya coos.

I catch the attention of one of the nurses and ask if they can let Joel come in. The nurses attending to me get me cleaned up as best they can and make sure I'm covered before they let him in. He walks up behind Tanya and wraps his arms around her. "He's beautiful."

A nurse swaddles the baby and then hands him to Tanya. I watch a family form right in front of my eyes while my heart shatters.

Tanya leans her head down and snuggles the baby. She then turns toward me. "Maclaren, are you sure you don't want to hold him?"

"I don't know." My voice catches and tears run down my cheeks.

Tanya walks over and I hold my arms out. She places the little bundle in my arms. I look into the tiny face of the little boy who's been growing inside me for the last eight months. He has Kyle's nose and eyes, but my mouth. I caress my hand along his little ear, a spitting image of mine.

"Hey, little man," I whisper. Kyle peers down at him and quickly wipes tears from his eyes.

"We've been thinking, and we would love for you to give him his middle name."

I look up at Tanya, surprised. She smiles. "He's a part of you. You deserve to give him a piece of his name."

Kyle and I haven't discussed this. "Braden," I blurt out. I quickly turn to Kyle. "Sorry. I just…if you hate it, we can pick something else."

"I like Braden," Kyle says softly.

"Lucas Braden Challinor," Joel announces. A look of pride lights up his face.

I look back down at Lucas and tears flood my vision. I lean in to give him a gentle kiss on the forehead. "Thanks for spending time with me. I loved every second of it," I whisper.

Twenty-One

It's late in the evening. The Challinors have taken Lucas to another room. I've had a chance to shower and chow down on the burrito Andi brought me from Chipotle. She and Travis left to grab their own dinner. While eating his own burrito bowl, Kyle's phone rings. Sliding it from his pocket, he glances at the screen and a smile lights up his face. It has to be Megan.

After his last visit here where he had mentioned Megan, Andi took it upon herself to stalk her to see if she would even be good for Kyle before sending a follow request and messaging her. Kyle was furious with Andi when he found out what she did. That was until Megan started talking to him more often. When Andi was in Michigan, they all met up. Andi nudged Kyle to ask her out, and he finally did.

"Hey," Kyle answers. He glances up at me. Part of me feels bad that he's sitting in a hospital right now and not out on what was supposed to be their first date. "Yeah, everything went good. He's here and healthy," Kyle says, setting his fork in his bowl. He pushes the tray table away, heading for the door. He stops, hand on the door handle. He looks at me. "Are you okay if I step out?"

I nod, not trusting myself to answer, a knot forming in my throat. I had been wondering if Megan knew anything about our situation. There was this fear that if she knew, it might ruin Kyle's shot with her. Those anxieties now can fade away. I'm so relieved Megan

makes him happy. He deserves it and being one of Kyle's best friends, I know Megan is the luckiest girl in the world.

Once I'm done eating, I dim the lights and turn on the television. Kyle walks back in, returning to his cold food.

"How's Megan?" I ask.

"Good."

"Kyle, I'm sorry I ruined your night."

Kyle's hand freezes, his fork hovering in the air. He looks at me. "Why would you say that?"

My lip trembles. "Because you should be dropping Megan off after your date. Not here."

Kyle shrugs. "It's okay. Megan understood. We'll get our first date next week."

It's silent. Kyle takes a few more bites before tossing the leftovers. He pulls a chair up to the bed. "The day I mentioned the pregnancy to Megan, I thought that I was going to have a coronary. She sat there for a fraction of a second, shrugged, and then asked if I wanted to go to the batting cages. I was flabbergasted. I explained the whole situation again, making sure she understood. All she did was roll her eyes and say, 'I got it the first time.'

"She's been sexually active in previous relationships," he explains. "She, however, was smart enough to use protection. That jab stung a bit, but she didn't care. She couldn't judge me for something she had also done, and she couldn't be mad at the fact that there was going to be a baby."

I'm quiet as I digest all of this.

"You didn't ruin my night, Mac. This is one of the best nights of my life," Kyle whispers.

Reaching over, I take Kyle's hand, giving it a tight squeeze.

The television casts a soft glow in the hospital room. I'm lying in bed when Andi tiptoes in, kicks off her shoes, and climbs into the bed.

"You need anything?" she asks.

I shake my head.

Soon, Andi is snoring lightly. I pick up my phone and scroll through my messages. I have a message from my mom, one from my dad, and even one from Dustin, but none from John. I click on our text conversation. The last text was from yesterday morning. Did I do something wrong?

Hi, I message.

The three little dots dance at the bottom before he replies, *Hey. How are you?*

Ouch.

He sends a sad face emoji.

Are you mad at me? I can't help but asking. I bite my nail nervously waiting for his response.

What? No! His name immediately flashes on my screen as he calls.

"Hey," I whisper.

"Hi." His voice is also low.

"Where are you?"

"At work."

"Oh."

"Why would I be mad at you?" he asks.

"You haven't spoken to me, and you never came back." A tear slides down my cheek.

"What are you talking about?" I hear a rustle and then a frustrated growl. My phone buzzes rapidly as several messages come in. I click out of the call to see them.

There is a picture of green goo, followed by *SLIME!! FYI, this is how it's supposed to go.*

How are you?

I take it you're sleeping. Good. I'll try and stop by before work.

Fell asleep, won't make it. I'll text you.

Maclaren?"

"Huh?" I sniffle, trying to hide that I'm crying.

"I really wanted to get back. I didn't realize my messages weren't sending."

"It's okay."

"Can you explain why I'd be mad?"

"Because I made you leave."

He chuckles. "You didn't make me leave. I understood. Everyone that needed to be in that room was in the room. How did it go?"

"Good." I take a deep breath. "He's healthy. Super tiny, but healthy." I pause. "His name is Lucas. Lucas Braden."

"I like it."

I swallow the lump in my throat. "They let us pick out the middle name. Even though I tried hard not to think of names, it's just the one that always floated through my brain."

"It's a good name."

"His cries were really quiet, like he didn't know how loud he was. He probably thought he was deafening."

John chuckles. "Cute."

"I held him," I murmur.

"Yeah?" John waits for me to say more.

I take a shaky breath. "He's perfect. I could have held him forever." I begin to weep.

"Maclaren, what's wrong? Do you need the nurse?" Kyle asks from the couch, the leather squeaking as he rises and comes to my side. I shake my head. Andi also stirs beside me.

"Mac, you're going to survive this. Take a deep breath," John murmurs. But I can't. I drop my phone and bury my face in my palms.

"John, she'll call you back," Andi says. There's a brief pause while John talks on the other line. "We got her." Another pause. "Yeah, I'll let her know." She hangs up and sets the phone next to her. She wraps her arms around me and pulls me close toward her. I shimmy over and then feel Kyle's weight on my other side. He loops his arm around both of us.

Twenty-Two

I spend a little over twenty-four hours in the hospital. My dad is there to take me home. He grabs my bags as I face down the stairs. I've been dreading this part, but the alternative was my mom's house, and I didn't want to be there, away from my bed, my room, and my stuff. However, looking up, I'm rethinking my plan. I hear someone descending and I step aside to let them pass.

"Hey there," Dustin greets me. *He's here?*

My eyes instantly well with tears and I wrap him in a hug. "Hi." My voice cracks. "What are you doing here?" I say into his shoulder. His arms slip around my back.

"Was having a crappy day and I figured I'd make myself feel better by visiting someone who was having what I thought was also a crappy day." I let out a little gasping hiccup. "Clearly I'm mistaken, because you seem to be in high spirits."

Dustin lets me cry on his shoulder until I gather myself. I wipe my eyes and look at him. There is a large wet stain on his shoulder, most likely comprised of tears and snot. "Sorry."

"Eh, it'll dry." I glance over at the stairs. "Ready?" He extends his arm. I lace my arm through his and together we begin our ascent.

I feel like I'm moving in slow motion. Slower than slow motion, if that is a thing. By the time I reach our landing I'm drenched in sweat and ready for a shower. My dad is waiting at the door. I keep hold of Dustin's arm until we're inside.

"I'm gonna go rinse off. Can you stay?"

Dustin looks at my dad for permission, and he nods.

"Are you sure though? I can come back."

"I'm sure. Here, I'll show you to my room."

Dustin follows me. I go to my dresser and grab some clothes. I tell Dustin to make himself at home before I make my way to the bathroom.

When I come back, Dustin is sitting at the edge of my bed. He pulls out an earbud as I walk in. "That's making yourself at home?" I ask.

"I never knew Jiminy Cricket could be used as an expletive. What was going on in there?"

My cheeks flush. "You heard that?" I sit down next to him, ignoring his question. I slide over until I'm resting against my headboard then pat the space next to me, inviting Dustin to do the same.

"I'm going to have to keep that one in my arsenal," he remarks, sitting next to me.

"You're welcome. Whatcha listening to?"

He hands me an earbud and I slip it in my ear. We sit silently listening to music. When I glance over at Dustin, his jaw is clenched and he's staring at his phone. I lean my head against his now dry shoulder. "Wanna talk?" I whisper. His shoulder rises with his shrug. I stay leaning against him until my eyes grow heavy. The next thing I know, Dustin is gently shaking me.

"Hey, I sent you a link. Take a listen to it when you're fully awake."

"Wait, no. Sorry. Please stay. You can talk to me."

"I'm good, Mac. Thanks for letting me chill. I'll catch you later, kay?" He turns and heads out the door. My body is achy and I can feel sleep trying to take over. I grab my phone, open John's text

message thread, and type *911-D* before sinking down into
my bed and falling asleep.

I don't know how long I'm out for, but when I wake up, I hear
voices coming from the living room. When I get to the end of the
hall, the voices become clearer. Kyle is telling my dad about baseball
camp. They pause when they see me.

"Hi. How are you feeling? Did you get some rest?" Kyle asks.

I nod and take a seat by him on the couch.

"You kids hungry?" my dad asks.

"Starving," I answer.

"Anything sound good?"

I shrug. "Surprise me." I get up and head back to my room.
"You can come too," I call out to Kyle.

I curl up on my bed and flip on the television. Kyle comes in and
takes a seat on my bed. When I look over at him, all I can focus on is
his nose, now knowing what it looks like on a much tinier face. I
sniffle a few times. My brain won't stop bringing up images of
Lucas. I squeeze my eyes shut, willing them to stop before my heart
explodes.

A soft knock on the doorframe has me wiping my eyes. I peer
around Kyle to see John.

"Hey." My voice cracks.

Kyle moves off the bed, clearing the space for John.

"Hi. Thought I'd stop by and check on you. I was also a little
confused by your text earlier."

Our heads turn as a knock comes from the front door. We
overhear my dad making small talk with the delivery guy, no doubt
agreeing with him that the stairs are brutal and then tipping him an
extra few bucks for making the climb. My dad brings the box and
some plates into my room and asks what we want to drink.

"We have Dr. Pepper, cherry Bubly, or lemonade," I inform the boys. My voice hitches at the end and my hand drifts to my belly. I take a shuttering breath.

Concern flickers across my dad's face.

"I-I just want water," I whisper.

The boys let my dad know their preferences and then head for the pizza.

We're all eating silently when I hear Andi at the front door next. "Hello, Mr. Young."

"They're in her room."

I wait for Andi to come bouncing in, but instead I hear the bathroom door close.

"When nature calls," I mutter, taking another bite of pizza.

"Holy cow!" The door hinges squeak and then Andi is standing in my doorway holding up what resembles Depends in front of her face. My face heats instantly. "Are you seriously wearing these?" She drops her arms, and her cheeks turn bright red. "Hello, everyone."

"Those are quite a turn-on," I hear from the hall. Dustin steps up behind Andi. I set my pizza down and shield my face with my covers.

"Shoot me now," I groan.

"I'll just…" Andi trails off, throwing it back in the bathroom.

"Is that still up for grabs?" Dustin asks, followed by the scrape of the pizza lid. I slowly peek out to see Dustin shoving pizza in his mouth.

I turn to John suddenly. "My text earlier."

"Huh? Oh yeah, what's 911?"

Andi walks back into the room, her eyes hyper-focused on me. I shake my head. "It was for Dustin." Her shoulders instantly relax.

"What?" Dustin looks between John and me.

"911 is the code we use when one of us is having a crisis," Kyle explains. "I can't believe you taught it to them."

"I didn't, hence the confusion. I was so out of it this morning."

"Who's having a crisis?" Dustin asks.

"You, apparently," Andi answers.

"I think I would know if I was in crisis, and I don't think I am." Dustin pats himself down and wiggles and shimmies before looking at me. "I was in crisis?"

How do I explain? "Well, it's like…like…"

"What was going on this morning?" Andi asks, staring at Dustin.

"Nothing," he says. Andi continues staring. "Seriously, nothing."

"He came over and said he had a crappy morning. I was a sucky friend and fell asleep, but something was still off when he left."

"Hence 911," John concludes. I nod.

John and Dustin exchange glances. I catch the subtle shake of Dustin's head. Andi catches it too.

She narrows her eyes. "You know, we don't lie to each other. Spill."

"It's nothing," Dustin states. His voice takes on a dangerous edge, like the day I made the comment about smoking. Whatever is going on, Dustin is not going to talk and pushing him is probably a bad idea.

"Dude, I'd be careful with how you answer," Kyle warns.

Andi opens her mouth to say something but I immediately spit out, "Hey, who's in the mood for ice cream?"

"Sounds great," Dustin comments and walks out of the room. I ease myself off the bed to find Dustin rummaging through our freezer. He must sense I've walked up beside him because he says, "There is nothing up here."

"I know. If we really want ice cream, we have to go out."

"Too bad there are no ice cream delivery services. Did someone mention that those stairs are brutal?" Dustin winks.

"I've heard rumors." I nudge him with my shoulder. "Let me grab the others and we'll go."

"Mac, I don't think that's a good idea," my dad calls from the living room. I look over at Dustin and roll my eyes. I head toward my bedroom anyway.

I hear the pop of the footrest and the creak as he gets out of the chair. He beats me to the hall, blocking my path.

"Peanut, you just had a baby. I think you should stay home and rest."

"Dad, I'll be fine. Please?" My eyes fill with tears. "You know Andi will look out for me. Kyle, too. I don't want to sit here."

My dad lets out a heavy sigh and relaxes, but as I step past, he catches my shoulder. "I want you to be careful."

"I will." I raise up on my tiptoes and give him a quick kiss on the cheek and then continue down the hall.

"You better not let anything happen to her, you hear me?" my dad threatens Dustin.

"Yes, sir," Dustin responds.

We all congregate on the landing. Kyle, Dustin, and Andi head down first. I take John's hand and start down the stairs. I'm not going much faster than I was this morning. We're halfway down the second set of stairs when John lets go of my hand and loops his arm around my waist, providing extra support.

"Mac, are you sure about this?" Worry laces every word.

"Yeah. I need out." I ignore every signal my body is giving me to turn back and continue down the stairs. If I go back to my room, I know my thoughts will wander and I don't want that.

When we step into the ice cream parlor, there is a decent line and the few tables are occupied. I look over the menu while we wait, though I can't help my eyes from drifting to Kyle's profile.

An image of Lucas flashes in my mind, making my heart ache. John leans over and whispers, "You don't look good."

"I'm really sore and my legs are tired," I confess, leaving out everything else.

John maneuvers me in front of him and loosely wraps his arms around my waist. "I've got you."

Andi turns. "I can't even. You two are adorable," she squeals. Kyle glances over and the corner of his mouth turns up in a grin. I know if Lucas ever smirks like that, all the girls are going to fall for him. Suddenly, it feels like the wind is knocked out of me. A small whimper escapes my lips. Kyle's face falls with worry, while John's arms tighten around me.

In a flash, Dustin ducks under the nylon rope. I hear a clatter and then a thud. I turn to catch Dustin righting a chair. He gives an apologetic shrug, wincing as he does, to the guy who was also going for the open table. He points at me and waves me over. John releases me and I make my way over.

"Thanks," I say, sitting. "Is your shoulder okay?"

"I'll live."

I settle my emotions marginally once we get our ice cream and I can just listen to my friends chatter. I take another bite as the little bell on the front door chimes. A young couple walks in, the man holding an infant car seat. I gasp and break down in tears.

"Oh my gosh, what happened?" Andi reaches over and pulls me into her arms. I can't answer. I just turn and bury my face in her neck. "It's okay. It's okay," she consoles.

I finally manage to mumble, "Are they gone?"

"Who?" Andi asks.

"They're walking out," John replies, already knowing who I'm talking about.

"I wanna go home. Like, now." I shoot up out of my chair, leaving my ice cream on the table. I keep my eyes on the pavement as I head back toward Andi's car.

It's quiet as Andi parks and I get out. I don't have it in me to climb the stairs.

"Come here." John scoops me up into his arms. I wrap my arms around his neck and bury my face into his shoulder.

John stumbles on the stairs at one point but catches us before we fall. I hear a chorus of gasps.

"You good, man?" Dustin asks.

I tighten my grip on John's neck. I turn my face up so he can hear me clearly. "You okay?"

"Yeah, sorry about that. You?"

"Good."

John ignores everyone else and continues up the stairs a bit slower, focusing on every step he takes. Right before we make it to the landing I ask John to set me down at the door.

John shakes his head. "I'm making sure you get securely in bed."

"John, my dad will freak. Please?" My voice catches.

He sighs but eases me to my feet. He keeps a firm hold on my waist, making sure I'm steady. I give him a quick hug and then open the door. I walk inside, tears pooling in my eyes.

"That was a fast trip. Everything okay?"

I shake my head, making a beeline for my room.

"All right. Thank you guys for being here, but I think it's best to call it a night."

"Mr. Young, if it's okay—"

"I said she's done, Kyle. Good night." The finality in my dad's words does not elicit an argument from anyone. Their feet shuffle out and then the deadbolt squeaks as my dad locks the door.

I curl under my covers as tears spill down my cheeks. I feel like there's a weight sitting on my chest, making it impossible to breathe.

"Oh, Maclaren." My dad sits next to me, stroking my hair. "I'm right here, peanut. I'm not going anywhere." I sit up and wrap my arms around my dad. He engulfs me in a hug, squeezing tight. He stays with me until I start to drift off.

My dad is sitting in the living room when I walk out the next morning. I go to the kitchen trying to decide what I want for breakfast.

"Do you want me to make you something?"

I open the freezer, thinking we still have some frozen waffles, when I spot the little bowl of ice cream, a receipt wrapped around it. Taking the ice cream out of the freezer, I unravel the receipt, noticing Dustin's scrawled handwriting. *Didn't want it to go to waste. Sorry for making you worry about me. I'll be fine.*

I stick the ice cream back in the freezer, forgetting all about breakfast, and return to my room.

"Peanut, are you all right?"

"Yeah," I call out.

I sink back into bed and pull up my text message thread with Dustin.

Are you sure? I type.

?

You're fine? Because it didn't seem like it. And I epically failed you yesterday.

I wouldn't say epically, but... A winky face emoji follows.

I'm grateful for texting because he doesn't see my lip tremble or the tear that leaks out.

Kidding, BTW! Please don't be crying. You're crying, aren't you? Yep, you're crying. It was a joke, I swear.

I know.

You're my most favorite clinic girl ever. Stop crying. SERIOUSLY! STOP IT! Right now.

I sniffle and try to rein in my emotions.

Are you still crying?

Who said I was? You just assumed.

Sorry, he says, followed by a frowny face. *But was I wrong?*

I hit the little shrug emoji.

Mac? Sorry!

No biggie. Thanks for the ice cream.

Do you need anything? How are you?

I don't respond. I set my phone on my nightstand and curl up.

Kyle drops by in the afternoon, bringing with him my favorite dish from Pita Jungle. We eat in the living room in silence. I set my container on the coffee table and square my shoulders.

I swallow. "Are you okay?"

Kyle glances over at me. "Yesh," he answers, mouth full of food.

"You're not upset? You're okay with the decision we made?"

Kyle drops his fork into his bowl. He looks at me. "I think the Challinors are extremely lucky, and I think we made the best decision we could."

"You're *for sure*, for sure? You're okay not being a dad? No waking up in the middle of the night, no diapers to change, no feeding schedule?" *No first smile, no little coos, no new baby smell.*

"Mac, I mean it. I'm good with our decision and seeing the Challinors with Lucas made me way more confident in our choice.

They are going to be great parents. They were so happy and we were able to do that for them." He pauses. "Are you okay with it?"

I shrug. Hot tears begin to roll down my cheeks. Kyle pulls me into his side.

"We did the right thing," he says adamantly.

Twenty-Three

It's been a week since Lucas was born and I've kept to myself, not letting anyone visit, only texting if someone reaches out. The only phone call I've taken was from my mom. The conversation was short, but there was no bickering at least. That same weight from the first night I came home sits on my chest. My dad is still at work and it's too quiet in the apartment. I quickly rinse off and put on clean clothes and drive over to John's.

When I knock on the door Eric answers quickly and then darts off. I step inside and close the door. "Who was at the door?" Marie calls out.

"It's Mac," I say, feeling tears gather as I climb up the stairs. John is reading on his bed when I knock on the doorframe.

"Hey." He looks up and smiles.

I can't keep my emotions at bay and begin to sob. Hurrying over to the bed, I crawl into his open arms. He holds me tight, stroking my hair. "It's okay," he whispers.

"John?" I blubber.

"Yeah?"

"I don't think I'm surviving. This really hurts." I take a shuttering breath. "I wasn't prepared for this and I really tried."

"You did the best you could," he whispers.

"Did I? Did I do the right thing? God isn't disappointed in me or anything?"

"What? No."

"How do you know? I mean, what if he was supposed to be mine? What if I was the one who was supposed to keep him?"

"Do you feel like you were?" John asks and holds me a little tighter. "Like, deep down, do you feel like you were the one who was supposed to raise him?"

Through the whole pregnancy I knew I wasn't ready to be a parent. I know I'm not ready to be a parent now. "No," I breathe out.

"Mac, you did the most selfless thing. It's going to take time to heal, but I don't think you made the wrong decision, and I don't think God is disappointed in you for the choice you made. You chose to carry a little life and created a family. There is no way God could be mad at that."

"I don't know…"

"You told me the Challinors go to church, right?" I nod. "If you ask them, I bet they would say that you gave them the best gift of all and that God provided in unexpected ways. To them, you are part of a miracle."

His words bring a fresh torrent of tears.

"You may not feel like you're surviving, but trust me, you are. You're doing amazing."

I lift my head. John reaches for my cheeks, wiping tears away the tears there. His thumb traces the dark circles under my eyes. "Oh, Mac…" He frowns. I nestle back into his chest, listening to the steady rhythm of his heartbeat. I feel myself start to slowly drift off and I shift a little to wake myself up.

"Uncomfortable?" he asks.

"Falling asleep."

"I know. You need to."

"But…" I can't formulate an argument, not with his body heat warming me like a cozy blanket and the gentle motion of his hand rubbing concentric circles on my back.

This is the first time in a week I feel rested when I wake up. I sit up, rubbing my eyes. John moved me at some point. I glance around the room, but he isn't here. I head downstairs, following the commotion in the living room.

"What? No! Wait, am I dead?" Andi exclaims.

"Don't worry, you'll respawn," Dustin consoles her.

"So, I died. I hate this game."

Andi is sitting criss-cross on the floor, squinting at the screen. Eric is a couple feet away, fingers furiously hitting buttons. Dustin and John take up the couch. I walk over and pass in front of Dustin, who smiles when he sees me. I sit between them, John reaching over and squeezing my knee. "Did you sleep okay?" he asks, turning his attention to me.

I nod.

"This is the absolute worst!" Andi drops her controller and then turns toward the couch.

"You're definitely going to die if you look this way," I say.

"I'm pretty sure I'm *dead* dead. Right?" She twists to look at the screen.

"Yup," Eric confirms.

Andi gets up and, before I have time to react, hugs me tightly. "I've been so worried about you. Then when I stopped by your apartment and you weren't there, I freaked. You doing okay?" She leans back to study me.

"I'm doing." I shrug.

"You're going to have to start taking my phone calls. I move into my dorm room next week. I can't just pop over if I don't hear from you."

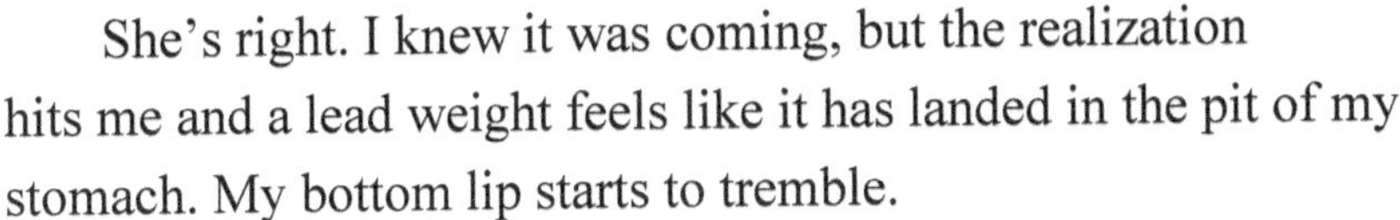

She's right. I knew it was coming, but the realization
hits me and a lead weight feels like it has landed in the pit of my
stomach. My bottom lip starts to tremble.

"Hey, it's not a big deal."

I clear my throat. "It kind of is, though."

"Andi, don't worry. She now has us. We will be horrendously
annoying and won't leave her alone. She will be so sick of us."
Dustin looks over and winks.

"He's right." John nudges my shoulder. "She's stuck with us."
With me, he mouths. My lip curls up in a small grin.

Dustin didn't lie when he said they would be annoying. Text
messages come every day, checking in. If I don't answer, it's usually
followed by a phone call. The past few days, all my texts have been
one-word answers or a quick thumbs-up.

Not that they need to worry. Mostly all I've been doing is sitting
on my couch and bingeing Project Runway, like now. The blinds are
drawn, the only light coming from the television. A knock on the
door interrupts my show and I groan, hoping whoever it is will go
away. Another knock comes, more forceful. I get up and open the
door.

"Hey, hey," Dustin greets me.

"What are you doing here?"

"You've got to stop ignoring your phone," Dustin says, pushing
past me into my apartment and taking a seat in my dad's recliner.
John follows behind him and gives me a little nod. I shut the door
and curl up on my couch again. John sits on the floor in front of me.

"How's it going?" He reaches up and smooths some of my little
flyaway pieces of hair down.

I shrug, then hit play. The designers are all in the studio working away. I scooch over and rest my head on John's shoulder. He turns, giving me a gentle kiss on the top of my head.

"It's much comfier up here," I whisper.

I sit up and slide over, making room for him. Once seated, I cuddle into his side. He drapes his arm around me and focuses on the television screen. "So, what are we doing?"

"Making clothes, dummy," Dustin quips.

I quickly explain the challenge. Out of the corner of my eye I see Dustin pull his phone out of his pocket. He types a quick message and then drops it in his lap.

"Oh my gosh. One of them messaged 911, didn't they?"

"The question is, which one?" Dustin says.

"It was Kyle," John confesses. "Followed shortly by Andi."

"They *both* heard from me today." Granted, that was hours ago. "I haven't completely ignored my phone," I snip.

"Look, isn't the rule that if someone sends a 911, you answer it?" Dustin has turned to stare at me.

"Yes," I huff and begin to bite my nail. John takes my hand, lacing his fingers through mine.

"We're still new to this process. I'm sure when we become pros we'll know to bring some sort of comfort food or flowers or whatever depending on the situation. You're going to have to give us a pass here. We're trying." John squeezes my hand.

"I'm—"

"Don't say fine, Mac." Dustin's tone becomes biting.

I inhale deep. "What's your problem?"

"Nothing."

I catch John studying Dustin, a slight frown on his face. There's a hint of worry in his eyes and his brows are furrowed.

"You're the one who came over. I didn't ask you to and you waltzed right in, might I add. You don't get to now tell me I can't say I'm fine."

"Okay, well maybe realize other people have stuff going on in their lives too. Maybe just be honest, because one"—he holds up his index finger—"friends don't lie and two"—he lifts his middle finger—"despite what we're feeling, we came over because we care about you. Jeez."

Dustin gets up and walks out the front door. Tears prick the corner of my eyes and I try to clear the sudden lump from my throat.

"Give him a minute. He's had a rough day."

"I'm really trying. I just—I can't breathe sometimes. My heart feels like it might splinter apart and I…I…"

"Mac, it's okay. You don't have to defend yourself, but he's got a point. You don't have to lie to us. We know every day isn't going to feel fine. Just let us know. Maybe we can come up with a sliding scale, like today is definitely a one, where you didn't leave the house, didn't comb your hair, and didn't shower. If you have a decent day and you run one errand, then it's a three." His shoulder lifts as he shrugs. "Fair?"

"Fair."

"Do you want us to leave? We were just instructed to make sure you were alive, not barge in and take over your living room."

"No, you can stay. I just… I'm not fun company right now," I mumble. "If Dustin wants to stay, we can order food. Are you hungry?"

"I already ate. Have you eaten?" John glances at the kitchen where my dad's coffee cup and plate from breakfast still sit in the sink. I've snacked a little but haven't eaten a full meal.

"Haven't been super hungry."

"If it's a matter of not wanting to go out, we can DoorDash something." Dustin's voice makes me jump. He must have come in while we were talking.

"If you guys already ate, it's fine."

"What sounds good?" Dustin asks.

I think for a moment. "Chinese?"

"Perfect." Dustin places an order. "It will be here in twenty-five minutes. I left a tip. You can add a little for the stairs if you feel like it." There is a hint of a smile as he says this. "You ready, John?"

"Wait, you don't have to go." My voice cracks.

"Mac, it's all good. Text us if you need us. Make sure to eat and we will talk to you later." Dustin twists the door handle and opens it slightly. "Oh, and please let me know whether Natasha wins or loses. She seems like such a crybaby."

"She is, and I will."

Dustin turns and walks out. John stands. "We did ride together, so I have to go. I can come back though."

"No, it's okay. It was good to see you. I'll text you."

I walk John to the door and give him a hug before settling back on the couch.

Twenty-Four

I'm surprised to hear my phone buzz at four in the morning.

Everything okay? I ask.

Feel like a drive? Dustin asks.

I sneak out of my room and down the stairs, waiting on the curb until Dustin pulls up. I notice the tension in his body as I climb in. Was he this tense earlier?

Dustin doesn't say anything as he winds through the complex, just turns up the music. We drive in silence for a while, which makes me nervous. I reach over and turn down the radio. "Dustin, what's wrong?"

"I just needed out for a bit. How are you?" He peeks over at me.

"You saw me earlier. You know how I am."

He gives me a look. "You didn't answer earlier. If you're not talking, neither am I."

"Okay, that's lame. There has to be a reason you asked if I wanted to tag along. Spill."

"Did it ever occur to you that maybe I don't want to talk?" he snaps.

Tears instantly spring to my eyes. I quickly turn to the window and try to discreetly wipe my eyes.

"Mac, hey, I'm sorry." There's a pause. "Mac?"

"Hm?" I keep my back to Dustin.

"Please look at me."

"You can take me home," I say as fresh tears gather in my eyes. "I'm sorry."

I realize we are pulling into the parking lot of John's work. I see a couple people outside, one of them being John. Dustin parks and I immediately climb out of the vehicle. I head straight for John, but Dustin catches up and grabs my wrist. "Mac, please."

I whip around. "Let go," I yell.

"Look, I just don't think you need to hear about my day right now."

"I said, *let go*." I jerk my arm and Dustin releases his grip.

"Hey, what is going on?" John asks, coming up behind me.

"How much longer are you here?" I turn, asking John.

"A while. Can someone fill me in?"

I cross my arms. "Dustin's being a complete jerk and has decided I'm not worthy enough to hear about his day. Even though something happened and he is clearly upset," I shout.

"I just thought it would be good to chill and drive around. Figured we'd come keep John company. I wasn't expecting to talk."

I ball my hands into fists while hot tears fall. "That's crap and you know it."

"Okay, well, I see the plan is going smoothly," John quips.

I narrow my eyes at him. "What?"

"Nothing," Dustin says.

"I thought you wanted her to know."

Dustin shrugs, but his jaw tightens.

"I'm so lost. What is going on?"

John turns to me. "You remember when you two met?"

"The party?" I try and think back to the night on the porch.

"Nope. When you got your lovely nickname." I tilt my head. John continues, "Dustin—"

Dustin jumps in. "I wasn't there because I was sleeping around." He winks at me. "I was there getting a few other tests done."

John interjects, "Everything came back clear, but a few weeks ago—"

"And long story short, I went back in for some screenings," Dustin interrupts again. "I'm waiting on the results, but we're not worrying about it. So, how's work?" He nods at John.

"Wait, what?" The whole conversation makes no sense. If he wasn't in there being tested for a sexually transmitted infection, then what would he be in for? I sift through everything I read through when I was looking up the clinic. "Oh my gosh." My eyes instantly fill with tears.

"Maclaren, we're not crying about this," Dustin snaps.

I go to wrap Dustin in a hug, but he shoves me hard, making me stumble back a few steps.

"What the hell, man?" John is immediately in front of me, angling himself between us.

Dustin turns, raking his hands through his hair before dropping them at his sides, clenching and unclenching his fists.

"It's fine," I say.

"It most certainly is not!" John yells.

I step around him and approach Dustin slowly. "Dustin? I'm sorry. I just reacted. That wasn't fair."

Dustin doesn't move but I can see his shoulders begin to shake.

"May I give you a hug?"

Dustin doesn't say anything but turns and I hesitantly step forward. I bring my arms around his neck and after a moment he leans in, wrapping his arms around me.

I hold him, letting him cry on my shoulder, returning the favor from weeks ago. I try not to think of the fact that Dustin may have cancer. If I let my thoughts wander, I will break down and he doesn't need that right now. He needs stoic, unemotional Mac. Why did he have to get stuck with this version of me? To bring him comfort, I whisper the words John has so often repeated to me. "You'll survive this. No matter what the outcome is, we got you." My phone buzzes in my pocket, but I don't release my grip.

When Dustin finally steps back, he turns away from me, wiping his eyes. I look around but John is nowhere to be seen. I slide my phone out of my pocket.

Had to head back in. Please let me know everything's okay. If things don't settle—911, okay?

"You ready to go?" I ask.

Dustin nods.

"Hungry?"

Dustin shrugs.

"Waffles?"

Dustin doesn't respond, just turns and heads toward his truck. I climb in and buckle. Dustin sticks the keys in the ignition and then drops his hand.

"Did I hurt you?"

I don't say anything. Instead, I stare at him, completely confused.

"Did I? I mean, you just had a baby." Dustin lets out a string of profanities.

"Woah, Dustin. I'm fine. Really."

"I'm so sorry."

"Like I said, I reacted. I shouldn't have done that."

"My reaction was way worse. I felt the impact. John should have beat me to a pulp for that." Dustin drops his head into his hands. "I can't believe I did that."

"Dustin. Please look at me." I shift in my seat and wait. When his eyes finally find mine, they are rimmed in red. "I'm not hurt. You did nothing wrong. What you're dealing with is intense and—"

Dustin shakes his head. "It's not an excuse."

"Um, do you want to chalk it up to hormones? Any time I overreacted, that's what I did." I give him a smile.

Dustin rolls his eyes. Sighing, he starts, "Maclaren—"

"Nope. You feel bad. I'm not hurt. We can both be emotional wrecks. Moving on. Now, waffles?"

"Waffles."

As Dustin backs out, I message John. *He's okay. Getting waffles*, I say, adding a little heart emoji.

It's silent at the table as the waitress delivers our food. I grab the syrup and pour it over my waffle. I quietly ask, "When do you get your results?" I release the handle, halting the syrup flow and set the bottle down. Dustin grabs it, quickly pouring syrup in a zig-zag over his own waffle.

For a second, I don't think Dustin heard me because he simply cuts into his waffle, taking a bite. I'm not sure if I should ask again or just let it go.

"Later today," he answers, cutting another small piece.

"You'll let me know?" I glance up at him. He sets his fork down and quickly swipes at his eyes. He nods and resumes eating.

"Um…I saw AJR is doing a concert here. We should definitely go."

Dustin shrugs.

I realize depending on results, Dustin might not be able to go. I internally chastise myself. I quickly take a bite of waffle, letting silence settle over the table again.

"Oh, she won." I point my fork at him.

Dustin stares at me.

"Natasha."

Dustin shakes his head.

"The designer, from—"

"*Ohhh.*" His mouth quirks into a half-smile.

"She cried." I chuckle. Dustin joins me.

Dustin drops me off and I head back to my room and take a short nap. I spend the rest of the day checking my phone for any message from Dustin or John with results from Dustin's tests. I'm lounging on the couch when my phone chimes.

CLEAR.

That one word from Dustin brings tears to my eyes. I fall back on the couch, breathing a sigh of relief.

I'm still riding that high later that evening when my dad comes home.

"Hey, saw these rather pathetic looking gentlemen outside. Thought they could use a good meal. I hope you don't mind." My dad steps into the kitchen, Dustin and John trailing behind him.

I squeal and attack Dustin. Dustin catches me and spins us before setting me down.

"I'm not even going to ask," my dad mutters.

"How do you feel? I bet you feel amazing!" I shake his shoulders. "Am I right?"

Dustin laughs. "I feel pretty good."

"This is good, isn't it?" I turn, expecting John to match my enthusiasm. He's not there. I spin, looking for him, but my dad nods toward the front door. I leave Dustin with my dad and head to the front landing.

I find John leaning on the porch rail looking out at the parking lot. I rest my hand on his back, stepping to his side. "Hey."

John swallows. He takes a deep breath. "Hi."

"What's wrong?"

He shakes his head.

"You can talk to me."

I begin rubbing little concentric circles on his back.

He clears his throat. "Sorry, it's just been a stressful couple of weeks. I guess it finally caught up to me."

"What's made it stressful?"

"Let's see, my friend was worried he had cancer, my girlfriend just had a baby, and Jonah got his hands on my math notes, so now I'm screwed on my homework." He blows out a breath.

"Man, do you think you'll fail the class?" I bump his shoulder. Classes began this week.

He turns his face toward me, his lips pursed.

"Oh, was the homework not the most stressful thing? Those other two seemed measly." I wink.

"This isn't funny," he says.

"You're right. Cancer isn't funny. It's scary." Tears gather in my eyes and I blink hard. "You've also spent quite a bit of energy making sure I've been okay, and I'm a freaking mess. I'm sorry I didn't notice you were struggling." A tear escapes and slips down my cheek.

John reaches up, swiping it away with his thumb. "You had other things going on."

"You know you can talk to me, right? If there is ever anything, I'm here."

"I didn't say anything about Dustin, because it wasn't my business to tell."

"I get that." I pause. "You called me your girlfriend."

His eyebrows scrunch together as he tilts his head. "Yeah?"

"I guess I didn't—um, okay." I bite down on my thumb nail.

"You sure? You look a little freaked out."

I drop my hand and wind my arms around his waist. Looking up into his deep-blue eyes, I've never been more sure of anything. I stretch up on my tiptoes and kiss him. His lips are frozen under mine for a split second before they come to life.

Someone gags from behind me, and John and I snap apart.

"Get a room." Dustin winks. I glance at John and watch his cheeks turn bright red. "Everything good, man?"

John nods.

"Dinner's ready," he informs us. He turns, heading inside. John slips his hand in mine and leads me into my apartment.

ONE MONTH LATER

Andi calls me Thursday evening announcing she will be in town for the weekend and tells me to polish off my bowling shoes. She invites Travis, John, and Dustin too. As I'm getting ready I hear my phone chime from the bedroom. I finish curling my hair, quickly adding some hair spray before grabbing it from my purse.

I stop dead in the hallway when I see the email. *ONE MONTH UPDATE*, the subject reads. Instantly, my heart stops and all the air evaporates from the room. This is an update from the Challinors about Lucas. When we were first looking into adoption, I thought it would be good to maintain a relationship with the baby. It's why we chose an open adoption. Now I'm petrified. I knew letting him go would be difficult, but I wasn't expecting the amount of pain it would cause. I'm not sure I'm ready to read how he is or look at photos. How often does he move and kick now that he has more room? Are his cries still quiet? Is he a good sleeper or does he keep Tanya and Joel up all hours of the night?

"Hey, hey," Travis calls as he knocks and opens the front door. "Andi's running late. No surprise there, but she told me she was your ride and figured I could pick you up and—"

"Trav, I-I can't breathe." I fall to my knees in the middle of the hallway, hands pressed to my chest.

"What's wrong?" Travis squats in front of me, studying me like he's trying to find an injury.

"They—they sent… It's an email and—"

It's like a puzzle piece clicks together in Travis's head. He sits down criss-crossed next to me. "You're not alone. I'm right here. Mac, look at me."

I look up to see him staring at me. "Hey. You're safe, okay?" I nod. "I want you to close your eyes and think of three things that make you happy, that make you feel calm." My ragged breathing echoes in the small hallway. "You got it?"

I shake my head.

"One thing then. Tell me what it is."

"Drawing," I manage to say.

"Okay, good. What do you draw?"

"C-clothes." I take a small breath.

"What would you say your favorite article of clothing to draw is?"

"Depends."

"Do you draw on an iPad or paper and pencil?"

"Depends."

"Which do you prefer?" He raises his eyebrows, expectant.

"S-sometimes it's nice to create designs the old-fashioned way, but there's so much more you can do on the iPad." I take a huge gulp of air. Travis smiles.

"All right. What's another thing that makes you feel calm?"

I take a deep breath in through my nose and out through my mouth. I do this a few times before answering, "John."

As if on cue, the door bursts open and John rushes in.

"What happened?" John runs over to me, immediately dropping to sit beside me. I grab his hand and interlace my fingers with his.

"I-I got an email from the Challinors." Upon saying it, it feels like an anvil drops on my chest and my breathing seizes again.

"John's right here. You're in a safe place. Try and take a nice, slow breath. Who are—"

"The adoptive parents," John answers, squeezing my hand. "It's an open adoption and Mac can receive email updates and send them as well. She also has the option to schedule visits with them. I think this is the first one."

I nod, glancing over at John. His hair has a bit more product in it, so it doesn't look unruly. He's wearing a short-sleeve button-down shirt and dark-washed jeans.

"You look nice," I say, trying to focus on something other than the crushing weight I feel. "Why?"

"I decided to go to church today." John shrugs.

Travis sits there for a moment, watching me. When he's sure I won't hyperventilate, he stands. "I'm going to let the others know we won't make it to the alley. I'll be right back."

Travis heads for the front door, phone to his ear. I change positions so I can sit cross-legged on the floor. I lean into John, and he wraps his arm around me. "I didn't expect this," I whisper.

"It's scary," John says.

"Let me check," Travis says as he walks back in. He veers toward the kitchen and I hear cupboards opening, then the water dispenser on the fridge. Travis rounds the corner and extends a glass of water to me. I take it, immediately draining half of it.

"Do you want Andi and Dustin to come over or should we just call it?" he asks me. "We can plan something another time."

"I want to see Andi."

"She wants to see you," Travis relays.

"Can Dustin pick up Freddy's on the way? Maybe we can just watch a movie instead," I suggest.

Travis nods. He says a quick goodbye to Andi and then sits back down with John and me.

"We don't have to keep sitting here." I push myself up, the boys following. "I'll be out in a sec," I say, handing John the glass of water and heading back to my room. I quickly change into an oversized T-shirt and gym shorts. When I come out, hushed whispers fill the air. I pause at the end of the hall, listening for a moment. What they say makes me interject.

"Wait, what about a panic attack?"

John and Travis both jump.

"I think that's what happened," Travis says, a hand to his chest since I scared him. "I've had a few and they suck. I just thought it would be helpful if someone knew."

"Does it always feel like that? Like…like…" I don't even know how to describe the feeling.

"It's different for everyone. For me, I always get really hot, my heart races, and I feel super nauseous. Sometimes, I actually throw up. I've never really felt like I couldn't breathe. I know that's a symptom though."

I nod. "I'm kind of glad you walked through the door when you did," I murmur.

"Me too. How are you feeling?"

The front door opens. I look down at my lap, biting on my thumb nail. "Today was a solid three. Maybe almost four until…"

Travis looks perplexed.

"That's good," Dustin says, setting the food on the coffee table. "It's been a while since you've even approached a four."

"It's the scale. You know, one is bad and five is good," Andi explains. Travis nods, understanding dawning on his face.

The five of us chat after the movie, but I can't get my mind off my phone. I haven't touched it since the panic attack, and my heart starts to race all over again as the home screen lights up. They're texts

from Kyle. I wonder if he's already checked the email. If he has, I should too.

"Mac, the great thing about email is you can check it whenever *you're* ready," John whispers.

I peek over at him. "I don't know if I'll ever be ready." At least if I open it now I have a room full of people to support me and make sure I keep breathing. However, it's also a room full of people who will watch me have a breakdown.

Before I can second-guess myself, I open the email. There is a short message and then an attachment. I quickly scan the short paragraph, take a deep breath, and then press the little paperclip icon. Pictures flood the screen, and immediately, hot tears run down my cheeks. I quickly close out of them and switch to Kyle's text message. He read the email and attached a couple of his favorites.

I press the heel of my hands to my eyes, willing the tears to stop. Just a short glimpse of Lucas and I can already see the changes. He's a little bigger, with cute round cheeks. In one it looked like he was smirking. Kyle makes that same face. It feels like someone is stabbing my heart. I try to take a breath in, but it only seems to intensify the pain.

"Mac, hey." I whip my head up, hearing Kyle's voice. Andi sits down next to me with her phone extended, Kyle on the screen. "Hi. Are you okay?"

"No," I blubber. "Did you see them?" Which seems like a dumb question because I know he did.

"I wasn't thinking when I sent my favorites. I didn't realize it would be this hard for you." Kyle swipes at his eyes.

"And you?" I sniffle. "Answer honestly."

"I was excited."

"He was," Megan pipes up from the background before coming into frame. "Like a little kid on Christmas."

I give them a small smile.

"It's probably very different for you," Megan says.

At this, fresh tears start to fall. I pull up the pictures again and scroll through them, finding the ones Kyle sent over.

"Mac, seriously. If this is too much, you don't have to look at them. I'll make sure to wait until you reach out before I send any or make any comments."

"I can't believe you didn't send this one." I hold up my phone to show Lucas in a little baseball onesie. I tilt it so Andi can see.

OMG, she mouths. *So cute.*

I'm studying the picture when something on the dresser catches my eye. I zoom in and see picture frames, but can't see what's inside them. I scroll through all the pictures again, focusing on the background. I find one with Tanya in a rocker, the dresser closer. I zoom in and there, sitting on the dresser, is a picture of Kyle dressed in his baseball uniform. Next to that frame is one of me. I'm smiling so big. Andi took that photo earlier this summer when we were sitting out by the pool, feet in the water. My belly is huge. Out of the frame, making his way over to us, is John. I can't believe the Challinors have pictures of us in Lucas's room.

"Mac?" Kyle asks.

"There are pictures of us," I say, switching back to my email.

I hit reply and type out a short message, then send it off before I lose my nerve. I close everything and then turn my phone off. I'll check for a response later. Right now, I just lean into John and let him hold me close.

NOVEMBER BREAK

It's November break and Andi, Travis, John, and myself are all over at Dustin's playing *Super Smash Bros.*, with Kyle and Megan joining us virtually. After taking a bathroom break, I hurry back to the living room but pause when my phone buzzes in my back pocket. I slide it out, quickly checking the notification. It's an email. I quickly swipe down to delete what is presumably junk mail, but when I see the subject line, my heart stops. I immediately turn my phone off and head back toward the couch. I pick up the controller. "Sorry, let's do this."

Dustin starts the game and the seven characters go back to battling. I try to focus on the game, but I can't stop thinking about the unopened email waiting for me. The Challinors sent an update with an attachment, meaning there's likely pictures. The screen blurs as tears build in my eyes. I take a deep breath and blink hard. On screen Yoshi dashes across a bridge and pelts Princess Peach with a turtle shell.

"Hey!" Andi turns and punches Travis in the shoulder. He lets out a little chuckle, already moving on to his next victim.

My character, Bayonetta, stands frozen, while Luigi rushes toward her. I feel like the air is being slowly pulled from the room. Luigi halts inches from Bayonetta.

"Mac?" John asks.

I press my hands to my chest, trying to keep my heart from exploding. I can't take a full breath. John scoots closer to me, reaching out. I jerk away from him. He holds up his hands in surrender. "Okay."

I stand, my vision spotting as I do. I keep one hand on my chest and move one hand to my belly. It feels like I'm breathing through a straw. John comes and stands in front of me but doesn't reach out. I hate that my brain reacts this way.

"Hey, Mac, you're back at work, right?" Travis asks casually. I glance down at him. "Yes or no?"

I nod.

"How many days did you have to work this week?"

I hold out four fingers.

"Were any of them long shifts?"

I take a small breath. "No."

"Who was the worst customer you had this week?"

I think about this. As I do I reach for John's hand. He knots his fingers in mine and gives my hand a squeeze. "Um…the guy on Tuesday, with the online order." I take another small breath.

"What happened?"

"He c-called and said we gave him the wrong pizza, when I'm the one who checked him out and repeated his order."

"What about your best customer?"

I'm finally able to suck in a full breath. John sighs in relief. I step close to him and rest my head on his bicep. "There was this cute little old couple that ordered a small pizza to split. The man was so sweet. He escorted his wife to the table, got her drink for her, and then bought her a cookie for dessert. She lit up when he brought it to her. It was adorable." I smile, remembering.

"Have you ever seen them before?" Dustin pipes up.

I shake my head. "I kind of hope they come in again though."

I move and sit on the couch, picking up my controller.
John sits down beside me, pressing his leg against mine. "Sorry," I whisper.

"Okay, shall we see if Andi can truly wipe the floor with us or what?" Dustin asks.

"Bring it on," Andi says.

We all turn our attention back to the screen. We alert Kyle and Megan we're starting and the game continues. I pull out my phone and send a quick text. Travis's phone buzzes. He glances over, quickly unlocking his screen. He reads the text and gives me a quick thumbs-up before focusing back on the game.

CHRISTMAS BREAK

Talking Stick Amphitheater, an outdoor concert venue, is teeming with people. The lawn, which provided the cheapest tickets and the only tickets we could afford, slowly begins to fill up. It's a very different atmosphere than where I started my morning.

Since John has been going to church here and there, I asked if I could join him one Sunday. He tried to hide his shock, but nodded and asked why I was interested in coming. I told him it seemed like it was becoming more important to him, plus the Challinors go to church. Maybe it would be good to get a glimpse at what Lucas would experience.

John's church has two services on Sunday. We went to the last one, picking up coffee beforehand. I relaxed some when I saw many people wearing jeans and T-shirts. Of course, some of the older folks still wore more dressy attire. John found us seats near the back. They started the service by having everyone stand and sing some songs. I wasn't really sure why they did that. I made a mental note to ask John. They had a little time to greet people and then collected an offering. Again, another question for John. Then the preacher gave a sermon, they prayed, and did something called communion. Add that to the list of questions.

Overall, it wasn't a horrible experience. John explained everything the best he could on the way home. I bet it's different if

you grow up in a church environment. It made me wonder how Lucas will experience church.

Now, sitting on the large blanket we have spread out over the grass, I glance down at my outfit. It's not that much different than what I wore this morning, except I put a little more effort into my hair and makeup.

Kyle and Megan sit near the opposite edge of the blanket. They came for the holiday break. Classes start up again mid-January and they'll be flying back tomorrow.

Dustin plops down beside me. "Where's everyone else?" I ask, glancing around the large lawn, not seeing Andi, Travis, or John.

"They're comin'," Dustin remarks.

My phone chimes and as I reach for my purse, I catch Kyle slide his phone out of his pocket. I'm hoping it's a group text from Andi, even though deep down, I know it's not. Sure enough, when I pull up my notifications an email from the Challinors is waiting in my inbox. The air begins to feel thin and I'm having a hard time breathing. Kyle's eyes shoot to me.

I give him a weak smile. Standing, I search the crowd for one person. He should be visible; his height makes him stand out.

"Mac? What can I do?" Dustin asks, standing next to me. It's still weird that he calls me by my name now. There are days I miss Clinic Girl, his little nickname for me.

I shake my head. My eyes catch a glimpse of John's blond hair, and my feet start moving.

"What's wrong?" Andi asks, seeing me approach. Travis frowns. John's brow instantly furrows.

"Let's take a walk." I grab John's hand, leading him away from the crowd. Part of me wonders if I should bring Travis along. He's so good at coming up with questions to distract me. It always amazes me how he can stay so calm. The one time he had a panic attack in front of me, I was anything but calm.

Travis and I were at Andi's, waiting in her bedroom for her to finish getting ready. A loud clatter came from the bathroom. She quickly yelled out to make sure Travis was okay, which I thought was odd.

"I'm good," Travis called back.

When I looked over at him, he was pale, and beads of sweat were beginning to form on his forehead. He moved from her bed over to the floor by her small cylinder trash can.

"What's happening? Should I get Andi?"

Travis shook his head. He placed his head in his hands, cursing under his breath.

The night I had my first panic attack came flooding back to me. Travis gets nauseous. He doesn't have trouble breathing.

My heart raced as I tried to think of what I could do. I'm horrible at coming up with questions for people; it's why I hate small talk. He needed a distraction.

"Did you know Andi peed in the wave pool at Sun Splash our junior year of high school?"

Travis glanced up at me.

"Yep, we had guzzled large vanilla Cokes from QT earlier and she followed it up with a bottle of water. The waves had just started and I said something to make her laugh. Suddenly, she grabbed my arm and yanked so hard, I thought my shoulder was going to dislocate. When I asked where we were going, she just told me away from there. Once we were far enough she asked if I thought it was true that they put chemicals in the pool to detect urine. By that time, I was laughing so hard I had to go too."

Travis stared at me.

"I don't even think Kyle knows that. So, I wouldn't say anything to her unless you really need ammo."

Travis pushed himself to his feet and walked back over to the bed. A few moments later, Andi walked in. She studied Travis for a heartbeat, then grabbed her purse.

"Ready?" she asked, heading toward the hall.

I got to my feet, following behind Andi.

Travis stopped me at the door. "Certain noises trigger it. Thanks for the story. It helped."

That moment plays on repeat in my head as John interlaces his fingers with mine. We find a secluded alcove near the entry gates and tuck away into it.

"Try and take deep breaths," John says. He draws me close, enveloping me in a hug, his hand rubbing up and down my back.

I cling to him, closing my eyes. I breathe in through my nose and out through my mouth a few times. "I'm excited for tonight. The band should be amazing." I take a breath. "You're here." Another breath. "My design classes start next week."

John's chest rumbles as he chuckles. "I'm not sure the last one makes you calm."

"It's exciting though."

After delivering Lucas, I took the first semester of college off. During my time off I've been designing outfits like crazy. Surprisingly, quite a few of them are maternity pieces. Over the holiday break I decided it might not be a bad idea to enroll in a few classes at the community college to try my hand in fashion design. As I thought, my mom disapproves of my career path. On our last call she told me as such, encouraging me to take some classes that were a bit more practical. But as my dad has pointed out, everyone needs clothes. Especially, as I've learned, pregnant women. It can't get more practical than that. Maybe she'll see that one day.

I pull away just enough to peer up at John. His beautiful blue eyes stare back at me, filled with concern.

"You okay?" he asks.

Nodding, I push up on my tiptoes and give him a quick kiss. "Ready to head back?"

"Only if you are."

"I am." I step away, interlacing our fingers and leading us back toward our group.

The lawn is a sea of people which makes it nearly impossible to find everyone. Kyle spots us and waves. He catches my eye as we approach. *Good?* he mouths.

I nod. I'm not sure if this feeling will ever go away. Every time a notification comes in, everything seems suddenly overwhelming. All I know is, I'm definitely not the person I was a year ago. I'm different now.

Having Lucas and giving him up for adoption was the hardest thing I've ever done. I'm so incredibly grateful for the Challinors for creating the perfect home for him. Even though the updates are hard, they are so rewarding. It's nice to be able to see the little boy I carried inside me grow up. Lucas has a piece of my heart and always will.

Tanya and Joel are naturals when it comes to parenting. I had told Tanya that she was meant to be a mom, and she is. Lucas is the luckiest kid. Tanya writes that in every single one of her emails. She said it in her first update.

When I responded to that update and asked why she had pictures of me and Kyle in his bedroom, she explained that we are his biological parents. She wanted Lucas to know everyone who loved him, from the very beginning. She tells him stories of the meetings they had with us and of the stories we share when we email. Kyle shares more about his life than I do right now, but I'm working on it.

I'm sure eventually I'll be able to see a notification and not feel like my world is ending. One day, I'll be overjoyed when those updates come in, and it doesn't seem impossible now with my friends and my boyfriend, who've all supported me along the way.

Sometimes you have to work at making a sour situation a little sweeter.

Music

Here is list of all (most) of the songs referenced and a few extras.

Songs Referenced by name
"Whenever, Wherever" Shakira
"I Knew You Were Trouble" We Came As Romans
"Tainted Love" Cover by Soft Cell & Marilyn Manson. Originally sung by Gloria Jones
"We Don't Talk About Bruno" *Encanto*
"Run the World (Girls)" Beyoncé
"Survivor" Destiny's Child

Girl Power/Labor Playlist
"Diva" Beyoncé
"I Am Woman" Jordin Sparks
"Baby" Justin Bieber, Ludacris
"Push It" Salt-N-Pepa

Bands Mentioned
The Cab
Arrows in Action
Heroes Like Villains
AJR

<u>**Songs I figured Mac and Dustin would listen to**</u>
"Five Minutes to Midnight" BOYS LIKE GIRLS
"The Great Escape" BOYS LIKE GIRLS
"Pretend.Release.The Close" Emarosa
"A Toast to the future kids!" Emarosa
"Tear Me to Pieces" Story Of The Year
"Tell Me I'm Alive" All Time Low (E)
"Safe" All Time Low

Note: You've Got Mail is a fictious band, but be on the lookout for them in upcoming books ☺

Acknowledgements

First and foremost, my Heavenly Father, who gave me this gift to create.

To my mom for reading *every* variation of this manuscript and to my dad for helping me set up a little contraption so I can make the book edges pretty.

To my brother, Tim, for reading through the beginning and providing very helpful feedback. To Mikalah for tolerating him. I've heard he likes to read a sentence out of context and ask for your opinion. I wish I could say this will never happen again, but that would be a lie.

To Jen, Jamie, Liz, Diane, Amanda K., and anyone else who read early versions of the manuscript and provided feedback. You all shaped the story and I'm extremely grateful.

To all those who made Mac and Dustin's musical taste what they are. Sarah and Holly Franklin. Chase Partee, for burning me a plethora of CD's (if you don't know what that is, ask a grown up). Finally, to Jared Morton for introducing me to Punk Goes Pop. The We Came As Roman's version of "I Knew You Were Trouble" is my favorite.

To the wonderful, amazing, smart, and talented Makenna Albert. Your editing skills are impeccable and I'm so happy we got to work together again. This story wouldn't be the same without you! Also, that title is all because of you. Thank you for brainstorming with me.

To Jamie Joiner for the beautiful cover art. I'm obsessed with it! I am so grateful we bonded over books while on Winter Retreat and became fast friends.

Finally, to you. Yes, you. I'm so thankful you took a chance on this book.

Karen Ramsey is an Arizona native. She comes home every night to her toy poodle, Pumpkin. When she's not crushing it at her day job, she's writing. Her blog can be found at caffeineandfaith.com. Since growing up in church she feels her life is powered by faith and caffeine keeps her going. She often wonders if there is a Starbucks Anonymous and should she attend, seeing as how when she walks into her neighborhood Starbucks she is greeted by name, no matter what time of day it is. She self-published her first book, *Enjoy the Little Things,* in 2023.